Blowback

Books by Peter May

The Enzo Files
Dry Bones (formerly *Extraordinary People*)
A Vintage Corpse (formerly *The Critic*)
Blacklight Blue
Freeze Frame
Blowback

The China Thrillers
The Firemaker
The Fourth Sacrifice
The Killing Room
Snakehead
The Runner
Chinese Whispers

Other Books
The Noble Path
Hidden Faces
Fallen Hero
The Reporter
Virtually Dead

Blowback

The Fifth of the Enzo Files

Peter May

Poisoned Pen Press

Copyright © 2011 by Peter May

First Edition 2011

10 9 8 7 6 5 4 3 2 1

Library of Congress Catalog Card Number: 2010932095

ISBN: 9781590588413 Hardcover
       9781590588437 Trade Paperback

Poisoned Pen Press
6962 E. First Ave., Ste. 103
Scottsdale, AZ 85251
www.poisonedpenpress.com
info@poisonedpenpress.com

Printed in the United States of America

This book is dedicated to the memory of my friend and mentor,
Tom Wright

Acknowledgments

I would like to offer my grateful thanks to those who gave so generously of their time and expertise during my researches for "Blowback". In particular, I'd like to express my gratitude to **Michel Bras**, three-star Michelin chef and owner of the "eighth best restaurant in the world", for giving me unfettered access to his kitchen, and feeding me some of the best food I have ever tasted; pathologist **Steven C. Campman, M.D**, Medical Examiner, San Diego, California; **Grant Fry**, Lead Forensic Specialist, Orange County Sheriff-Coroner Department, California; **Patrick Nolan**, Ponderosa Kennels, Maryland, USA; **Linda Sperco**, Blue Ribbon Dog Sports Coaching, New Jersey, USA; **NDZ**; **Bob Dartnel,** managing director, Foster & Freeman Ltd., Evesham, England; **Karteek Alahari**, Oxford Brookes University, England; and **John Hally**, my brother-in-law, and former pupil of Hutchesons' Grammar School, now resident in upstate New York, USA. I would also like to offer my thanks and congratulations to **Rudolph Chelminski** for his excellent book, **"The Perfectionist"**, on the death of Bernard Loiseau. I found it to be both an inspiration and an indispensible reference book on the history of modern French cuisine.

La nature parle et l'expérience traduit.
—John-Paul Sartre

Prologue

Dominique slipped the two wooden stakes under her arm and zipped her standard issue waterproof jacket up to the neck. It was still winter cold. Wet now, although the snow remained thick on distant volcanic peaks. She pushed off up the track through the trees. Pine needles lay thick in the mud, the smell of them filling damp air, a powerful, bitter scent of decay, like the smell of death that awaited her at the end of her climb. She felt the chill anticipation of it in her bones.

Beyond the treeline the hill rose steeply. The little track, bounded by a crumbling dry stone wall, followed its ragged contour before turning sharply to circumvent a stand of dark trees. There it rose again toward the summit where the hill flattened out and stretched away into the misted distance of the high plateau.

Dominique stopped at the turn and, looking back, was surprised at how far she had climbed. She stood, breathless, for a moment, and saw the blue flashing light of her van at the foot of the track, and the string of parked vehicles that snaked up the narrow road beyond it toward the *auberge*. She saw a group of tiny figures clustered on the road, an upturned *parabole* beaming its signal to the gods of some edit suite in Paris where its images, accompanied by some well-chosen sound bites, would be dissected for ease of digestion. A great story! A tragedy! A shock *aperitif* for prurient consumers of the evening news all over France.

Wearily the young gendarme turned to face the last few hundred meters of her climb. As she neared the summit she saw, at last, the old ruined stone *buron* breaking the horizon. It was hard to believe now that such a place had once been inhabited. But only in summer, with the beasts feeding on the great banks of wild flowers and sweet grasses that blanketed the plateau. And maybe then, with its soft estival winds and its unbroken views across the roof of France, it was a good place to be. An escape from the world below. A sense of elevation. Of godliness.

But today clouds sat low on the peak, drizzling their misery on the world, losing distance in grey mist. And Dominique saw two figures in dark, shiny waterproofs huddled in the shelter of the wet stone, one sitting on broken rocks, bent over, head in hands. The other stood by the opening that led to the shadowed interior of the *buron*. Its stone roof appeared almost intact, crumbling *lauzes* that kept out the light but let in the rain, supporting a chimney that had not felt the heat of a fire in years. A second, more dilapidated, roof rose at an angle above it, shelter for the animals when the weather closed in.

The standing figure stepped forward to shake Dominique's hand. A familiar face. He was a big man, broad as well as tall, but diminished somehow by grief. His dark blue *béret* was pulled down low on a furrowed brow, from beneath which grim eyes met hers.

Dominique glanced at the seated figure, and saw the torment in the woman's briefly upturned face, before it fell back again into black despair. It was the merest of acknowledgments, but no shake of the hand. The gendarme turned back to the man. "Show me."

He nodded and bowed his head to duck beneath the lintel as she followed him into the darkness beyond. Their shadows fell across a mud floor where water lay in pools, reflecting broken light from the doorway. A mess of footprints pitted the mud. Dominique unclipped the flashlight from her belt and let its beam wander back through the dark until it found the twisted figure of a man in a tracksuit half-lying in a pool of rainwater turned red by his blood. She felt a short, sharp, involuntary intake of breath briefly inflate her chest. Ten years in the *gendarmerie* and this was her first murder. While she had, in that time, pulled horribly mutilated corpses from car wrecks, nothing had quite prepared her for looking into the dead, staring eyes of a man whose face was known in every household in France. A face marred by a single bullet wound in the dead center of his forehead. The bullet had passed straight through. She saw the white, grey mess of brain streaked amidst his bloodied hair, and down in the mud, and felt her stomach heave. She let her eyes follow the beam of her flashlight around the body, just barely in control. She heard the quiver in her own voice. "No gun?"

"None that I could see."

"Anything missing?"

"He always wore a belt with a pouch to carry his *portable* and his *Thiers*. It's gone."

Dominique glanced at him, and felt a tiny frown settle across her eyes. "You think someone killed him for his cellphone and his knife?"

The man shrugged, a helplessness in the slight movement of his shoulders.

Dominique felt the first flush of nausea subside. She tipped her head toward the door. This was a crime scene. She knew well enough that nothing should be disturbed until the experts arrived. She followed the man outside, and took the stakes from under her arm to hammer them into soft ground with the mallet she had brought from the van. One on either side of the entrance. Then she stretched a length of blue and white tape between them and watched as it flapped and fibrillated in the breeze.

"Who found him?"

"I did." The man turned painfully blue eyes toward the soft brown of hers. "He left to go for his run as usual, immediately after the lunch service."

"He went running every day?"

The man nodded. "Always the same route. Down the road from the *auberge*, then up through the trees to the *buron*, and along the ridge and back down toward the main road." He sighed. "When he wasn't back by four we started to get worried. Elisabeth was scared in case he'd had a fall."

"Wouldn't he have phoned?"

"If conscious yes, I suppose he would."

"Why didn't you phone him?"

"I did. There was no reply. That's why I went out looking for him."

"What made you look in the *buron*?"

"I didn't at first. When I couldn't find him I backtracked and checked inside." He drew in his lips to contain his emotion. "It's not an easy thing to find your little brother like that."

Dominique nodded. She couldn't really imagine how that must have felt. "What about all these footprints?"

"There seemed to be a lot of them. Certainly more than he could have made himself. And I guess mine are among them now, too."

"Did you touch the body?"

"No. I approached close enough to see that he was dead. I mean, that was obvious. Then I went back down to the hotel and called you people."

Dominique let her gaze fall on the forlorn figure of the woman on the rocks.

The man answered the unasked question. "She insisted on coming back up with me. Said she wouldn't believe it if she didn't see it for herself. She was very nearly hysterical." His mouth settled in a grim line. "Catatonic now."

Dominique walked toward the edge of the track where it began its descent through the falling gloom toward the smudged line of trees below. The arrival of darkness would make access difficult for the *police scientifique*. It would be morning before a proper search of the area could begin. The vehicles on the road had their lights on now. She turned back toward the figure of the man to find him watching her. "How did the press get here so quickly?"

A look of sad resignation flitted across his face. "They were already here. Marc had invited them all down from Paris. He loved to entertain, to be the center of attention. And, of course, no journalist in his right mind would refuse an invitation to dine at the table of Marc Fraysse."

"What was the occasion?"

He hesitated. "He was in deep despair. Maybe you were aware of the speculation in the media. That Marc was about to lose a star."

"Would that have been so bad?"

The man's smile was wry and sad and filled with disbelief. It conveyed with its simple turn of the lips all the history and sophistication which he possessed, that a country gendarme could never acquire. It verged on the patronising. "It would have been *everything*. Everything he had dedicated his life to achieve. It would have been shocking, humiliating, devastating."

Dominique knew that she must appear gauche and guileless to this man, but pressed on. "So why did he invite the media?"

"He said he wanted to make an announcement."

"Which was?"

The dead man's brother laid his open palms out before him. "He never made it. We'll never know."

Chapter One

He had bearded and washed the scallops, wonderful fat, succulent *noix St. Jacques* that the fishmonger in the covered market across the street had reserved for him. They purveyed the delicious aroma of the sea without a hint of fish. He had sliced them in half, along the round, with a razor sharp knife to make medallions, then left them to drain on kitchen paper, their milky sweet juices absorbed by the softness.

Now he plated up the salad. A few fresh green leaves. Lettuce, baby spinach, rocket, and a drizzle of thick, sweet dressing made with a syrupy balsamic, carefully gathered in a corner of the plate. He turned back to the stove. His Calphalon nonstick *sauté* pan was smoking hot. Tiny pools of bubbling melted butter and shimmering olive oil ran across its surface as he tipped it one way, then the other, before dropping in the *St. Jacques*. The sizzling sound of searing scallops filled the room along with their sweet smell. Sixty seconds, and then he flipped them over, pleased with the caramelised crust on the cooked side. Another sixty seconds, and he slipped a thin metal skewer through the side of the fattest of them, deep into its center, before extracting it quickly and raising it to his lips. The merest touch told him that the scallops were warmed to the middle, and therefore cooked. But only just.

Quickly he arranged five medallions in an elegant heap next to the salad on each plate and swivelled toward the table, one in each hand, to deliver them to the two facing place settings. He had already poured tall glasses of chilled, crisp Gaillac *blanc sec* from Domaine Sarrabelle. Hélène looked wide-eyed at the plate in front of her and breathed in deeply. "My God, Enzo, they smell fabulous. You'd have any woman eating out of your hand if you served up food like this every evening."

Enzo grinned. "Maybe that's the idea."

Hélène raised a sceptical eyebrow. "Hmmm. If only."

"But in any case, I'd rather you ate them off the plate than out of my hand, *commissaire*. And quickly. They won't keep their heat for long in these temperatures." No matter how high he had turned up the central heating, the pervasive cold of this early onset winter weather seemed to fill the apartment. Only the heat of the oven and the gas rings seemed to hold it at bay. As he sat down to slice through a scallop and spear a forkful of salad, he glanced from the French windows across the square toward the floodlit twin domes of Cahor's gothic Saint-Etienne cathedral. The rain slashed diagonally across his line of sight, and he almost imagined he saw an edge of sleet in it. Which would be unprecedented for late October in this ancient Roman city.

"Delicious."

He turned his head to find Hélène beaming at him, as his *St. Jacques* melted in her mouth. She washed it over with a sip of *blanc sec*, then dabbed fine, full lips with her napkin.

She was still a handsome woman for all her forty-odd years. Hair normally piled up beneath the hat of her uniform, tumbled in luxuriant elegance across square shoulders. Only the sixth woman in the history of the *République* to be appointed Director of Public Security to one of the country's one hundred *départements*, she had never quite seen the joke in Enzo's refusal to call her by her name. He referred to her always as *commissaire*, as if it were somehow amusing. She had reflected, more than once, that it might also be a subtle way of his telling her that their on-off relationship was doomed never to progress to intimacy.

She popped another *St. Jacques* in her mouth. "I'm afraid there are still no developments in our attempt to identify who's been trying to kill you."

Enzo studied her thoughtfully, distracted by the delicate caramel flavour of the scallops mixing with the sweet, vinegary flavour of the balsamic, and the crisp, slightly bitter tang of the greens. He prepared his palate for the next mouthful with a generous sip of wine and shrugged dismissively. "Well, it's over a year since the last attempt. So maybe whoever it was is already dead, or behind bars." But he knew that was unlikely. With four of Roger Raffin's celebrated cold cases already solved, and only three remaining, someone out there would be increasingly anxious to stop him.

Hélène, too, looked less than convinced. But she decided on a change of subject and slipped the last morsel into her mouth before taking a piece of bread to mop up the juices that lingered tantalisingly on her plate. "Where's Sophie these days?" She glanced around the apartment almost as if expecting to see her suddenly appear.

"Ah," Enzo said. "I'm glad to say I finally persuaded my daughter to resume her education. I was very disappointed when she dropped out of university to go and work at Betrand's gymn."

"Oh?" Hélène feigned interest. "What's she studying?" And she was surprised to detect a hint of evasion in Enzo's response.

He leaned across the table to take her empty plate and carried the two of them back to the breakfast bar. "Oh, she's away on a *stage*. Just a few weeks' work placement." He paused. "I'll be with you in a moment."

And he turned his attention to the main course. A *filet mignon de porc* which he had marinated in a hoisin, five-spice, and honey sauce, and then roasted in a hot oven. He removed it now from the tinfoil he had wrapped it in before cooking the *St. Jacques*, and cut it into moist, tender discs which he arranged on a warmed plate. Over the meat he drizzled a reduction of the marinade, then served the cubed, honeyed roast potatoes which had been crisping in the oven on a bed of rosemary.

"*Voila!*" He delivered his plates to the table like a magician presenting the denouement of a complex trick. He grabbed a bottle of red and expertly removed the cork. "Some oak-aged syrah to go with it. Enough strength and fruit in it, I think, to stand up to the sweetness of the pork." He poured them each a glass.

"*Mon dieu*, Enzo!" Hélène surveyed the plate in front of her, breathing in its aromas. "*Are* you trying to seduce me?"

He grinned. "It's not exactly three-star Michelin quality, *commissaire*. But anything that can persuade you to slip out of your uniform for the night has to be not bad."

She smiled demurely, knowing that his flirtation was empty of intent, but enjoying it all the same. Her knife cut through the meat as if it were butter. A little sauce, a cube of honeyed roast potato. She closed her eyes to savour the taste. "You missed your vocation in life."

Enzo laughed heartily. "It's just a hobby, *commissaire*. I'm not at all sure I would have wanted to spend my life slaving seven days a week in a hot kitchen like Marc Fraysse."

She regarded his smiling face, his dark hair drawn back in its habitual ponytail, greying now, but not enough to hide the silver streak in it. His eyes sparkled with life and amusement, one brown, one blue, and she thought how handsome he was for a man in his fifties. "Is Fraysse the next on your list?"

His smile clouded a little, and he nodded. "Actually I'm leaving for Puy de Dôme in the morning." He paused. "An early start."

Which she took as a hint that he did not anticipate her staying the night. She raised the wine glass to her lips to mask her disappointment.

Chapter Two

A cold rain as fine as mist swept down from the extinct volcanos that ringed this vast plateau at the very heart of the country. The *autoroute* looped around the grey conurbation that was Clermont Ferrand, apartment blocks and factories climbing the hills around its northern fringes and vanishing in the fog like so many mirages in an industrial desert. Here, incongruously, was the home of Michelin, the tire manufacturer that had spawned the world's most prestigious guide to good eating. The *Guide Michelin* had been ranking French restaurants since 1933 with one, two, and three stars.

Enzo turned off the A72 which was headed east in the direction of Saint Etienne, and swung south toward Thiers, one of the five principal administrative towns of the *département* of Puy de Dôme. Dating back to the fifteenth century, this ancient *cité* was the cutlery capital of France, and home of the *Thiers* knife. Windshield wipers smeared his vision as the town emerged slowly from the mist and rain, rising up a steeply-pitched volcanic slope toward a ragged summit. Clusters of soiled white and pink houses were built into the gradient, four stories high at one side, two at the other. From the foot of the hill, the road snaked its way up between them, walls and windows and balconies rising up on either side of it like cracks and ledges in the walls of a canyon.

Narrow streets turned off left and right, up and down, leading away into the shadowed heart of the mediaeval city, where centuries-old cantilevered houses overhung cobbled squares.

As he neared the top of the hill, the town opened out into a balustraded *place* with a spectacular view over a jumble of red-tiled roofs toward the valley below. Homes clung precariously to rocky outcrops among the trees on the far side of a ravine that cut deep into the hillside. Enzo found parking for his beloved, mud-spattered Citröen 2CV below the square and walked up past an ugly, modern building that housed the *Hôtel de Ville*. A line of blue gendarmerie vehicles stood nose to tail along one side of the street.

The gendarmerie itself, next to the Café Central, lay on the other side of the square, a handsome building of yellow brick and white stone, inlaid with patterns of red. Enzo climbed a short flight of steps and walked through a tall, arched doorway into the reception area. A middle-aged gendarme behind the desk wore a dark-blue pullover with a single white stripe across chest and upper arms. He looked up. Whatever he might have expected to see, it certainly wasn't this tall, pony-tailed Scot in baggy cargo pants, hiking boots, and khaki anorak, a large canvas satchel slung over one shoulder. Curiosity raised a single eyebrow as Enzo gave him his best smile.

"I'm looking for Gendarme Dominique Chazal."

Curiosity gave way to mild suspicion. "Are you?"

"I am."

"And who should I say is looking for her?"

"Enzo Macleod."

The gendarme hesitated for a long moment, as if reluctant to submit to the notion that he might actually be a public servant rather than simply a wielder of power over the populace. Then he turned and disappeared briskly through a door behind him. It was less than a minute before the door opened again and a young woman in uniform emerged, wide-eyed and smiling. She reached across the counter to shake Enzo's hand.

"Monsieur Macleod."

Enzo tipped his head in acknowledgment, impressed by the warm firmness of her handshake.

"I've been expecting you for quite some time."

◇◇◇

Enzo followed her blue van north on the D906 toward Vichy, where the collaborationist régime of Marshal Pétain had once set up government during the Nazi occupation. Several kilometres out of Thiers they turned off east toward the small village of Saint-Pierre, a clutch of houses gathered around an indulgent church built from the local rusted ochre stone. The village nestled in the fold of a valley between two impressive volcanic crags, and just beyond it, a private road turned off to the right, flanked at its entrance by two stone blocks, each bearing a grey marble plaque chiselled with the monogram, MF.

The road climbed through a pine forest that rose darkly above it on both sides. After a couple of hundred meters, Dominique pulled off into a beaten parking area where a dirt track headed up through a fire-break in the trees. She was already out of her van and standing at the foot of the track before Enzo could get out of his driver's seat. "The Auberge Fraysse is at the top of the road, about a kilometre further up the hill. Marc used to go running every day in the afternoon. He came down the road to this point, and then followed the track up through the woods to the plateau."

Enzo slammed the door of his 2CV shut and peered up into the gloom. "And came back down the same way?"

"No, the track skirts the edge of the plateau and comes back down the south facing elevation to the main road. He would follow the road back round here, then on up to the *auberge*."

"He inherited the hotel and restaurant from his parents, didn't he?"

"He and his brother, Guy, yes. But Guy only got involved after Marc got his third star."

Enzo tipped his head toward the opening in the trees. "You'd better take me up."

It was steep, and hard going, roots and ruts making the track beneath the pine needles uneven and treacherous. Enzo could not imagine running up it. After a few dozen meters he was breathing hard. He looked up to see Dominique striding confidently ahead of him. She was a slim girl, somewhere in her mid-thirties he guessed, and the sway of her hips, and the alternate tensing of taut buttock muscles in tight-fitting uniform pants, combined to spur him past his age-induced pain threshold. Only the gun in its black holster attached to her white leather belt gave him pause for thought. Women with guns were not to be messed with.

Although the rain had stopped, the mist still hung in wreaths and strands among the trees like smoke, while rainwater slow-dripped from a million pine needles, soaking them as they climbed. As they emerged, finally, from the woods, Dominique turned to face him, barely out of breath. Enzo, red-faced and trying to control his gasps, struggled the last few meters to catch her up.

"Want to take a rest?"

"Nooo, no, I'm fine," Enzo lied. And then, casually, "Is it much further?"

"We're about a third of the way up."

His heart sank. He smiled. "I'm right behind you." And inwardly he cursed the stubborn male ego that refused to admit that he wasn't as young as he used to be.

It took them another fifteen minutes to reach the summit, and Enzo several more minutes to recover. He stood with one foot resting on the rock on which Marc Fraysse's widow had sat seven years earlier when Dominique first arrived at the scene. As he tried to subdue his breathing, he looked around. The *buron* was half hidden by the cloud that lay across the plateau. Here the mist swirled in pools and eddies that followed the contours of the breeze stirring among the tall wet grasses. Enzo let his eyes wander over the half-collapsed structure. "What was this place?"

"A *buron*. It's where a farmer used to bring his family, June through September, when he took his sheep or cattle up to the plateau for the summer grazing. You find them all over the Auvergne."

Enzo nodded. "In Scotland, they're called *shielings*. But it's the same thing." He stood up. He had been over the details provided by Raffin's account of the murder many times, but he wanted to hear it from the young gendarme herself. After all, Dominique Chazal had been the first law officer on the scene. "Tell me what you saw, Dominique, when you first arrived." And he listened intently as she took him through the events of that bleak February afternoon in 2003. The media parked up in the road at the foot of the hill. Guy Fraysse, and Marc's widow, Elisabeth, waiting for her by the *buron*. The body lying in a pool of rainwater inside, blood turning water red.

He watched the earnest concentration in her face as she worked to recall every detail. And he couldn't help but think that although it was not a pretty face, it was attractive in its plainness, devoid as it was of make-up. And that there was a beautiful serenity in the deeply warm brown of her eyes.

He followed her into the *buron*. "It was pretty much like this then too. Rainwater lying in pools in the mud. Only there was a mess of footprints."

"Which you identified?"

"There were five sets in total. Marc Fraysse himself. His brother. His wife. And two others that we were never able to identify. Presumably belonging to the murderer, or murderers."

"Or to anyone who might have taken shelter earlier in the day, long before Marc got here."

Dominique shook her head. "The forensics people didn't think so. They felt that the footprints were fresh, or at least made at the same time as the others."

"Casts were taken?"

"Yes."

"And the body was where, exactly?"

Dominique stepped deeper into the gloom. "Right here. Lying at right angles to the wall."

"Face down?"

"More or less. His head was turned to one side. The *police scientifique* found traces of blood and brain tissue on the back wall, and from the way the footprints were configured, it seemed as if he had been knocked back by the blast, banging against the wall, before tipping forward."

"You'll let me see the autopsy report? And the photographs?"

"I can show you a copy of the autopsy report, and pics of the crime scene. But the pathologist still has the originals of the photographs he took at the post mortem."

Enzo nodded then stepped back out into the mist, screwing his eyes up against the light. Was it getting brighter, or was it just the contrast with the dark interior of the *buron*? Whatever, it felt better to be out. There was a strange, pervasive presence within the tumbledown building. Enzo had felt it before at crime scenes, almost as if a victim's spirit could not rest, but haunted the place until the killer had been found. However, he knew that this was just the product of an over-active imagination.

He turned to find Dominique looking at him appraisingly. "Did you know him?" he said. "Marc Fraysse."

"I'd met him, yes. He was a local celebrity."

"He was celebrated all over France."

"And the planet. Chez Fraysse was voted the fifth best restaurant in the world the year before he died. But he was a local boy, born and bred. So he was ours. We felt that sense of pride in him that you would feel for a member of your own family. Marc, Guy, Elisabeth… everyone knew them."

Enzo smiled. "You were very fortunate to have a restaurant like that on your doorstep."

Her sudden laughter, and the patent amusement in it, took him by surprise. "Oh, I never *ate* at Chez Fraysse!" She punctuated her words with more laughter. "The cheapest menu was a hundred and fifty euros back then, Monsieur Macleod. Do you think I can afford that on a gendarme's wages?"

"Surely a woman like you has a man who would be prepared to spend that on her?"

Her smile faded a little, and he saw her eyes cloud like cataracts. "Never knew one who would," she said. She struggled to rediscover her smile. "If you're finished here, we should go back down the hill."

But Enzo stood his ground. "One last thing." He glanced around, as far as the mist would allow him to see. "His belt and pouch were missing, yes?"

"That's right."

"And never found."

"No."

"Did you search for them?"

"We did. A dozen officers combed an area of about five hundred square meters around the *buron*, and the whole length of the track. We found nothing. Not even a cigarette end."

He turned his gaze back on her, and found her looking at him, head dipped slightly, so that she appeared to be looking up from below her finely arched brows. Her eyes were wide and shining again, and full of warmth. He said, "This is the first time in any of my enquiries that I've had this kind of cooperation from the police."

She grinned. "Just don't tell my superiors."

"Why? I mean, why are you being so helpful?"

She shrugged with a kind of casual innocence. "When I took the call from Guy Fraysse to say that his brother had been murdered up here on the hill, I was twenty-eight years old. It was my first murder." She smiled. "And last." She paused. "I hope. Anyway, although I was nominally in charge of the case, being the first officer on the scene, it was really taken out of my hands. Marc Fraysse wasn't just a chef. He was a celebrity. France's favourite son. I had *procureurs* and *juges d'instructions* and commissioners of police descending on me. This was far too important a case to be left to some hick gendarme." He detected the merest hint of bitterness in her tone. "But for all the high flyers who arrived in Thiers in the days that followed, not one of them was able to throw any light on the murder. And when the publicity finally faded away, so did they." She drew a deep breath. "I would like to know who murdered him, Monsieur Macleod. And if *you* can't find his killer, I don't think anyone ever will."

By the time they got to the bottom of the track the cloud, if possible, had settled even lower across the hilltops, and the *buron* had vanished from view, almost as though it had never existed, and the murder of the most celebrated chef in France had been the figment of someone's colorful imagination.

Dominique opened the door of her van. "Do you want to take a look at the evidence and reports?"

Enzo nodded. "Yes, I do. But not now. I want to go and check in up at the *auberge* and meet the family first. I want to get a feel for the place. And the man."

Chapter Three

On the road up to the hotel, Enzo passed a group of workmen hammering in snow-poles. They stopped and watched as he drove by. One of them nodded when Enzo caught his eye. A big man, unshaven, with dark, haunted eyes. Their pick-up was parked at the roadside a few meters further on, and beyond that the road suddenly opened out on the left, the ground falling away steeply, fifteen or twenty meters to a stream in spate at the foot of the gully. A low, white-painted wooden fence acted as a barrier. A little further on the land rose sharply, and a waterfall dropped sheer from the rocks to a pool of bubbling, frothing effervescence that fed into the stream.

It was through the trees above the waterfall that Enzo caught his first glimpse of the *auberge*, home to Chez Fraysse, one of the world's most celebrated restaurants. As he rounded the bend in the road, it swung into full view. Enzo's initial reaction was one of disappointment. He had not been sure what to expect, but the square, stolid stone house with it's steeply pitched *lauze* roof did not quite measure up to his image of a three-star Michelin establishment. But then, for most of its life it had just been a rural *auberge*, an *étape* on the road for the travelling salesmen who had once plied their trade along the old D2089 between Clermont Ferrand and Saint-Etienne. It wasn't until he pulled into the paved parking area beneath plane trees that spread their branches to offer summer shade that he realized how deceptive that first impression had been.

The stonework of the original house had been sand-blasted to its original rusty yellow, and meticulously pointed. Graceful conservatories had been appended to the south and west, with tasteful stone-faced extensions built out to the north and east. The east-side extension linked up with an L-shaped out-building, converted to guest rooms, forming three sides of a courtyard shaded by a huge chestnut tree shedding brown leaves on shiny cobbles. There were more bedrooms in a converted barn on the west side of the car park, with beautifully manicured terraced gardens descending to an outdoor swimming pool. High end guest rooms for a three-star restaurant so remotely located were a must. Not only to provide overnight accommodation for those who wished to drink and drive, but in combination with the restaurant to maximise the high income stream which would mean survival in a tough business.

As he followed the path around to the front of the house, Enzo saw why Marc Fraysse had chosen to stay here and remodel the property he had inherited. It sat proud on an outcrop of rock, the land falling away sharply below it to the forest and a spectacular panorama across what seemed like the entire Massif Central. Even on a day like today, you could see all the way across to the snow-capped mountain ranges of the Auvergne and the dominating shadow of the Puy de Dôme volcano, pushing almost five thousand feet up into the clouds. Both conservatories provided unfettered access to the view, and it was behind their protective glass that Marc Fraysse had established the restaurant's two dining rooms, even at the risk of distracting from his *cuisine*. The view alone would have been worth the money. In summer their glass frontages could be removed to provide a real sense of dining al fresco.

The main entrance was now at the front side of the east extension, and Enzo found himself sucked through its revolving door into a brightly lit reception area with glass on three sides. A thin, attractive woman in her mid-forties, sitting behind the reception desk, offered him a welcoming smile.

"Can I help you?"

"I believe Madame Fraysse has reserved me a room." He saw the merest flicker of a shadow momentarily mar her smile.

"Ah, Monsieur Macleod. Yes, we've been expecting you." She reached beneath the desk and produced an electronic key card, slipping it into a shiny holder embossed with the initials MF, beneath which his room number, 23, was printed in curlicued gold. "It's on the first floor. To your left at the top of the stairs. One of our suites."

Enzo took the card. "Thank you."

"Shall I send someone to get the luggage from your car?"

Enzo raised his canvas overnight bag. "This is it, I'm afraid. I travel light."

Her eyes blinked at the bag and back at him, but her smile never faltered. "Of course. I'll let Madame Fraysse know you've arrived. She'll receive you in her private rooms. The double doors at the far end of your hallway. She'll call you when she's ready."

Madame Fraysse was a strikingly handsome woman in her late fifties. Fine silken hair the color of brushed steel was drawn back from a delicately featured face and arranged in an elaborate bow of black ribbons at the back of her head. She had the palest of green eyes and full, lightly colored lips that stretched back across perfect white teeth as she smiled her welcome. She oozed class and money, and Enzo thought that her taut, wrinkle-free complexion, and too-perfect teeth, probably owed much to cosmetic and dental surgery, betraying a certain vanity indulged by wealth. She offered him a firm handshake and ushered him into her private apartment.

Enzo said, "I very much appreciate you giving me this kind of access, Madame Fraysse."

She waved him into an oxblood leather armchair, and lowered herself into another one opposite. "I would do anything, Monsieur Macleod, to find out who murdered my husband. The police have been worse than useless. And your reputation goes before you."

Enzo glanced around the sitting room. There was a spartan quality to it. The hard, cold shine of varnished floorboards; plain walls hung with frameless modern abstracts which no doubt had cost four and five, perhaps even six, figure sums; an unyielding leather suite; Venetian blinds on curtainless windows. Polished pieces of antique furniture stood around the room like staff awaiting instructions that would never come. There was no fireplace, and although the room was heated, there was something of a chill in the air. "I don't want to raise your expectations too high, madame. There seems to be very little evidence to go on in this case. And a complete absence of apparent motive."

"But you have already solved four of the seven cases in Roger Raffin's book, haven't you?"

"More or less, yes. But of all the cases he wrote about, this seems to me to be the most puzzling. Why would anyone want to kill a man who seemed to be universally loved?"

There was an awkward silence.

"Are you asking me?"

"I suppose I am."

"Then I have to tell you that I haven't the faintest idea, Monsieur Macleod. In many ways Marc was a weak man. He *wanted* people to love him. He *needed* their love. And he would do almost anything to win it. But he was funny, and generous, and never had a harsh word for anyone. He hadn't an enemy in the world."

"I read that he was prone to depression."

She pursed her lips a little. "He was, yes." Enzo detected a reluctance in the admission. "Marc was a man of extremes, you see. Extreme ambition, extreme hard work. And extreme depression when things went wrong. But that was rare. Mostly he was up, extremely amusing, and extremely gregarious. And, of course, extremely talented. Not only was he a unique and wonderful chef, but he was a wonderful motivator of people. Everyone who worked for him would have followed him to hell and back. And there were times, monsieur, as he fought for recognition, and toiled to create Chez Fraysse, that we spent more time in hell than anywhere else."

"Your husband inherited the *auberge* from his parents, didn't he?"

"Yes. Both he and his brother, Guy."

"So it's jointly owned."

"Yes, although it was barely worth a thing when his parents died. Passing trade had virtually dried up with the opening of the A72 *autoroute*. Business had been dwindling for years, and the property was in a poor state of repair. It was only Marc's growing reputation, with the awarding of the stars, that saved us from complete obscurity. And then, of course, the winning of the third and final star elevated us to another level altogether. Everything seemed possible, then." She waved an arm vaguely around her. "All that you see here was only possible because of Marc's brilliance in the kitchen."

"Guy never cooked?"

"Oh, he and Marc trained together, yes. Both of them had learned at their mother's apron, but it was their father who sent them for formal training. Which was ironic, since he never worked in the *auberge* himself. It didn't make enough money, you see. Just provided the family home and a supplementary income. Old Monsieur Fraysse travelled around France selling shoes. And it was in a restaurant in Clermont Ferrand, where he had eaten regularly for years, that he obtained apprenticeships for his sons in the kitchen of the Blanc brothers."

Enzo nodded. The Blanc brothers had, at one time, probably been the best known culinary siblings in France, even more renowned than the Roux brothers, or *les frères* Troisgros. Sent by their father to train under the best chefs in the country, they had returned to Clermont Ferrand to elevate the family kitchen from its humble origins offering cheap meals for working men and women to a three-star Michelin restaurant that had brought the food critics salivating all the way down from Paris.

Almost as if she read his mind, Madame Fraysse said, "I think Papa Fraysse thought he might follow in Monsieur Blanc's footsteps, and that Marc and Guy would return like the Blanc brothers to transform the fortunes of the *auberge*." She sighed deeply, something approaching amused melancholy in her eyes. "He must have been bitterly disappointed when Guy dropped out to go off and train as an accountant. And, of course, he never lived to see any of Marc's stars."

"So the restaurant is only worth what it is today because of Marc?"

"Marc's cuisine, yes. But Marc had no head for figures. It wasn't until he won his third star that the fabric of the building itself was really transformed. That's when Guy came to join us, and it was Guy who achieved that transformation." She stood up, then, and wandered toward the window. She wore black pants that stopped several inches short of the ankle, and black leather boots beneath them. Over her white blouse she wore a long black shawl that she gathered around her now, as if cold, folding her arms and gazing from the window at the view of the Massif. "We had worked hard, with limited resources, to turn the *auberge* into a place that would impress a Michelin inspector, but it was Guy who really made the difference. He has a wonderful business sense, Monsieur Macleod. He used Marc's reputation to raise the money needed to turn us into a hotel-restaurant that would one day be rated fifth in the whole world."

Enzo heard the pride in her voice, and saw it in her eyes as she turned back to look at him, arms still folded imperiously across her chest.

"And the multi-million euro business it is today," she added, almost as an afterthought.

"Do you have children, Madame Fraysse?"

"Two, yes. A boy and a girl. Both away at university."

"Training to follow in their father's footsteps?"

Her laugh betrayed genuine amusement. "Good God, no! They grew up seeing first hand just what a damned hard life it is running a hotel and restaurant. It's much more than a career, you see, monsieur. It's your *life*. And no escaping from it." She laughed again. "And like most of the younger generation today, my children don't really want to work at all. They'll probably be perfectly happy to fritter away the next few years in education before inheriting a business that will keep them in the style to which they have become accustomed. No doubt they will either sell up or get others to run it for them." She met Enzo's gaze directly. "Do you think me very cynical?"

Enzo gave a tiny shrug of his shoulders. "You know your children better than I do, Madame Fraysse." Yet he couldn't help wishing that he had been able to persuade his own daughter to finish her degree rather than go to work in a gymnasium. Generalisations were dangerous things. "But I think that in order for me to make any real progress in this investigation, I am going to have to get to know your husband as well as you did."

"Not an easy thing, when he has been gone seven years."

"That's why I have to rely on you. And Guy, of course. How did you first meet Marc?"

She smiled, and her eyes glazed over with distant memories. "We were just kids, really. I think I was seventeen, and training to be a nurse at a hospital in Clermont Ferrand. Marc and Guy were in the middle of their apprenticeships with the Blanc brothers, and having a pretty hard time of it from all accounts."

For a moment, Enzo felt as if she had left the room, transported back in time to relive those precious memories of a youth long lost. There was a lengthy silence, but he didn't dare break it. Then she smiled again, as if returning from a journey that had taken only seconds in reality, but hours in her mind. She was back.

"Some of the other girls and I used to sneak out of the nurses' home at night to meet up with the boys from the restaurant. They all lived in the hotel in some horrible cramped rooms up in the attic, and they had to sneak out, too. There was a park near the university, Jardin Lecoq, and an old boat shed on the lake. That's where we used to meet up and have secret meals. The boys always cooked for us. Best food we'd ever had." She laughed. "There were a lot of teenage hormones being given free rein in those days. But Marc was hopeless. So shy. Guy was much bolder, much more sure of himself. But it was Marc I always had the soft spot for."

"You were married young, then?"

"Good heavens, no! We all went our own ways, and it was some years before Marc and I met up again. I was over thirty when we got married."

"And Guy? Did he end up marrying one of the nurses, too?"

But Madame Fraysse just shook her head. "No. Guy never married. I don't know why. Just never met the right woman, I suppose."

Enzo scratched his chin thoughtfully. "Would you say that Guy dominated his younger brother?"

Madame Fraysse thought about it for a moment. "In many ways I guess he did. In the old days, certainly. He was older, more outgoing, never short of confidence. I suppose Marc must have aspired to be like him. But in the end, it was Marc who had the talent and the drive to make the most of it. Guy would probably still have been working in some grey accountant's office, wasting his life counting other people's money."

For some moments, Enzo was lost in thought. Memories he hadn't entertained for years flickered on the periphery of his consciousness, like an old black and white movie seen out of the corner of the eye.

"Monsieur Macleod?"

He looked up, surprised.

"Are you still with us?" Her smile was a little forced.

"I'm sorry. Just running some thoughts through my head." He made himself focus again. "What did Marc do when he wasn't in the kitchen?"

Madame Fraysse laughed again. But there was no amusement in it this time. "When was he *not* in the kitchen?" She perched herself on the edge of the armchair opposite again. "When Marc got his third star, Guy got the money to build him his dream kitchen. You'll see it shortly. Extended out from the original house, but mostly hidden from the view of the clients. He had an office built on to it, with picture windows looking into the kitchen so that he could always see what was going on. He spent a lot of time there, planning menus, taking phone calls. He was the darling of the Paris media, you know. They couldn't get enough of him. And he was always making early morning dashes up to Paris to record some radio or TV show, then driving like a maniac back down the *autoroute*.

"And then, of course, he ran. Every day. He was fanatical about his fitness. So many chefs die young, Monsieur Macleod. All that butter and cholesterol in French *cuisine*. That was one of the reasons he worked so hard to develop the low-fat *style Fraysse*, as he liked to call it. Food that used few of the fatty ingredients of traditional French cooking, but which was still served with wonderful sauces that fizzed with flavour and life. Only the best, purest ingredients were good enough for Marc. He really elevated the preparation and cooking of food to a pure art form."

There was no disguising her undying admiration for her late husband, almost as if she were defending him from attack. And there *had* been those critics, Enzo knew, who had not admired the *style Fraysse*, and who had taken no small delight in saying so.

"He also had a small office up here in the apartment, just off our bedroom. You can see it if you like."

Enzo stood up. "I'd like that very much."

He followed her through an open doorway to the bedroom. More austerity. An uncomfortably high-looking bed with antique head and footboards, a couple of pink Chinese rugs the only compromise to comfort on the otherwise hard, polished surfaces of the floor. A dresser with a large, circular mirror sat in the window space, and an enormous dark-wood *armoir* stood against the far wall.

"All his clothes still hang in the wardrobe," she said. "I never did have the heart to throw them out." She stopped to open one door of the *armoir*, revealing a row of pants and jackets hanging neatly on the rail. Polished shoes lined up beneath them, and shelves up one side contained scarves and hats, gloves and sweaters. She reached in to touch a Paisley-patterned silk scarf lined with cashmere, stroking it fondly. Then she grasped it and raised it to her face, breathing deeply. Her smile was bittersweet. "I can still smell him on it. Even after all these years. It's strange how we leave something of ourselves behind us, so long after we are gone. A scent, a strand of hair. It's comforting, really, to think that we don't just vanish entirely without trace."

No, Enzo thought. Only some murderers manage that.

She pushed open a door to an adjoining room. "He had his *petit bureau* in here. His little private den."

Enzo followed her in. It was a small room with one single tall, arched window facing out on the view. A roll top desk was pushed against the wall beneath it, mahogany filing cabinets on either side, one topped with an inkjet printer/copier. The rest of the room was bare but for a couple of armchairs arranged around a fireplace that looked and felt as if it hadn't seen flames since the flame of life had been extinguished from its owner. The walls were painted cream, the skirting boards and architraves a dark chocolate brown. Framed photographs of Marc Fraysse covered the walls. Press photographs, mostly. Marc pictured with celebrities, politicians, movie stars; engaging in a round table debate in a TV studio; in the kitchen, dressed in his chef's whites and tall hat. And in framed reviews, letters from Michelin, and a hand-written note from the late French president, François Mitterand. *Dear Marc, I have no idea how to fully express the pleasure I derived from indulging in the pure "style Fraysse" at Saint-Pierre yesterday evening. I am salivating still. Or, as my political opponents would probably have it… dribbling…*

Enzo studied a portrait of the young Marc taken by the celebrated Robert Doisneau. A chiaroscuro in black and white of a fresh-faced young man inclined to plumpness, dark eyes shining with life and humour. And something else. Something intensely felt, burning somewhere far behind them. The ambition, perhaps, the drive that had made him one of the world's top chefs in the years to come. Whatever it was, Doisneau had caught it. Magically. It had been the great talent of the man to capture what no one else even saw.

He turned, then, noticing for the first time another door, in the wall opposite the window.

"It opens off the hall," Madame Fraysse said. "He liked to come and go without going through the apartment." She cast a critical eye around the room. "It feels a little cold now." And Enzo realized she didn't mean the temperature. "I had it redecorated after his death. I regret that now. There was so much of him in here. But I just couldn't bear the constant reminder. Now, it might have been a comfort."

She turned toward the roll top and drew back the lid to reveal a cluttered desktop, shelves and brass-handled drawers ranged along behind it. It was a handsome piece of furniture

"But I never cleared out his desk. So many personal things. It didn't seem right."

Among all the papers lay a titanium MacBook Pro laptop computer, and next to it a white pearl fountain pen, intricately worked in what looked like matte silver. It stood in an elegant desk stand. Enzo lifted it up and removed the cap to reveal the engravings on its silvered nib. "It's a beautiful pen."

"It's a Dupont Taj Mahal. The workings are in palladium. It's softer than platinum, and more beautifully colored, don't you think? It was one of a limited edition of a thousand."

Enzo raised an eyebrow. This was no ordinary pen. "Must have been expensive."

"I think, monsieur, you could have dined at Chez Fraysse every evening for a week, and still had change. After he gained that third star, nothing was too good for Marc. Only the finest pen was good enough for writing on the finest paper." She lifted up a sheet of stationery from the desk. "You only have to touch it to feel the quality. He had all our stationery watermarked with the MF logo." She held it up to the light, and Enzo saw the pale graphic representation of the intertwined M and F subtly embedded in the fabric of the paper.

"He hand wrote each day's menu himself, sitting here at his *bureau*." She slid open the top drawer of the right-hand filing cabinet and extracted a sheet from one of a dozen or more suspension files. "He kept all the originals. A kind of archive." She passed it to Enzo, and he was struck by the distinctively ornate flow of the handwriting, the light and heavy lines of the palladium nib, the flourish at the end of each word. Like the work of an artist: *la tarte aux cèpes de pays à l'huile de noix; rafraîchie d'un bouquet parfumé.* A mere forty euros for this appetizer on the *à la carte.*

Enzo handed it back to her. "Makes me hungry just to read it."

She smiled. "Don't worry, Monsieur Macleod, we have a place set for you to eat with us tonight *en famille* in the kitchen." And he found himself a little disappointed that he would be eating in the kitchen rather than the dining room. The fare would probably be somewhat different.

He turned back to the desk, fingering things, as if the touch of them might bring him somehow closer to the dead man. A paper punch, a ruler, an eraser. He lifted the lid of the laptop and noticed its power cable snaking away to some concealed power point behind the desk. "Did he use the computer much?"

"Oh, yes, he spent a lot of time on it. He loved his email. He was forever writing to somebody, and his inbox always seemed full. He used his browser to scour the web in search of ideas. Novel ingredients, novel recipes. And, of course, critiques of his food, articles about himself. He needed the reassurance of constant praise, you see. Sadly, it didn't matter how many good critiques he received, one bad one would send him spiralling into a depression for days."

Enzo closed the lid again and noticed that the laptop sat on a large blotter covered with scribbles, the idle doodling of a dead man. But here were words, too, and names. The initials JR, their contours inked over again and again till they were almost unreadable. A phone number that began with the digits 06. A cellphone number. The phrase, *la nature parle et l'experience traduit,* written in Marc Fraysse's distinctive hand. *Nature speaks, experience translates.* A quote, Enzo knew, from Jean-Paul Sartre. His thoughts were interrupted by the door from the hall opening behind them. Both he and Madame Fraysse turned to be greeted by the grinning, florid face of a large man losing his hair.

"Ah, Guy. You're just in time to meet Monsieur Macleod."

"They told me you were up here." Guy extended an enormous hand to crush Enzo's. The sleeves of his voluminous khaki shirt were rolled up to the elbow, the tails of it out over well-worn denims, and he wore a pair of scuffed sneakers. Not the image Enzo had had in mind of one of the world's most successful restauranteurs. "A pleasure to meet you, Monsieur Macleod. We have heard a great deal about you." There was a twinkle in his blue eyes, and an openness that immediately drew Enzo. "Has Elisabeth been filling you in?"

"She has."

"Good. Well, we're both entirely at your disposal. We want to get to the bottom of this, Monsieur Macleod. It's been too long, and there is still no closure."

"Well, I hope I'll be able to do that for you, Monsieur Fraysse. But there are no guarantees, I'm afraid."

"No, of course not. And it's Guy, by the way. You don't mind if I call you… Enzo, isn't it?"

"Yes."

"I hate formalities. And I'm sure my sister-in-law would prefer you to call her Elisabeth."

A glance at Elisabeth's frozen smile told Enzo that perhaps she wouldn't. He decided to stick with Madame Fraysse.

"At any rate, if you are finished here, I'm sure you would like to see the kitchen," Guy said.

"Very much."

"Good. It's a bit special. I'll take you down. But first I want to show you my pride and joy."

Enzo heard Madame Fraysse's barely audible sigh. "His wine cellar."

Guy beamed. "Exactly. I have more than four thousand labels, Enzo, and nearly seventy thousand bottles. You couldn't put a price on the collection. I have vintages down there that will *never* be drunk."

Enzo frowned. "Why not?"

"Because they're far too valuable to waste on a moment of fleeting pleasure."

◇◇◇

The cellar was accessed through a stout oak door off the reception area, just a few paces from the west-facing dining room. Guests were already assembling in the lounge to order aperitifs and await that day's *amuse-bouches*, spoonfuls of flavour served on lacquer platters, whatever the chef might have dreamed up during the afternoon to whet the appetites of evening diners.

Guy flicked a light switch at the top of a flight of wooden steps leading down to the cellar. Lamps flickered and shed soft light on rows of wine racks stretching off into the chill gloom below them. The cellar was enormous, filling the footprint of the entire house, hacked out of the bedrock on which the foundations had been built. The floor was stone flagged, and the walls themselves bedrock rising to stone founds.

Guy's voice boomed and echoed as he led Enzo down the steps. "The temperature down here never wavers," he said. "Summer or winter. Better than any air-conditioning. A constant twelve degrees centigrade. Perfect to keep the wine in best condition." He started off along a narrow passage between two towering rows of racks. "When success came we spent money on three things. The building itself, Marc's kitchen, and my cellar. And I'm pretty sure I've assembled one of the best in France." He stopped and turned to confront the following Enzo with a mask of incomprehension. He shook his head. "The strangest thing. Marc was possibly one of the best chefs this country has ever produced. He had an impeccable palate. Incredibly discerning. He should have revelled in the *dégustation*, the tasting of the wines. But he didn't drink. Only the odd glass. He had no interest in wine. None. Quite extraordinary."

Enzo nodded his agreement. "Yes." How anyone, never mind a three-star chef, could not enjoy a glass of good wine was beyond him.

"You're a wine man yourself, I take it?"

Enzo grinned. "One of my great pleasures in life, Guy, is to sit back and enjoy a bottle of fine wine."

Guy's beam stretched his face. "Excellent! A man after my own heart, then. I know that you are here on… what shall we say… rather unpleasant business. But we'll break open a few good bottles as compensation while you are. And have some damned good food, too. Marc would have approved of that." He paused. "You're from Cahors, aren't you?"

"That's right."

"Yes… the black wine of Cahors. The Malbec is a difficult grape, but when it's crafted properly the results can be magnificent." He reached up and carefully drew out a dusty bottle. "Château La Caminade. Ninety-five. Wonderful with a *civet de sanglier*. The blood of the earth mixed with the blood of the wild boar. But I'm sure you've had many a bottle of La Caminade."

"I have." Enzo felt his mouth water with anticipation.

But to his disappointment Guy slipped it back into its rack, and headed off among the canyons of wine. Once again he stopped, stooping this time to very carefully extract a bottle from one of the lower racks. He turned, holding the bottle in both hands, to present the label to Enzo. "What, I am sure, you won't have tasted before, is one of these."

Enzo peered at the faded and browning label and raised his eyebrows in surprise.

Guy roared with laughter. "Shocked?"

Enzo couldn't help but laugh. "I am a little."

"Never expected a dyed in the wool Frenchman to have a Californian vintage in his cellar, did you?"

"I certainly didn't."

Guy turned the bottle to look at the label himself. "Opus One was the brainchild of two of the world's great winemakers, you know. Baron Philippe de Rothschild and Robert Mondavi. They hatched the idea between them in Hawaii in 1970, and this was their first vintage, more than thirty years old now, but still wonderful. Cabernet sauvignon blended with sixteen percent cabernet franc and four percent merlot. It cost three hundred and fifty dollars when they first produced it. You can imagine what it is worth now."

"Only as much as someone is prepared to pay for it."

"True. But let me assure you Enzo, there are many people who would pay plenty for a bottle like this. Just to experience those flavours. That wonderfully evolved, intense and fragrant nose of cedar, black fruits, smoked meat, leather spice. So full of fruit and soft tannins, but still elegant in its complexity."

Enzo felt saliva filling his mouth again. It was almost as if Guy were tormenting him on purpose, tantalising him with the promise of something he would never deliver. The Frenchman slipped the bottle back into its resting place, and set off again at pace. Enzo struggled to keep up.

"So many wines to choose from. You could debate with yourself all day which one to have." He stopped at the end of a row. "I do understand, you know, that the cellar is ostensibly for the pleasure of our diners, that we offer them possibly one of the best wine lists in the world. But they are like my children, these bottles. Every last one of them. I hate to see them opened at the table of strangers. It's like a little part of me dies each time one is drunk."

He turned to his left and drew out a bottle at chest height. "Now this…" he swivelled, beaming, toward Enzo, "…is something you are only ever likely to see once in a lifetime. And most people never will. I have all the best vintages here from Bordeaux and Burgundy, from '59 to 2005. Cheval Blanc, Ausone, Haut Brion, Lafite, Margaux, Petrus…" He paused, eyes wide and shining with excitement at the recital of these unsurpassable vintages and labels, as if in owning the bottles he owned everything else about them, too. "But this… this is special."

He turned the label toward Enzo with reverential hands.

Enzo's eyes opened wide. "Château Latour, 1863," he read. The label was only barely legible.

Guy almost trembled with the excitement of holding it. "Here. Take it." He held it out toward Enzo, but the Scotsman shook his head.

"I couldn't. What if I dropped it?"

Guy laughed heartily. "I would dispatch you in swift order to join my brother, wherever he might be." He almost thrust it at Enzo. "Go on, take it!"

Enzo tensed as he grasped the bottle firmly, the glass cool on the skin of his palms, the smell of age rising from its label, and it felt like holding history in his hands. Such a bottle would never even appear on a wine list. No one could put a price on it. And yet Guy had acquired it, probably at auction. So he had put a price on it then. He wondered what it was, but knew Guy would never tell.

Guy watched him intently, knowing exactly how Enzo must be feeling, enjoying it, even second-hand. He took the bottle back, and Enzo breathed a sigh of relief, which Guy detected immediately. He grinned. "Like I said. There are some bottles that will never be drunk, simply treasured by their owners. Sometimes the joy of collecting is almost better than drinking." He fed it gingerly back into its cradle and turned to Enzo, the tension of the moment evaporating into the cool air. He smiled. "Let's show you the kitchen."

Chapter Four

Sliding glass doors parted to usher Guy and Enzo into the kitchen. Enzo had been unsure what to expect, never having been in the kitchen of a three-star restaurant before, but this surpassed anything he might have imagined. It was vast. A huge rectangular space divided in two halves. One half was shared by a servers' station where the cheese trolleys were loaded and the coffees made, and by the *boulangerie-patisserie* which baked the bread and prepared the desserts. The other half was where the serious cooking was done. There were hotplates and gas rings, ovens, freezers, larders, and a charcoal grill. A dazzling array of shiny, stainless steel surfaces.

The whole kitchen was alive with activity. Extractors hummed and timers pinged, and an extraordinary number of men and women in white, sporting long green aprons and tall white hats, moved among the preparation and cooking areas with all the sure-footedness of a well-choreographed ballet company. Evening service was imminent.

"There are anything up to twenty chefs working here at any one time," Guy said. "Although the bulk of them are *stagiaires*. Most trainees spend a season here, learning from the bottom up. But we have short term trainees, too, who normally come to us on release from college courses. The *stagiaires* get all the donkey work to do. Chopping vegetables, preparing stocks, jointing the birds, trimming the meat, washing the floor." He wandered across the space that divided the two halves of the kitchen, where a long, low, marble table was laid out with three place settings. Beyond it, floor to ceiling glass windows gave on to what Enzo assumed must have been Marc's office.

Servers in loose black tops and pants glided in and out bearing large silver trays loaded with *amuse bouches* prepared in the *patisserie* to serve guests in the lounge. Enzo was aware of curious eyes flickering in his direction, then away again. There couldn't have been anyone in the kitchen who did not know why he was here.

"The organisation of the kitchen is fairly simple," Guy said. "It is divided into four. The larder, or *gare manger*; the vegetable section; fish and meat; and the *boulangerie-patisserie*. There is a chef in charge of each, the *chef de partie*. Then there is the *sous chef*, or *second*, the *chef de cuisine*, and, of course, *the* chef himself. *Le patron*."

"And who is *le patron* now?"

"Let me introduce you."

Guy led Enzo across to where a work station was being set up with wooden chopping board, knives, and condiments below a blindingly bright heat lamp. The chef behind it, dressed all in white, was nearly extinguished by the light. A man in his early forties with a neatly trimmed ginger moustache and amber-flecked green eyes, he was almost painfully thin. Enzo wondered how anyone who enjoyed his food could be so emaciated.

"This is Georges Crozes. He was Marc's *second*, promoted to chef when Marc died."

Georges wiped a bony hand on a clean *torchon* dangling from his apron strings and reached over stainless steel to shake Enzo's hand. He had unsmiling, guarded eyes. "*Enchanté, monsieur.*" But Enzo felt that he was less than enchanted to meet him.

Guy seemed oblivious. "Traditionally, when a three-star chef dies, Michelin takes away a star. They say it is a mark of respect for the deceased chef, since how could someone else immediately fill those three-star shoes? In reality, it usually means huge loss of income for the widow or whoever has inherited the restaurant." He beamed appreciatively in the direction of Georges Crozes.

"However, because of the circumstances of Marc's death, they made an exception for us. And it is very much down to Georges that we have retained that third star ever since."

Enzo said, "I understood that Michelin was thought to be on the point of taking away one of Marc's stars anyway."

Guy flicked him a glance. "A rumor. Whether it was true, we'll never know. At any rate, Georges was his *protégé*, schooled in the *style Fraysse*, and although he has introduced his own individual slant on things, it is still essentially Marc's *cuisine* that we serve here. And since we still have those stars…" He shrugged to indicate he believed his point had been made.

"Monsieur Fraysse, your evening meal is ready."

Enzo turned to find an older man smiling benignly at them. He was tall, a man in his sixties, almost completely bald, with a tightly trimmed silver moustache. He was dressed all in black like the other servers, but had the relaxed demeanour of someone in charge.

Guy nodded. "Thank you, Patrick."

Patrick waved an open palm toward the marble table and Enzo saw that it was now laden with food. There were a large breadbasket with four different kinds of bread to be broken by hand and eaten with the fingers, bowls of salad and pasta, and a large steaming dish of freshly cooked mussels in a cream and garlic sauce.

Elisabeth Fraysse bustled out of the office as Guy and Enzo took their seats, and she sat opposite them while Patrick placed clean plates in front of each.

"Did you get that bottle I asked for?" Guy asked him.

Patrick made a small bow, for all the world like a well-practised butler, or an old family retainer. "I did, Monsieur Fraysse. I've had it breathing for you."

Guy grinned at Enzo. "A little something to celebrate your arrival."

As they loaded their plates with salad and pasta, and large scoops of shiny, gaping mussel shells revealing succulent orange *moules*, Patrick brought a bottle to the table and held it with the label toward Guy, bringing a smile to his employer's face.

"Perfect." He turned to Enzo as Patrick poured him a mouthful to taste. "A 1993 DRC Grand Cru, La Tâche. Domaine de la Romanée Conti. Most people believe you should only drink white with fish and *fruits de mer*, but a good *pinot noir* will go with most seafood and is particularly good with *moules*." He put his nose in the wine glass, breathed in, swirled it, breathed in again, then took a small sip to wash around his mouth. "Oh." His eyes almost closed in ecstasy. "This is going to be so very good."

Patrick filled Enzo's glass, then Guy's, but Enzo noticed that Madame Fraysse was drinking only sparkling mineral water. Guy raised his glass to touch Enzo's, and they sipped at the pale liquid red. Its wonderful spicy light fruit filled Enzo's mouth, and he caught Guy watching him for his reaction. "I hope," Enzo said, "that watching me drink this doesn't induce you to die a little."

Guy laughed. "Never, when a bottle is shared with a friend. What do you think?"

"I think it's an extraordinary wine, Guy."

"What do you taste?"

It was, it seemed to Enzo, almost like a test. What did he *really* know about wines. He took another sip to roll around his mouth and said, "It's light, elegant. But still rich. Full of plum, berry, and a touch of vanilla. Aged long enough, I guess, for most of the tannins to have turned to fruit."

Guy grinned infectiously. "Spot on. You know your wines, Enzo. Not bad for a Scotsman."

"Maybe we'll try a whisky tasting some day, and we'll see how *you* get on?"

Guy threw his head back and roared with laughter. "And I'll bet there's a thing or two about drinking whisky that you could teach me."

Enzo smiled. "You would win that bet."

He turned to the *moules*, breaking off a piece of bread to dip in their creamy juices, then extracting the first of them with his fork and popping it into his mouth. It was so soft and tender and full of flavour that it seemed to simply melt on his tongue. He used its empty shell as pincers to pick the others from their shells, savouring each one in turn, and cleansing his palate from time to time with some wine and the mildly dressed salad on his plate.

He looked up to find Elisabeth Fraysse watching him. Her smile was a little embarrassed, as if she had been caught spying on him. "I see you enjoy your food, Monsieur Macleod."

Enzo grinned. "I do." He patted his middle. "A little too much sometimes." He mopped up more juices with another piece of bread. "What sort of waiting time is there for reservations at Chez Fraysse?"

"It's about six months these days," Madame Fraysse said. Enzo's hand froze midway to his mouth, juices dripping from his mussel shell.

"You're kidding? How can anyone know what they will be doing or where they will be in six months' time."

Guy said, "People who reserve with us know exactly where they'll be and what they'll be doing. They'll be eating here."

Enzo nodded thoughtfully. "You spoke earlier about trainees being with you for a 'season'. What length is a season?"

"April to November," Madame Fraysse said. "When Marc was alive he insisted we stay open all year round. But it was hopeless in the winter. When the weather was reasonable we could still only half-fill one of the dining rooms, even with three stars. When the weather was unreasonable, we would have cancellations. We get a lot of snow here in the winter months."

Guy said, "After Marc died we took the decision to close from the end of October to the beginning of April. And we still make more money than most other restaurants do in a whole year."

"We're closing for the winter at the end of next week," Madame Fraysse said, almost pointedly. As if warning him that his time there would be limited.

Enzo found himself momentarily distracted as he met the eye of an attractive young woman working behind the nearest stainless steel counter, where she was squeezing swirls of cream from a dispenser on to the tops of hollowed-out round courgettes filled with a steaming savoury stuffing. She had beautiful brown eyes and long blond hair piled up beneath her tall chef's hat, accentuating fine cheekbones and the elegant line of a delicate jaw. The hint of a smile played around full lips, and Enzo felt his heart leap. Then her eyes dipped again to the courgettes.

"Shutting down in the winter also means that we stay true to the philosophy of Marc's cuisine," Elisabeth Fraysse was saying. "Perhaps even more than he did himself. Because, you see, out of season it was impossible to acquire the fresh herbs and vegetables that he insisted on using. Of course, he had evolved winter menus, but they were never quite the same."

Guy said, "He only ever wanted the freshest of vegetables, prepared in the simplest of ways, so that they retained the essence of their true flavours. Which, of course, he enhanced with the herbs and wild flowers that only grow in these parts. The vegetable sauces and reductions and *purées* with which he decorated his plates were not just for presentation. They brought unique flavours to the plate to complement the meat or the fish. Of course, he was inspired by others, like Michel Guérard and the brilliant Michel Bras down in the Aveyron, but his *cuisine* was very much his own, developed from that wonderful palate of his."

"And the herbs and flowers from his *potager*," Marc's widow added. "We've developed and expanded the kitchen garden that Marc started all those years ago. He would have loved what we've made of it. We have a gardener who looks after it full time now."

"But, of course," Guy said, "most of what it produces is not available in the winter. Which is one reason we never opened a restaurant in Paris. It would have required too great a compromise to the *style Fraysse*."

Following a selection of local cheeses, washed down with the last of the DRC, desserts freshly prepared by the chefs of the *patisserie* arrived at the table. Wisps of steam rose from a cylinder of *fondant chocolat* placed in front of Enzo. A *boule* of creamy home-made vanilla ice cream sent rivers of molten heaven down its sides to marble the hot chocolate that oozed from its interior as Enzo broke into it with his spoon.

As he savoured its understated sweetness, he once more caught the eye of the blond girl behind the stainless steel. This time she was plating up perfect moulds of steamed *chou fleur* on pools of a syrupy mushroom and herb reduction. The evening service was in full flow, and Enzo was struck by how smoothly it was all going, each of the chefs contributing his or her own part to the well-practised choreography. Servers drifted in and out, food wafting past on steaming plates on their way to the dining room. Requests for service, or orders called, were delivered with impeccable politeness.

Trois foies gras, s'il vous plaît, greeted by a chorus of *oui*'s.

Service, s'il vous plaît, answered by the unhurried arrival of a black-shirted server. Nobody seemed rushed, or stressed. It was not like any kitchen Enzo had ever been in.

The girl was still smiling at him, and Enzo stole a glance at Guy and Elisabeth Fraysse to be certain they hadn't noticed. He reached into his satchel and took out a small notebook, and began scribbling in it, as if he were taking notes. He smiled at Madame Fraysse. "There's a lot to take in on my first day. I don't want to forget anything." On the facing blank page he wrote in large numerals the number 23. And as he slipped the notebook back into his bag, he tore out the page, covering the sound of it with a theatrical cough. "Excuse me." He put his hand to his mouth and crumpled up the page in his fist so that it was well hidden. Then he secreted it into his pocket.

He sipped his coffee, barely listening to the conversation at the table, which was desultory now, the subject of Marc Fraysse exhausted for the moment. He made eye contact with the girl several more times before refusing Guy's offer of an *eau de vie*, and rising stiffly to his feet.

"It's been a long day," he said. "And I had an early start this morning. I think I'll head for bed now, if you don't mind. Thank you so much for a wonderful meal."

Guy and Elisabeth rose, too. "It was nothing very special," Guy said. "Except for the wine, of course." He shook Enzo's hand. "See you in the morning."

Elisabeth offered him a cool handshake. "Goodnight, Monsieur Macleod. Why don't you join me for breakfast in the dining room tomorrow?"

Enzo was slightly surprised. "I would like that very much." He nodded. "Goodnight." And as he passed the stainless steel counter where the blond girl was still working, he dropped the scrumpled up page from his pocket on to the floor, catching her eye one last time to direct her toward his note. As the sliding glass doors opened to usher him out of the kitchen, he glanced back to see her stoop quickly to recover it and slip it into a hidden pocket somewhere beneath her apron.

Chapter Five

Enzo stepped from the shower, drying himself with a big, soft, warm towel before slipping into his robe and rubbing his hair with a hand-towel. He ran his hands through it then, sweeping the thick strands of it back from his brow to fall in ropes across his shoulders.

He looked at himself in the mirror as he brushed his teeth, lips pulled back to reveal a row of fine, white upper front teeth, the buzz of his electric toothbrush filling the bathroom. He had been blessed with strong teeth that had required little dental care over the years. But the years had been less kind in other ways. He could see the crows' feet gaining definition as they fanned out from the corners of his eyes, the deepening crease down the right side of his forehead and upper cheek where he slept on it. Some mornings before movement brought blood back to his face, it looked almost like a scar.

He could see the faintest discoloration now in the whites of his eyes, but he had long stopped being aware of the contrasting colors of his irises, the genetic inheritance of Waardenburg Syndrome. His jawline was holding up well, but there was a certain lack of definition now about his neck, and if he failed to shave for a few days he could see that his bristles were starting to silver, like the hair on his head. One day, he guessed, his distinctive white stripe would be lost forever.

He rinsed his mouth and padded bare-foot back through to the living room. A comfortable three-piece suite was arranged around a widescreen LCD TV, and the late evening news was playing on FR3. Thick-piled carpet led through an open arched doorway to the bedroom where the covers on his king-size bed had been turned down by the maid sometime earlier in the evening.

A soft knock at the door startled him, although he had been expecting it for some time. His heart beat a little faster as he crossed to the door and opened it a fraction. Out in the darkened hallway, he saw the pale, nervous face of the blonde. She glanced anxiously back along the hall before he opened the door wide to let her in.

She hurried into the room, bringing with her cold air from somewhere outside. As he closed the door behind her, she flung her arms around his neck and reached up to kiss him. He kissed her forehead and took her face in his hands, turning it up toward him to look at her. "What on earth have you done to your hair?"

She pulled away. "Oh, papa! It's obvious, isn't it? If I hadn't dyed it, they'd have seen my white streak, and they would have known I was your daughter the moment you arrived." It was the one symptom of Waardenburg that he had passed on to her.

He took her hand and led her to the settee. "Come and sit down, Sophie, and tell me all about it. Do you want a drink?"

She flopped into the soft embrace of the settee's upholstery. "Oh, God, yes! I could murder something with alcohol in it. I've hardly had a drink since I've been here! Four weeks, and it feels like four months. Peeling bloody vegetables and washing floors. This is the last time I ever go undercover for you."

Enzo smiled as he opened the refrigerator and took out a bottle of chilled Chablis. "It'll do you good. You'll find out what real work's all about."

Sophie glanced around the suite. "I see *you're* really slumming it." She watched him uncork the bottle and fill a single glass. "Are you not having one?"

"Just brushed my teeth."

She pulled a face. "Yeh, toothpaste and Chablis. Doesn't really go, does it?" She took the glass from him and he dropped into the armchair opposite.

"So tell me."

She shrugged and sipped her wine. "Not much to tell, really. That letter of introduction you got from your friend at the catering school in Souillac really did the trick. They took me on for the full five weeks, no questions asked. But there's nothing to do here, papa! You spend most of the time working, and the rest of the time cooped up in a tiny room in the staff annexe watching a crappy TV set that looks like its broadcasting a snowstorm. And the food? You'd think because you're working in a three-star kitchen you'd eat well. But all our meals are cooked by one of the *stagiaires*. Pretty bloody awful. We all have to take turns. Even me. So you can imagine!"

Enzo could, only too well. He wrinkled his nose.

But Sophie wasn't finished. "And the social life is *zero*!"

"You aren't here to socialise. You're here to be my eyes and ears behind the scenes, to pick up the kind of things no one's ever going to tell me."

"I didn't know it was going to be like this, though. I thought it would be fun. Roll on next week!" She took a lengthy draught from her glass.

"That's Chablis, Sophie. You don't drink it like lemonade."

"You do if you haven't had a decent drink for a month."

Enzo sighed. Sophie was almost twenty-four now, but it was hard to believe sometimes that she wasn't still sixteen. "Have you learned anything at all?"

She pursed her lips in a secret little smile and tilted her head to one side. "Maybe."

"Sophie!" Enzo was losing patience.

Sophie tucked her legs up under her and leaned on the arm of the settee. "Well… a lot of gossip, I guess. Folk just love to blether."

Enzo couldn't resist a smile. From the time she had started to talk he had spoken only English to her. He knew that she would be steeped in French language and culture as she grew up, but he had wanted her to absorb at least a little of her cultural heritage. And, of course, the English she had learned was *his* English, peppered with Scottish words, and flavoured with a gentle Scottish accent, like the warm scent of whisky on a summer's evening. "And what have they been *blethering* about?"

"Oh, this and that." It was clear she had something to tell him. Something she was pleased with. But she wasn't about to blurt it straight out. "And the *sous chef's* taken a fancy to me."

"Oh, has he?" This was not what Enzo wanted to hear. "Well, I hope you're not encouraging him."

She cocked an eyebrow. "Philippe's a good looking guy."

"What about Bertrand?"

"What about him?"

"You're not cheating on him, are you?"

A petulant little pout pursed her lips. "I'm not here to take lectures from you on cheating." She saw immediately how she had hurt him, carelessly, thoughtlessly. And she immediately relented. "I'm sorry, papa. I didn't mean that like it sounded."

Enzo nodded, but said nothing.

"Anyway, I'm not cheating on anyone. It's just nice to be getting a bit of attention, that's all." She sipped on her wine again. "Everyone who was here when Marc Fraysse was still alive really loved him. I mean, no one's got a bad word to say about him. Apparently he was endlessly patient with the *stagiaires*. Unlike his successor."

"You don't like Georges Crozes?"

She shrugged. "He's okay, I suppose. Bit of a cold fish. But he's good, you know? Everyone respects his talent. It seems like Marc really thought the world of him. But he's got a temper on him. He can lose it sometimes. And you don't want to be around him when he does."

"What about Marc himself? Any stories, anecdotes, observations?"

Sophie smiled. "He had a bit of a passion for the horses, apparently."

Enzo frowned. "You mean he went horse riding?"

Sophie laughed. "No, papa! Don't be silly! I mean he liked betting on them. It seems he drove into Thiers most mornings to the PMU to place a few bets on that day's *courses*."

Enzo nodded thoughtfully. "And Guy? What's he like?"

"He's a lovely man, papa. Treats everyone like a member of the family."

"What about him and Elisabeth? Is there anything between them, do you think?"

Sophie raised her eyebrows in surprise. "Romantically, you mean?"

"Or sexually."

She shook her head. "I don't think so. If there is, they keep it incredibly well hidden. They are more like brother and sister. Except that she's a lot more aloof. Treats the staff like the staff. Likes to be called *patronne*, or Madame Fraysse. Guy is happy for everyone to call him Guy. Which everyone does. Except for Patrick, of course. He's been with the family for years. Ve-ery old fashioned. But nice." She took another sip from her glass. "Apparently Marc had everyone just call him Marc, even the *stagiaires*. Which is unheard of. The chef is *always* called *chef*."

"And Georges?"

"Oh, he's *chef*. No doubt about that. You wouldn't last long if you called him *Georges*."

Enzo regarded his daughter thoughtfully as she drained her glass. "So what is it you haven't told me yet?"

Sophie pouted. "Oh, papa, you're no fun. How did you know?"

Enzo laughed. "Sophie, you're like an open book."

She frowned. "If I was, I wouldn't have been able to work undercover here for four weeks without anyone knowing."

Enzo smiled indulgently. "No, you're right. I'm sorry." He gazed at her fondly. So much of her mother in her. The mother he had only really got to know vicariously in the bringing up of her daughter. "So what is your little secret?"

"A pretty open secret really." But she grinned conspiratorially, leaning forward slightly, as if they might be overheard. "Georges' wife, Anne, works as a receptionist at the hotel. You probably met her when you checked in."

Enzo recalled the slim, handsome woman behind the reception desk. A woman in her forties, he would have guessed.

Auburn hair drawn severely back from a pale face, strong features enhanced by the merest touch of make-up. Her smile had been warm enough. But he remembered, too, the momentary shadow which had dulled it when she realized who he was. "Anne." He repeated her name, as if trying it out for size. But, in truth, it was the technique he employed for defeating his poor memory for names. Once repeated, forever remembered.

"Everyone who was here at the time reckons Anne Crozes and Marc Fraysse were having an affair." Sophie sat back in the settee, pleased with herself. "Which, if you were looking for motive, would provide plenty for either Georges or Elisabeth."

Sophie stayed another half hour, drinking more of his wine, regaling him with tales of her four weeks in the kitchen, demanding news of Cahors, wanting to know if he had seen Bertrand. But his mind was only half with her. If it were true that Anne Crozes and Marc Fraysse had been having an affair, then it would be reasonable to assume that if everyone else knew about it, then both Elisabeth and Georges must have suspected it, too. But while motive was significant, Enzo was always careful not to attach too much importance to it. Real, hard, forensic evidence was much more compelling, and often led in a direction that belied motive. Moreover, it was equally true that while everyone around you knew that your spouse was cheating, you were very often the last person to know it yourself. And, even then, the last one to admit it. Lending veracity to the old adage that there are none so blind as those who will not see. Still, it was food for thought.

Sophie was suddenly on her feet. "I'd better go."

Enzo followed her to the door, where she stopped, turning to look at him earnestly. "Have you seen Charlotte?"

"Out of bounds, Sophie."

"Oh, papa…"

"Goodnight." He opened the door and pushed her gently out into the darkness of the hallway. She hesitated a moment before turning back to kiss him lightly on the cheek. "You can't just accept it. You've got rights. And he's my blood, too."

But she was away before he could respond, and he saw her hurrying off along the carpeted passageway to be absorbed by the dark, his mind a complex confusion of thoughts he had successfully been keeping at bay. Until now.

As he turned to go back into his room, the merest hint of a movement at the opposite end of the hall flickered in his peripheral vision. He stood stock still, heart thumping, and peered into the darkness, eyes growing accustomed to the lack of light as he did. But there was nothing. No movement. No sound. After several long moments, he began to doubt that he had seen anything at all. He returned to his room and shut the door firmly behind him.

Chapter Six

Sunlight flitted about the vast landscape spread below them as clouds scudded across a sky torn and broken by a cold northwest wind. The rain and low-hanging cloud of the day before was gone, and from their table in the south conservatory dining room, the view was breathtaking, as if seen from some hidden vantage point in the sky itself.

"Saint-Pierre," Elisabeth said, "is the closest you can get to heaven without passing through the gates." She smiled. "So they say."

"It's aptly named, then," Enzo said. "If this is, indeed, where St. Peter resides, then we must be at the very gates themselves."

Elisabeth tilted her head and broke off a piece of *croissant* with long, elegant fingers. "Marc would certainly have had you believe that. He loved this place, you know. He had our bedroom fashioned from the room which had once been his parents'. He was born in that room. And his children were conceived there, too." The brightness in her eyes clouded a little. "He might well have died there, had he lived." And then her face broke into an unexpected smile. "If that doesn't sound a little too... Irish, you would say, yes?"

Enzo grinned. "Yes." He dipped his *croissant* into his *grande crème* and had raised it halfway, dripping, to his mouth, before realising that Elisabeth was watching him. Perhaps, he thought, his predilection for dipping *croissants* in his coffee was not quite *de rigueur* in a three-star restaurant. But it was too late now, and his momentary pause had allowed the coffee to soften the soaked segment of *croissant* to the point where it broke off and fell back into his coffee cup, splashing and staining the pristine white linen around it.

He felt his face reddening. "Excuse me." He dabbed at the tablecloth with his napkin.

He wondered if her smile was just a little patronising. "Don't worry, Monsieur Macleod, Marc would have approved. He loved to *tremper* his *croissants*." It almost seemed like a way of affirming her husband's humble origins while placing herself on a slightly higher plane.

A young female server approached the table with a replenished *pichet* of freshly squeezed orange juice. She hovered it over Elisabeth's glass. "Madame Fraysse?" But *la patronne* simply dismissed her with a wave of the hand, and the server immediately shrank away to present herself at Enzo's side of the table. "Monsieur?"

Enzo gave her a friendly smile. "No thank you."

The girl bowed and moved discreetly away. Enzo glanced at Elisabeth, but the widow was now gazing from the window at the view below, lost in some distant thought.

He said, "In everything I have read about your husband, the speculation about Michelin being poised to remove one of his stars is ever-present. Did Marc really believe that was about to happen?"

She turned a weary expression toward him. It was a subject which had almost certainly worn thin. "I don't know that he believed it. But he was certainly afraid of it." She sipped at her steaming herbal *tisane*. "It is the nightmare of every three-star chef. The achieving of each star is a long hard road of blood, sweat, and frustration, Monsieur. Of terrible uncertainty in an uncertain world. Each star won is a cause for celebration. When you have one you want two. When you have two, you want three. But when you have three, there is nowhere to go but down. It was Marc's constant dread that he would lose a star. It drove everything he did, almost to the point of obsession."

"But where did the speculation come from? Michelin?"

"Oh, no. Michelin would never be so indiscreet. It originated entirely in the media."

"Something must have given rise to it."

She sighed. "It was all sparked, seemingly, by a single, malicious article published by one particular Parisian food critic. A freelance critic, Monsieur Macleod, who writes for several of the more distinguished Paris publications, but also has his own online blog. An unpleasant man."

"You knew him personally?"

"I didn't, no. But Marc did. He and a few other Michelin-starred chefs were frequently criticised in his columns. He was, and still is, a fierce critic of the Michelin system, and likes to think that he alone should be the judge of good taste in French cuisine." She paused, some dark thought passing like a shadow across her face, reflecting the shifting patterns of light and shade in the landscape beyond. "There was an enmity between him and Marc which dated back to the time when he was awarded his third star."

Enzo frowned. "You told me yesterday, Madame Fraysse, that your husband did not have an enemy in the world."

Her smile was rueful. "With the sole exception, perhaps, of Jean-Louis Graulet. But Graulet didn't murder Marc, Monsieur Macleod. He was in Paris the day that Marc died."

Enzo finished dipping the remains of his *croissant* in his coffee and poured himself a fresh cup from the fine Limoges china jug on the table. He sipped on it thoughtfully. "Did Marc have a biographer?"

"No, he didn't. But he talked several times about writing a memoir. An autobiography."

"A lot of people in his position would hire a professional to ghost write something like that for him."

"Oh, not Marc. He would have wanted to do it himself."

"And did he?"

"Not that I know of. I went through all his papers and his computer disks at the time, but there was nothing." She paused. "Strange, though."

"What is?"

"He had trouble sleeping in the last months. I used to wake at maybe two or three in the morning to find his side of the bed empty and cold. Then I would find him in his *petit bureau*, huddled over the computer on his desk, tapping away. He was always strangely evasive when I asked him about it. I always had the impression that he was, in fact, writing his memoir and for some reason didn't want to tell me. A surprise maybe. Which is why I searched for it after his death. But I guess I was wrong."

Enzo scratched his chin thoughtfully and realized he hadn't shaved that morning. "What do you think he *was* doing on his computer, then, in the small hours of the morning."

She shook her head. "I haven't the faintest idea, Monsieur Macleod."

Chapter Seven

Dominique's office was small, but unusually well-ordered. Crime prevention posters, calendars, newspaper cuttings, official documents, all were pinned in neat groupings to the yellowing cream-painted walls. Her desk was a paragon of good organisation: in-trays, out-trays, a spotless blotter, a computer screen angled against the wall, and a mouse with mat and keyboard placed side by side in perfect alignment. An empty coffee cup sat on a cardboard coaster. The polished surface of the desk itself was unmarred by unsightly rings or watermarks.

It was, in its own way, a reflection of Dominique herself. Small, but almost perfectly formed. Only now, in the confines of her office, did Enzo realize just how small she was. At least, in comparison to his six feet, two inches. Outdoors they had both been dwarfed by the landscape.

Her chestnut brown hair was pulled over in a side ponytail and pleated, before being drawn back across her head and pinned in place. It was executed with immaculate precision, allowing for the wearing of her hat when necessary. Enzo wondered why she would have gone to such trouble when there was no man in her life. That's what she'd told him, hadn't she? That she was single. Or had he misunderstood? He replayed their conversation on the hill from the previous day. No. She had told him she had never known a man who would spend the kind of money on her that would buy a meal at Chez Fraysse. But still, his original impression persisted, emphasised by the lack of a ring on her left hand, and he wondered if it was just his imagination that she had made an effort to present herself more attractively today.

Unlike yesterday, she wore a little make-up. A slight *rouge* coloring of her lips, and a smudge of blue on the lids of her brown eyes. That touch of color somehow lifted her face out of plainness. The collar of her pale blue blouse was immaculately pressed and turned out over the neck of her darker blue jersey with its white stripe and rank epaulettes. Her black holster seemed very large, resting on slim hips, and her pants were tucked into ankle-length boots. Her eyes were filled with their usual warmth, and her cheeks flushed a little as she rounded her desk to spread out a selection of photographs for him to look at.

"These are the casts we took of the footprints in the *buron*. You can see how much shallower the treads are on Marc Fraysse's running shoes. All the other prints seem to have been made by either hiking boots or gumboots."

She cross-referenced the photographs of the casts, with pictures of the prints left in the mud.

"These are Guy's prints. And Elisabeth Fraysse's." She traced their tracks with the tip of finger. "Madame Fraysse didn't venture far inside. These are Marc's prints. They are all over the place, and here's where they back up against the wall when he was shot. But there doesn't seem to have been a struggle."

Enzo looked at the two unidentified casts. "These are both smaller than either Guy's or Marc's. Did the Fraysse brothers have particularly large feet?"

"No, they were both average."

"So either or both of these unidentified sets could have been made by a woman."

"Or a man with smaller feet. Or a boy. A teenager, maybe. They are only one size smaller."

Enzo studied them in silence for a long time before Dominique reached for a stapled document of a dozen or more pages.

"The autopsy report," she said. "You can keep that if you like. I made a copy for you."

Enzo glanced up to find her big brown eyes examining him closely, and for a moment his stomach flipped over. It was extraordinary how a mutual attraction could be conveyed without a single word. Of course, it was always possible to misread the signals. He smiled. "I really appreciate that, Dominique. Thank you." He riffled through the pages until he came to the pathologist's description of the wound.

Dominique pressed close against him so that she could read as he did. And he felt the distant pangs of arousal that her proximity excited. He forced himself to focus.

The wound is centered 6.5 centimetres from the top of the head, and on the midline is an 8 millimetre round defect surrounded by a 3 millimeter-wide collar of abrasion. Surrounding the wound is sparse stippling in a 5 centimetre by 4 centimetre distribution.

"What causes the stippling?" Dominique glanced up at him.

"Bits of gunpowder hitting the skin and causing abrasions. The closer the gun the more dense the stippling. Any more than about two feet, or sixty centimetres, away and there wouldn't be any."

"So this was close."

"Probably about thirty centimetres." Enzo turned then to the description of the exit wound.

The exit wound was centered 7 centimetres from the top of the head, 1 centimetre to the right of the midline, and measured 1.5 centimetres with no evidence of abrasion, soot, or stippling. As this was a perforating wound, no projectile was recovered from the body. The projectile entered the head through the location described, caused an inward-beveled and comminuted defect of the frontal bone, passed through the left cerebral hemisphere, causing a wide hemorrhagic and disrupted path surrounded by contusion, and exited the occipital bone through an outward-beveled bony defect in the location described. The direction of the projectile was backward, slightly downward, slightly rightward.

"Hmmm." Enzo re-read it thoughtfully.

"What?"

"The path of the bullet. Someone shooting you would generally raise the gun, at arm's length, to eye-level. Theirs. For the bullet to have taken a slightly downward path would suggest somebody taller than the victim."

"Or someone standing on higher ground."

"As I recall, the interior of the *buron* was pretty flat."

She nodded. "Yes, it is."

"Sadly, however, there is nothing very conclusive in the trajectory, Dominique. Marc Fraysse might have cowered as he raised his hands to protect himself, so that his killer was shooting slightly downwards."

He turned back a page, to the preliminary description of the body as a whole.

Dominique peered at the report. "What are you looking for now?"

"To see what the pathologist says about the hands." Almost as he said it, he found the relevant passage.

"Blood blowback on the backs of the hands and fingers," Dominique said. She was still intimately acquainted with the details of the case. "Blood spatter blowing back from the entry wound was identified on the backs of his hands and fingers, as if he had his hands facing the shooter, raised to shield himself."

Enzo read through the pathologist's description for himself. "You said the pathologist still has the pics?"

"Yes."

"Would there be any chance of acquiring them? Just for a quick look."

"Sure. I'll ask."

He slipped the autopsy report into his satchel. "Did anyone look at his computer?"

"I believe someone from the *police scientifique* went through it. But it was never brought in for forensic examination."

"Why not?"

She shrugged. "I don't know. I guess no one thought it was relevant. Forensics is not my area of expertise, and the powers that be seemed to think that Fraysse was just the victim of a random crime. In the wrong place at the wrong time."

"You think he was murdered for his phone and his knife?"

"Personally, no. That never seemed to me like sufficient motive. But then some people don't seem to need a motive to kill." She laughed, a little self-consciously. "Not that I'm any great expert on that either. There aren't very many murders committed around here." She looked at him curiously. "What do *you* think?"

"I think the chances that it was a random killing are almost zero. No one would be waiting up that hill in the hope that someone might pass by with valuables to steal. Marc Fraysse took that route every day. Everyone knew that. So someone was waiting specifically for him. Whether they meant to kill him or not, that's another matter. But kill him, they did." He perched on the edge of Dominique's desk and found her a willing and attentive audience. "The fact is that eighty percent of murder victims know their killer. Of those, sixteen percent are related to their killers. And half have a romantic or social relationship with them. It's something you have to keep very much in mind when you're looking at a murder."

"I thought your specialty was forensic science. The evidence."

"It is. But in the absence of evidence you have to look for motive, then try and put the two together to nail your killer. In this case, because of lack of evidence, or any other evidence to the contrary, your superiors seem to have been very keen to write off a celebrity murder they couldn't solve by putting it down to a random killing. That kind of crime is almost impossible to resolve. It's a face-saver."

"So you think someone had a reason for wanting to kill him?"

"Or to threaten, or to harm him."

"Do you have some idea who that might be?"

Enzo smiled and shook his head. "No, I don't."

"So where will you begin?"

Enzo gazed thoughtfully from the window, across the square toward the balustraded view of the valley below. "In his computer."

Chapter Eight

He was not quite certain why he was reluctant to ask Elisabeth for permission to examine her late husband's computer. But lurking somewhere at the back of his mind was the fear that perhaps she might refuse him, in which case a valuable line of investigation would be permanently closed off. Why he thought it was even remotely possible that she might do that was unclear to him. But he didn't want to take the chance.

And so when he returned to the hotel he made sure that both Guy and Elisabeth were downstairs before he headed up, ostensibly, to his suite. Service staff were in all the rooms, making beds, cleaning bathrooms. Service carts stood about in the hallways, the sound of vacuum cleaners coming from several open doors. He slipped past his own rooms, nodding to a middle-aged lady in green and white who was taking toilet rolls from her cart to re-stock one of the bathrooms, and when she went back into the room, he turned the handle on the door of Guy's study to slip quickly inside.

He closed the door behind him and stood, with his back against it, controlling his breathing for several moments. It occurred to him how ridiculous this was. Why hadn't he just asked her? Still, he was here now. He crossed quickly to the bureau and rolled up the top. The MacBook Pro sat where he had last seen it, and he lifted the lid to press its power button. Its start-up chorus chimed loudly and he tensed, waiting nervously for it to boot up. When, eventually, the desktop loaded on to the screen, he sat down to look at it and take stock.

The first thing he checked was the Airport connection and was pleased to see that the computer was still connected wirelessly to the hotel's wifi system. So he was online.

From the dock along the foot of the screen he selected the mailer and clicked on it to load. The in-box was, as he expected, empty. He checked for *Sent* mail. Also empty. Then scrolled down a long list of folders in the left-hand window. A complete archive of all Marc Fraysse's emails, sent and received. There was an odd sense of prurience in going through a dead man's private correspondence, but Enzo had no time to dwell on it. He scanned the titles of the folders. Many of them were simply people's names. Jacques, Paul, Michel, Pierre. Others catalogued bills and invoices, correspondence with *amazon.fr*, exchanges between Fraysse and his website designer. There were folders filled with the emails that had passed back and forth between the chef and his various suppliers. Then one titled, *RECIPES*, which brought Enzo's scrolling cursor to a halt. Had a three-star Michelin chef really exchanged emails with others about recipes? He clicked to open it. Apparently he had. They were sub-divided into folders: *Boeuf, Agneau, Lapin, Cheval, Porc…* Enzo's cursor hesitated and hovered over the folder titled *Cheval*. It seemed inconceivable, somehow, that horsemeat would ever be served up to customers in a three-star restaurant. He opened the folder. Information across the top of the mailer told him that it contained nearly 600 messages. They had all been sent to a single address: ransou.jean@wanadoo.fr. None had been received in reply. Enzo double-clicked to open one, and was puzzled to be greeted by a series of apparently random letters and numbers:

PV: 18/12: 3e: 14: 150; 7e: 4: 130; 9e: 5,9,10: 200
D: 1re: 3,7,15: 125; 4e: 13: 175; 12e: 2,5,12: 150
L: 6e: 11: 200; 8e: 10: 125; 9e: 1,7,8: 150

There was no name and no signature. Enzo gazed at it uncomprehendingly, then checked the date that the email had been sent. 18th December, 2002. So the 18/12 was the date.

He checked the time at which the email was sent. 2:14am. He opened the next mail down. More of the same.

MB: 19/12: 2e: 9: 175; 5e: 3,6,9: 150; 6e: 16: 200...

This one sent on December 19th at 2:53am. Enzo frowned. These were not recipes for horsemeat. He opened several in quick succession, all filled with the same mysterious code. He had no idea what the letters indicated. *PV, D, L, MB*, but another thought was beginning to coagulate in the stream of information uploading to his brain.

Quickly he checked to make sure that the computer was still connected to the printer. It was. He turned the printer on, and winced at the noise it made during start-up, praying that it was still in use and that the ink had not dried up completely. He selected two of the *Cheval* emails at random and chose *Print*. The old ink-jet printer whirred and clattered and churned out two print-outs, faded but legible. He folded them together and slipped them into his jacket pocket, then returned to the computer.

He felt as if he had been in the dead man's study for an inordinately long time now, although in reality it had been no more than a few minutes. He pressed on. Scrolling rapidly through the Finder desktop, he clicked on the *Home* folder, which was named *frayssemarc*. Near the top of a column of folders was one named *Documents*. He opened it. It was filled with sub-folders whose headings seemed to indicate lists of recipes and ingredients. Opening up just a few of them confirmed Enzo's suspicions. So this, it seemed, was where Marc Fraysse had actually kept his culinary secrets. He stopped scrolling on one, mid-list. It was titled, simply, *Moi*. Me. He opened it. Inside was a single document called *moi.dssr*. Enzo had no idea what that was. He double-clicked it, and saw a piece of software called *Dossier* opening up on the dock. The document *moi.dssr* then appeared on the screen as a blank pane containing one large window, and one narrow one down the left-hand side, which was headed *Title*, and *0 entries*. A slide-out pane to the left of that contained one single icon called *Unfiled Entries*. Enzo felt a wave of disappointment. It seemed that the document was empty.

Instinctively he moved his cursor to click on *Unfiled Entries*, and suddenly a document entitled *Moi* appeared in the narrow window, and an icon of a padlock in the large one next to it. Locked. Enzo's eye flickered up to the top of the document and a toolbar, where he spotted the same padlock icon. He clicked on it, and a window dropped down asking for a password. Enzo took a deep, tremulous breath, and glanced at his watch. He must have been in here ten minutes now. There was no knowing where in the hotel either Guy or Elisabeth might be, and God knew how long it might take to crack Fraysse's password.

He drew his mouse across the blotter, and his cursor swooped down to the dock where he selected and opened the Safari web browser. When its window filled the screen with Marc Fraysse's homepage, he selected Google from the toolbar and typed into search: *most common computer passwords.*

Within seconds, more than thirty-three million links to sites on the subject appeared on his screen. He selected the top one, which took him to a magazine article which listed the ten most commonly used passwords. He raised his eyebrows in surprise. Were people really so stupid? The number one password was *password*. Then came *123456*, followed by *qwerty*, which on a French keyboard would be *azerty*. More in hope than expectation, Enzo began trying them out, one by one. Some seemed surprising, like *monkey* or *blink182*, or idiotic, like *abc123* or *letmein,* but none of them worked. He was not surprised.

He closed his eyes, his mind turning over furiously. Some people, he knew, used the names of their children, but he had no idea what Marc and Elisabeth's children were called. He tried *Elisabeth*, without success. Then Marc's first and second names separately, followed by his date of birth. Nothing. He sighed and sat back in frustration, and found his eyes wandering over the doodles on Fraysse's blotter. They came to rest on the quotation from Sartre: *la nature parle et l'expérience traduit.* As with the letters, JR, Fraysse had gone over again and again the initial letters of each word in the quotation, so that they stood out quite markedly. He didn't believe for one moment that Fraysse had done it consciously, but rather sub-consciously, perhaps while speaking on the telephone. But together, those initial letters produced the acronym *Inpelt*. It was a seriously long shot, but Enzo turned back to the keyboard and typed the letters into the password window and hit the return key. The large empty window to the right immediately filled with text, and the scrollbar revealed that there was a lot of it.

But Enzo had no time to scan even a few sentences. He heard the door opening into the bedroom next door from the living room beyond, and his heart pushed pulsing up into his throat. Someone was in the bedroom. Perhaps just the maid. But it was equally possible that it could be Elisabeth. What to do?

As quickly as he could he re-typed the password, which he had to do twice before it would lock the document. Then he shut it down. He fumbled in his jacket pocket for the memory stick he always carried with him and plugged it into the USB socket. When its icon appeared, he dragged and dropped the document on to it, and it began to copy. Infuriatingly slowly. He could hear the unknown person moving about in the next room. "Come on, come on!" he muttered under his breath, through clenched teeth. He stopped breathing as the progress bar moved painfully, protractedly, from left to right, before finally the transfer was complete and he sucked air back into his lungs. He ejected the icon and pulled the memory stick from its socket, stuffing it into his pocket and rising to his feet as the door from the bedroom swung open.

He turned, hoping to see the maid. But it was Elisabeth who stood there, her right palm placed flat against her chest. She seemed startled, even shocked, to find him there. "Monsieur Macleod!"

Enzo did his best to seem relaxed. "Just taking a look at your husband's computer, Madame Fraysse. I didn't think you'd mind."

"You startled me. The staff never come in here. So when I heard movement I thought perhaps we had an intruder."

Enzo grinned self-consciously. "Just me."

"It is customary, Monsieur Macleod, in polite society, to ask permission to view private belongings. Even those of a deceased person."

There was no mistaking the controlled anger in her voice.

"My apologies, madame. Since you had shown me in here yesterday, I didn't feel I was intruding on privacy. And I didn't want to disturb you."

"Well, you have. I have nothing to hide from you, Monsieur Macleod, and am happy to show you whatever you want to see. But, I *would* like to be asked."

Enzo nodded contritely. "I appreciate that, madame. My apologies again, if I upset or startled you." He glanced at the computer. "Shall I close it down?"

"No, that's alright."

They stood for a moment in awkward silence. Then Enzo forced a smile. "Well. I'll leave you in peace, then." He turned toward the door.

"Monsieur Macleod?"

He stopped, and turned, the door half open. "Yes?"

"Did you find anything?"

He frowned.

"On the computer?"

"Oh. No. Nothing of any significance." But he knew that the moment he was gone she could track exactly where he had been by checking the *Recent Items* menu. He wondered why it was that he didn't want to ask her about the emails, or tell her about the locked document. But instinct and experience told him that information shared could be information compromised. "I'll see you later."

And as he stepped out into the hallway, pulling the door shut behind him, he exhaled a deep breath of relief.

Chapter Nine

Enzo's laptop sat open on the coffee table, while he squatted on the edge of the settee waiting for the *moi.dssr* file to transfer from his memory stick to his hard drive. Sophie was curled up beside him, one arm draped idly over his shoulder watching the slow progress of the transfer. It was after eleven, and she had sneaked straight up to his room after the evening service.

"Won't you be missed?" he had asked her.

"Nah. Everyone's too tired to bother about socialising at the end of the day. And the only one who's liable to notice I'm not in my room is Philippe."

"Who's Philippe?"

"The *sous-chef*. I told you!"

"Oh. The boy who's taken a shine to you?"

"Yes."

"So how will he know that you're not in your room?"

"Oh, papa, stop being so suspicious." She had drawn a deep breath of indignation. "He quite often comes in to listen to music and chat."

"And that's all?"

"That's *all*." She had sighed, then. "Anyway, I've been playing a bit hard to get lately, so he won't be surprised if I don't answer when he knocks on the door."

Finally the file finished transferring, and he double-clicked on it. A message appeared informing him that he did not possess any software that would open it.

Sophie squinted at the screen. "So what are you going to do?"

"See if I can track down the software and download it."

She disentangled herself and lifted the computer on to her lap. "What's it called? I'll find it for you."

"It's called *Dossier*."

"No problem."

He watched as she focused on the screen, eyes wide and fixed on the browser, tapping on the keyboard in search of the software. She was a beautiful young woman. Even tired, and washed out at the end of the day, and without a trace of make-up. She had inherited her mother's fine, strong features, and her father's dark hair and Waardenburg streak, though concealed now by the blond rinse. He remembered how, in those first weeks after her mother had died, and she was just a wet, pink, crusty bundle, he had felt such resentment toward her. As if somehow it had been Sophie's fault that her mother had died giving birth to her. He found it difficult now, to believe that he had harboured such feelings. Of course, they had passed. And he had come to see her as Pascale's gift to him, a little part of her that would live on in her daughter. And perhaps, too, in Sophie's children, if she ever had any.

"What?" Sophie's question startled him. Her eyes had never left the screen.

"What do you mean?"

"I can feel your eyes on me."

He smiled. She was so much a part of him. "I love you, Sophie."

Her eyes flickered up from the screen, and he saw them grow moist as she met his. "I love you, too, papa." And she reached out suddenly and touched his face. He felt her fingers track lightly over his bristles. "Do you ever see Kirsty these days?"

He felt himself tense. "Occasionally. When I'm in Paris."

"She's still with Roger?"

He nodded. "You don't keep in touch with her, then?"

She shrugged. "No point. Since we're not sisters any more."

The revelation that his daughter by his first marriage was not his daughter after all, but the fruit of a fleeting affair between his wife and his best friend, had come as a shattering blow to Enzo. Sophie had greeted it almost joyfully. Kirsty was no longer her half-sister. She didn't have to share her father with anyone anymore.

"I need your credit card."

"What?"

"Your credit card. To pay for the download."

"You've found it, then?"

"Would I need your card if I hadn't."

Her logic was impeccable. Annoyingly, he could hear himself in it. They were far, far, too alike. He reached for his satchel and took out his wallet, and held out his card.

"Just read it out to me."

"Where did you learn to be so damned bossy, girl?"

"You, papa. Read!"

He sighed and read out the details of his card while she tapped them into the computer.

She hit the return key with a flourish. "*Et voilà!*" She beamed at him. "Downloading now." It took several minutes to download, and then Sophie installed it before passing the laptop back to her father. She squeezed up close to him so she could peer at the screen as he opened up *moi.dssr*, and entered Marc Fraysse's password to unlock the document. "What is it?"

"Wait…" Enzo scanned the first few lines, then scrolled quickly through several thousand words of text, stopping occasionally, scrolling back, then forward again. "Elisabeth was right," he said finally. "Marc Fraysse *was* writing a memoir."

"You mean like an autobiography?"

"Sort of, I guess. Although, this really just looks like notes and anecdotes. As if he was gathering his thoughts before getting down to the real meat of it, so to speak."

Sophie grinned. "As a chef *would* do."

Enzo scrolled back up to the top of the document, to a date and a place where, for Marc Fraysse, it had all begun. And the voice of the young Marc spoke across the years to Enzo and Sophie, as clear as if he had been there in the room with them.

Chapter Ten

Clermont Ferrand, 1972

I had just turned seventeen, and wasn't doing so well at school. I never did get my *Bac*. The truth is, I didn't see the point. I was going to work in the kitchen at the auberge. Everyone knew it. Mama, papa, Guy. So why did I need to know about about algebra and geography? What possible reason was there for learning about history. It was past, gone. Only the future mattered. And right now, I knew what my future would be. It was to follow in the footsteps of my brother. Footsteps that would lead me straight to the kitchen of *les frères Blanc,* where papa hoped I was going to learn how to keep him in his old age.

I didn't want to go. Guy had been there a year, and I had heard enough of his stories to know that however much I had hated school, I was going to hate Jacques and Roger Blanc a whole lot more.

School had broken up in July, and I had spent the summer working at the *boulangerie* in Thiers, treading water till I would go to Clermont Ferrand in October. The prospect of dragging myself out of bed at three every morning all through that summer to work in the stifling, flour-filled heat of the bakery had infused me with dread. In the event, I loved it. I loved being up and working while the rest of humankind was asleep. It felt, somehow, as if I had inherited the whole world, and had it all to myself. The *boulanger* was a grumpy old bastard to most people.

When I say old, he just seemed old to me. He was probably just in his early forties. But he never had a harsh word for me. He could see I loved my work, I loved being there, and I worked damn hard for him.

I also adored the fact that when everyone else was working during the day, I was free as a bird. Free to climb the hills and wander the plateau. Free, it seemed, for the first time in my life. The apprenticeship in Clermont was the only cloud on my horizon. In the early summer it seemed a lifetime away. But as the weeks passed, it started to loom dark, and ever closer.

For the first time in my life I had money in my pocket. Money earned through the sweat of my own labour, even if I did give most of it to my folks to pay for my keep. Of course, I also helped mama in the kitchen for lunch and evening service, but I was in bed by eight. And I slept like I have never slept before or since.

It seems strange to me now when look back on that time. But the fact was, I didn't really want to be a chef. Long hours of mind-numbing work in the cramped and claustrophobic heat of a restaurant kitchen was something I already knew about. And it wasn't how I wanted to spend the rest of my days. But when you are seventeen, and without qualifications, or ambition, life stretches ahead like a prison sentence. And you do what you have to. You do what you know.

I didn't realize it then, of course, but the twin tyrants of Jacques and Roger Blanc, though I would grow to hate them, were the ones who would give me both the skill and the motivation to be what I am today.

I remember well the day I left home. It was late October. The weather had turned and the equinoctial gales had already stripped the trees of their leaves. Cloud was settled on the plateau and a fine wetting rain colored everything black. It all seemed to bear down on me, like a pressing weight, and reflected the color of my mood. Papa had bought me everything I would need for my sojourn in Clermont. Laid out on my bed were two white chef's blouses, two pairs of grey and white checkered pants, and two pairs of rubber clogs. And that was it. My uniform for the next three years, a uniform that would be stained by sweat and by cooking and by hauling coal, and washed and washed until it was almost threadbare.

I remember looking at those things, and the open suitcase on the bed beside them. I remember looking around the room where I had lived my whole life up until then. Walls that bore witness to the scars of my childhood, walls which had seen all my tears and joys, my growing pains, my first fumbled attempts at masturbation. And those walls bore witness to the last tears that I would ever shed within them.

I looked from the window, then, at the view I had always taken for granted, and knew that I really didn't want to go.

Papa drove me to Clermont Ferrand in his old *Quatre L*. I was seventeen years old and I had never been to the city. It was a wonder to me. All those buildings that towered over you, casting their gloom on the rain-sodden streets. The traffic and the trams, and all those people. I had never seen so many people. It gave me a perspective on my life that I had never had before, and made me feel small, and terribly insignificant. My world had been the *auberge*, my school, my parents, my brother. Suddenly it all seemed like nothing at all.

I remember passing the Michelin factory on the way into town. The huge, smokey, industrial complex churned out the tires that turned around the wheels of France. Of course, I had heard of the *Guide Michelin*, but I had no idea then how those two words, and the stars that went with them, would shape my life.

The Lion d'Or stood in a narrow street off the grand Place de Jaude. The theatre was nearby, and the cathedral and the synagogue, so it was well-placed. The building dated from the nineteenth century, five stories high, and for decades had provided meals and accommodation for the VRPs, the *voyageur représentant placiers*, or travelling salesmen, who motored the length and breadth of this vast country peddling their wares. But the brothers Blanc had changed all that, bringing back from their respective apprenticeships a mastery of French cuisine learned at the feet of the then undisputed practitioner of the art, Fernand Point, in his hotel-restaurant, La Pyramide, on the banks of the Rhone.

They had transformed their parents' establishment, winning first one star, then two, in the space of just five years. And much of the resultant profit had been poured back into the building to raise it to quite another level. Its clientele no longer consisted of the chattering VRPs in their threadbare suits, but business-men, successful *commerçants*, politicians, some of whom were now making the trip from Paris just to eat and be seen there.

For the first, and last time in my life, I entered through the front door of the Lion d'Or. Monsieur and Madame Blanc greeted my father like a long lost friend, one of their oldest and best loved clients from the fondly remembered and informal days of the workmen's lunches. Papa kissed me then, on both cheeks, handed me my suitcase, and left.

When he was gone I was taken into the kitchen and intro-duced to Jacques and Roger. They were big men, both. Tall, corpulent, and perfectly intimidating. Roger sported classic French moustaches which curled up over each cheek. Jacques had a big, florid, clean-shaven, round face that seemed set in a permanent scowl. Each in turn, crushed my hand in his, watched by a gallery of silent apprentices relishing the arrival of a new boy, on to whom they could offload the most unpleasant of their tasks. Among them was Guy, of course, and he could barely conceal his glee.

"Your brother can show you the ropes and take you to your room," Jacques said.

The "ropes", it turned out, consisted of responsibility for the great cast-iron coal-burning stove that fuelled the kitchen, heating the ovens, and bringing the grills and hotplates up to searing temperatures. That meant shovelling the coal from the cellar below the kitchen into buckets, and hauling it up to keep the stove well stoked. It also meant scraping out the ashes from the night before, setting and lighting the firebox so that the stove was up to temperature by the time the chefs arrived at eight-thirty, a task I had to perform twice a day, for lunch and dinner services.

I was also to be responsible, every other week, for cleaning out the black, oily deposits of soot left in the firebox beneath the rings on which the Blanc brothers conjured their culinary magic. And I would have nothing more than a wire brush to do it with. Guy had been doing it for the last year, and was only too delighted to be passing it on to me.

He showed me the garbage cans I would have to empty, and took enormous pleasure in telling me how I would have to scour clean, wash and dry, every counter top and stove surface in the kitchen every night. And God help me if Jacques or Roger found a speck of dirt on them the following day.

And here was me thinking I had been going to learn about cooking!

I was to share, it transpired, a room up in the attic with my brother. A small, dark, dank room up in the Gods, with a tiny window from which you could just see the twin spires of the cathedral of Notre Dame de l'Assomption. You might have thought that having my brother for company would have softened the experience. But Guy couldn't be bothered with his little brother. He was offhand, almost cruel. Thick with all the other apprentices. And I felt shut out and desperately alone.

That night, after showing me our room, he and the others went off to gather in one of the other bedrooms to play cards. I asked if I could join them. But Guy just laughed and said no one would have any time for a kid like me. They played for money, and I was far too young. He left me to sit on the edge of my bed, staring gloomily into the darkness outside. Rain was battering against the window, and the wind seemed to whistle through every crack and slate in the roof. I don't think I'd ever felt so alone.

I had wept on leaving home. And I wept again now. Tears of loneliness and misery. And I pulled back the ice-cold sheets of the unforgiving bed I would sleep on for the next three years, to cry myself dry, so that my brother wouldn't hear me sobbing when finally he came to bed. Which is when I realized that my mattress was soaking. Drenched in cold water poured from tumblers by mischievous hands. I cursed aloud. And I could hear the stifled giggles of apprentices in the corridor outside.

Chapter Eleven

"Oh my God, papa, that's so sad. That was rotten of Guy. You'd think he would have wanted to look after his little brother."

Enzo looked up thoughtfully from the laptop and slid it from his knees back on to the coffee table. "Children can be cruel," he said. "Sometimes when you're young, you succumb to that inner cruelty. You do and say things that you never would as an adult."

He felt her eyes upon him. "That sounds like the voice of experience speaking."

His smile was forced, and a little sad. "Oh, I empathised with Marc alright. But Guy wasn't so bad, really. Just a bit insensitive, and playing to the gallery of his fellow apprentices. I had a worse experience, I think."

"When?" He heard the surprise in her voice, and he regretted speaking.

"It doesn't matter. It was a long time ago."

She grinned. "Well, if you were just a kid, then it must have been."

He turned to look at her and raised a cautionary eyebrow. "Be careful, young lady."

"And you don't have a brother."

There was a momentary hiatus before Enzo turned away and lifted the computer back on to his knees. "Anyway, it's going to take me some time to go through all this stuff."

He felt Sophie tugging on his arm. "Papa?"

"Forget it, Sophie."

But she wasn't about to. She grabbed his head with both hands and turned it toward her. "Are you telling me you've got a brother?" It was incredulity now in her voice.

He could barely meet her eyes. He was such a bad liar. "I'm not telling you anything."

"Damn you, papa!" She forced him to look at her. "I can't believe that I'm twenty-four years old and only now finding out that I've got an uncle."

Enzo pulled his head away. "It's not like that. He's not really my brother. He never was."

She grabbed both his shoulders and almost shook him. He felt the strength of her indignation in the grip of her hands. "Jesus Christ, papa! I've a right to know."

He retaliated with anger. "No you don't! You've no rights in my life."

"Of course I do. If you have in mine, then I have in yours." She was breathing heavily. "Tell me, papa! Tell me!"

He gasped his frustration and pushed the computer back on to the table, standing up and moving away toward the window. He shoved his hands in his pockets. "I wish I'd kept my big mouth shut."

"Why?"

"Because it's painful, Sophie, that's why. Because sometimes you just pack things up into little boxes and file them away in the darkest corners of your mind so that when you go trawling your past you don't even see them."

There was a long silence, then she said in a quiet voice, "I want to know."

Enzo gazed at the floor, then out into the darkness beyond the glass. But he was aware of Sophie's reflection in it, still curled up sideways on the settee, watching him. "My father was married before he met my mother. He had a son, Jack. When his wife died he was left to bring him up on his own. A bit like me with you. Jack was five when dad married my mom, and seven when I was born. I haven't spoken to him in thirty years. Not since dad's funeral."

"Why?"

"It's a long story, Sophie, and I really don't know that I want to talk about it."

He heard the frustration in her breathing. "Tell me what he did, then, that was worse than Guy with Marc."

"Oh, there were lots of things."

"But you were thinking of one in particular, weren't you?"

He refocused on her reflection in the window. "Goddamn you, Sophie! You don't give up, do you?"

"No." Her tone was stubbornly defiant. "So tell me."

He turned away from the window to meet her eye for the first time, and he knew there was no point in avoiding it any longer. In a careless moment he had let the genie out of the bottle, and there was no way now of squeezing it back in. He could have kicked himself. For almost forty years he had kept such thoughts to himself. No one knew about Jack. Not his first wife, not Kirsty. Only Simon, his boyhood friend and confidante, knew about Jack's existence. But Simon had betrayed him, fathering the daughter he'd thought was his. And so Simon, too, had been packaged up and dispatched to the darkest recesses of his mind, to be lost amongst the morass of other unwanted memories.

It was odd how powerfully he had identified with Marc Fraysse. Leaving home, the safety of everything he had known, starting an apprenticeship in a strange place amongst strangers, where his greatest enemy was his own blood. The emotions were the same, although the circumstances quite different.

His thoughts carried him back to his childhood among the crumbling Victorian tenements of the east end of Glasgow, the industrial powerhouse of his native Scotland, a tiny country which had fought for so many centuries to maintain its independence against the military and cultural domination of the English. The memory of those shabby red sandstone buildings of his early years was still very vivid to him. The Macleods had not been a wealthy family, which is why they had lived in the east end of the city. The prevailing wind came from the west, so all the filth from the factory chimneys got carried east. In those days the buildings were black with it.

Sophie's penetrating gaze brought him back to the present.

"Your grandfather was a welder in the shipyards. He was an honest hardworking man, who only ever tried to do his best for his family. God knows how he survived in the years between his wife dying and meeting my mom. Back then, a single dad had no support. I think my grandmother was the only one he had to help him out."

He crossed the room and perched on the edge of an armchair, hunched forward, leaning on his thighs, staring at the floor as if it might provide some kind of clearer window on his past. It seemed strange to be talking about his family after all these years.

"My mom's family owned a café. There were a lot of Italians in Glasgow at that time. I think many of them had been interned during the war and stayed on afterwards. Anyway, they all seemed to open cafés or restaurants. *Tallys*, the cafés were called, and no one made ice-cream like the Italians. My mom worked at the café, my dad at the shipyard, and between them they made enough for us to lead a reasonably comfortable life. There was no such thing as credit in those days. Not for the likes of us, anyway. You bought what you could afford, with the money that you had. But I don't ever remember going without. Neither me nor Jack. They were good folk, your grandparents."

He glanced up to find her watching him intently, transported back through the years to a heritage he had never spoken of, to a place and time in which the seeds of her own future had been sown.

"The thing was, my dad was ambitious. They both were. But not for themselves. For us. For me and Jack. They both saw it as their goal in life to make better lives for us than they'd ever had themselves. And that meant education. My dad was obsessed with the idea that the only way out of poverty was through learning. So we lived a frugal existence, and every spare penny they had went into a savings account to pay for our education."

Sophie frowned. "But there was state education in Scotland, wasn't there?"

Enzo nodded. "There was. In the nineteenth and twentieth centuries the Scottish education system was reckoned to be just about the best in the world. Everyone had access to it. Rich and poor. Why do you think so many inventions of the industrial age are attributed to Scots?"

"Oh, papa, not again!" Sophie sighed, and was almost tempted to join him in the incantation. She had heard it so many times. But nothing would stop him.

"Alexander Graham Bell, the telephone. John Logie Baird, the television, John Boyd Dunlop, the pneumatic tire, John McAdam, metalled road surfaces."

"Yes, yes… anaesthetics, bicycles, color photography, decimal points, radar, ultrasonic scanners."

He laughed. "Peter Pan. Sherlock Holmes. Damnit, even the concept of capitalism was invented by a Scot. And you can put virtually all of that down to the quality of the Scottish education system. So you can see why my father invested such faith in it." Enzo shook his head. "But the state system still wasn't good enough for his boys. He wanted to send us to a private school."

Sophie whistled softly. "That must have cost a fortune."

"It just about broke them. Jack was seven years older than me, so he went first. To Hutchesons' Grammar School, a private boys' school in the toffee-nosed south side of the city. Hutchie, they called it. It took the last three years of primary school, and five years of secondary. So Jack was going into his fifth and final year of secondary as I went into the first year of primary. When he finished, he was going to university. That was already ordained."

He remembered that first day at Hutchie as vividly as Marc Fraysse had recalled his introduction to the Lion d'Or. Trudging along Beaton Road on a wet September morning in his new uniform. The obligatory cap. The blazer. The short trousers that he would have to wear until the fourth year of secondary, chaffing his thighs red raw when wet. The knee-high grey socks with their blue band at the top. The belted blue raincoat that dwarfed the nine-year-old Enzo, turning him into a ridiculous caricature of some classic noir detective. He felt lost, having just left behind all the friends of his first four years at state primary. And he recalled how miserable he was.

"Anyway, Jack was the old hand, a prefect by then. A stalwart of the school rugby team, excelling on the sports field as well as in the classroom. I thought he would take me under his wing, show me the ropes, as Jacques Blanc asked Guy to do with Marc. What I didn't know then was that Jack's school life was one big lie."

Sophie tipped her head to one side, puzzled. "What do you mean?"

"I mean he'd invented a whole history about himself that bore no relation to reality. The boys who went to Hutchie came from all over the city. So they weren't in the habit of going back to each other's houses after school. But almost without exception, they came from middle and upper-middle class well-to-do families living in the poshest parts of town.

"The exception, of course, was Jack. And he couldn't bring himself to admit to his peers that his father was a welder and that his step-mother was an Italian. He was ashamed of where he came from. He was ashamed of us. So he'd made up a story about where he lived and who his parents were, and I guess over the years it had grown and grown, like all lies, until it was just out of control."

"Oh, my God. And suddenly his younger brother turns up at school, and the whole lie is in danger of crashing down on him." Sophie's eyes were wide at the thought of it.

Enzo said, "Yeah. A wee brother called Enzo. He must have been dreading the day I would start at Hutchie. But he'd never said a word about it to me at home. Maybe he thought I would just run straight to dad. He saved it all for my first day at school. He only had one more year to get through, you see. Then he would be away to university. Home free. No one would ever catch him in the lie then."

"What did he do?"

"I was barely through the gates when he grabbed me and dragged me into the gymnasium. He banged me up against the wall-bars and made it clear to me that I was to keep my little mouth well and truly shut. We were *not* brothers. There was *no* relationship between us whatsoever.

"And to make it clear to me what kind of hell I could expect if I made even the slightest slip, he'd arranged a little *bizutage* welcoming committee for me. A hazing, he called it. He and a bunch of other fifth formers grabbed me just after the bell had gone to end the first break. The playground had emptied and they carried me out into the quadrangle, or the quad as it was known. There was a pond right in the center of it."

His memory of the moment, the place and time, was acute. He could still see the colonnade that ran below the gymn, the cafeteria on the ground floor, with the science labs and art rooms above it, the classics rooms on the west side, where Latin and Greek were taught. And in the center of the quad, the Hutchiepond, as he came to know it. Two connected oblongs of murky water where lilies grew among the detritus of the playground. A strange feature for a boy's school, plucked from the mind of some deluded architect.

"They didn't!" Sophie gasped.

Enzo nodded, and couldn't resist a smile. "They did. Completely submerged, I was. Soaked and half drowned. And they all ran off, leaving me in the water to be discovered by my new form master who thought I'd got lost. Of course, I was sent home in disgrace. A stupid boy who'd fallen into the pond on his first day at school. It was unheard of."

He looked up to find Sophie stifling a grin. "Oh, papa. I guess it must have been awful for you at the time. But looking back, you've got to admit it was maybe just a little bit funny?"

Enzo grinned, too. "Sure." But his decades-long feud with his half-brother prevented him, still, from fully appreciating the joke. "I never did snitch on him. So the lie went undiscovered."

Sophie shook her head. "And that's why you haven't spoken to him for thirty years?"

"No." Enzo stood up and pushed his hands in his pockets again. "We spoke for the last time at your grandfather's funeral, though the feud between us dated from well before that. And it wasn't anything to do with that first day at school."

"What was it, then?"

"Like I said, it's a long story."

"I want to hear it."

"And if I don't want to tell it?"

"I won't let you not tell it. You know that. You'll never hear the end of it until you do."

Enzo drew a deep breath and closed his eyes, and was saved by a knock at the door. Three soft raps. He froze where he stood, and he and Sophie exchanged panicked glances.

"What'll we do?" Sophie whispered urgently

Enzo nodded toward the toilet door. "Go into the bathroom and stay out of sight. I'll see who it is and get rid of them."

She slipped off the settee and hurried across the room. As soon as she pulled the bathroom door shut behind her he straightened out the cushions where she had been sitting and crossed to the door as the knock came again.

With apprehension beating in his chest, he opened it a few inches to see Guy standing beaming at him from the darkness of the hallway. He had a conspiratorial air about him and was clutching a bottle and two glasses. Enzo let the door fall open a little wider and tried to adopt a casual air of surprise. "Guy?"

"I hope you weren't in bed." He glanced up and down then and grinned. "Ah. I see not. I hope you don't mind me disturbing you like this, Enzo. But this is a mirabelle that I don't share with just anyone." He held up the unlabelled bottle. "And I knew you'd want to try it."

Enzo didn't see how he could refuse the invitation without seeming churlish, and he needed to keep Guy on-side if he was going to make progress with his investigation. He forced a smile. "Just a quick one, then. I'm pretty tired." He held the door open to let Guy in, then shut it quickly, remembering the laptop, and moved hurriedly past him to close its lid and hide the screen.

"Doing a bit of homework?"

"Just checking my email and making a few notes."

"Elisabeth said you were looking at Marc's old laptop today. Find anything interesting?"

Enzo wondered why he would ask, when Elisabeth would surely have relayed to him the answer he had already given her to the same question. "Not really, no. Just looked back through some of his old emails. I tried to open a couple of files, but they were locked."

Guy nodded solemnly. "He was very secretive in some ways, Marc. There was a part of him he never let anyone into. Not even Elisabeth. I think he shared more secrets with that damned computer than he did with his family."

"Well, if he did, he didn't leave them accessible to anyone else." All of which was true. Still, Enzo felt he was indulging in a deception and felt uncomfortable with that. He changed the subject. "What's so special about the mirabelle?"

"It's made by an old farmer on the far side of the village. Wonderful stuff. You know, the government is taking away the inherited right to distill a certain quantity of your own alcohol each year, so whatever his secret is, it's going to die with him." He set the two glasses down on the coffee table and uncorked the bottle. He poured two small measures of the crystal clear liquid, and the perfume of mirabelle plums suffused the air around them. "It's about eighty percent proof, so go easy. It's got a helluva kick, but a taste to die for."

Each raised his glass, they chinked them together, then sipped in silence. The taste of the plums filled Enzo's mouth, and the alcohol burned all the way down to his stomach. It almost brought tears to his eyes. He blinked several times. "Wow!"

Guy grinned. "Told you it was good." And he sank down into the settee where Sophie had been sitting only a matter of minutes earlier. "Take the weight off your feet, man." He nodded toward the armchair opposite. "Elisabeth said you wanted to learn everything you could about Marc." He chuckled. "And I've got a few stories I can tell you."

Reluctantly, Enzo eased himself down into the armchair. There was going to be no easy escape. And Guy looked as if he was settling himself down for an extended stay.

◇◇◇

Sophie had long ago given up hoping that Guy would make an early departure. He had been regaling Enzo for some time now with stories of adventures that he and Marc had shared during their apprenticeship together *chez* Blanc. She had all but stopped listening, standing with her back to the wall, then slowly sliding down it to squat on the floor counting the minutes till she could get out of here, back to the staff annexe and her bed. She glanced at her watch. It was gone midnight. She closed her eyes and sighed deeply.

"The thing about Marc and Jacques Blanc was that they just didn't get on," she heard Guy saying. "Jacques hated Marc, and Marc was terrified of Jacques. Once Marc found his feet in the kitchen he'd become a bit of a smart ass. And Jacques, I think, figured he was trying to *péter plus haut que son cul.* Accusing the apprentices of trying to fart higher than their asses was his favourite insult." He chuckled. "The Blanc brothers had complete control over us, you see. You did what they told you, or else. And when you got asked to do something, they would stand over you and watch you do it. And, believe me, with just one of those sets of eagle eyes on you, it was only too damned easy to screw up."

Enzo nodded. He knew how difficult it was to do anything well under the watchful gaze of a critical eye.

"So there was this one time… Marc was busy charging the firebox with coal. It was right before dinner service, and Jacques suddenly barked at him. He wanted him to add some ingredient to a *jus* that had been reducing on the grill for over two hours, and he slapped it down on the worktop beside the stove. Marc stood up in a panic and lifted it up. Can't remember what it was now, but he had the ingredient in one hand, and a scuttle of coal in the other. 'Well, go on then, kid!' Jacques shouted at him. And in a moment of total confusion, Marc emptied the scuttleful of coal into the stockpot."

Guy roared with laughter at the recollection of it. "Well, I don't think I ever so Jacques Blanc so angry. A two-hour reduction totally ruined. And inexplicably. What on earth possessed Marc to do it, I'll never know. But in a fit of temper Jacques swept the pot off the stove, and it went everywhere. Damned lucky that nobody got scalded. Anyway, he refused to let anyone clean it up, and it got tramped all over the floor, and dried in on all the work surfaces, and burned on to the stove top. And when the dinner service was finally over, he brought a toothbrush into the kitchen and handed it to Marc. 'Use that to clean it up, kid,' he said. 'Every last drop of it. Even if it takes you all night. And if I find a single trace of it in the morning, you'll be out of here, sweeping the streets where you belong.'

"Well," Guy shook his head, "Marc *was* up all night. And Jacques got himself out of his bed several times to check on him. But in the morning, there wasn't a damn trace of it anywhere. I really think Jacques was quite disappointed. It would have been his perfect excuse to get rid of Marc once and for all."

Guy leaned forward and refilled the empty glasses on the coffee table before Enzo could stop him. Guy lifted his and took a mouthful. Enzo reluctantly followed suit. "But Marc got his revenge," Guy went on. "About a month later, we had a couple of days off and went up to Paris the two of us. First time there. Went on the train. Well, we visited the catacombs. You know, the bit that's open to the public, where they dumped all the bones from the cemeteries they redeveloped for housing. A spooky place. Human bones floor to ceiling."

Enzo nodded, his mind suddenly flooded with recollections. He knew the catacombs only too well.

Guy chuckled. "Marc managed to filch one of the skulls and sneak it out with him. About a week later, back at the Lion d'Or, Jacques had a big stock pot bubbling away on the stove. And when no one was looking, Marc slipped the skull into the pot. You can imagine Jacques' reaction when he went to check on the reduction about half an hour later, and saw a foreign object in there. And then his horror when he fished out the skull. None of us could look. He was apoplectic, demanding to know who was responsible. Of course, no one owned up, and he was never able to prove it was Marc, although I'm sure he knew it was."

He drained his glass. "I'm certain he must have heard us all laughing our asses off up in the attic that night and cursed the day he ever took on *les frères Fraysse*." He lifted the bottle. "Another?"

"No, no thanks," Enzo said hurriedly. "I'll not sleep if I do." He hoped that Guy would take the hint.

But Guy was lost in his memories again. "You'd have thought it would be Marc that would drop out and not me." He shook his head. "My problem was, I just didn't really have the talent. But Marc hated it. I mean he really hated it." Guy looked at Enzo, frowning at the recollection. "Until we came down one morning. And everything changed."

Enzo found his interest piqued, in spite of his pressing sense of Sophie still hiding in his bathroom. "How?"

Guy grinned. "I don't think any of us had ever seen the Blanc brothers smiling. But they were like two Cheshire cats that morning. The whole family was in the kitchen, the daily routine abandoned. They were opening bottles of Champagne. And, damnit, if they weren't pouring glasses for the apprentices, too. Unheard of, Enzo. Unprecedented." His eyes were wide and shining as he recalled the moment. "They'd just had a call from the director of the *Guide Michelin*. They were to be given a third star in the forthcoming edition. Well… the phone never stopped ringing. There was a constant procession of folk in and out of the kitchen. It was magical, glamorous. A crowning glory. Here were these two surly, bad-tempered brothers whose magic in the kitchen had elevated them to the status of superstars. And Marc saw that. And suddenly he knew exactly where he wanted his life to take him. He wanted that superstardom, too. More than anything. And it changed his life."

He sat for a while, still lost in the moment, then slapped his thighs and stood up. "A quick pee and I'll leave you in peace to get to your bed." And he headed for the bathroom door before Enzo could dream up some excuse for stopping him.

Enzo got slowly to his feet and waited for the commotion that was certain to follow. But all he heard was the sound of Guy urinating in the toilet and then flushing it. The sound of rushing water came from the taps, and then a few moments later Guy emerged to recover his bottle and the two glasses. Enzo was still tense, but Guy seemed oblivious.

"Listen, Enzo, I want you to have lunch in the dining room tomorrow. On me. The full three-star treatment, a true taste of the *vrai style Fraysse.*"

Enzo was both astonished, and excited. He knew that the full menu ran to nearly 200 euros. It was a rare privilege even to sit down to a three-star Michelin meal, never mind have someone else pick up the tab. "That's very generous, Guy," was all he could think to say.

Guy grinned. "See you tomorrow, Enzo. Good night." And he vanished off into the hotel.

Enzo closed the door behind him and hurried into the bathroom. There was no sign of Sophie. Where the hell had she gone?

He was startled by the sudden sound of the shower curtain on the bath being pulled roughly aside, and a pink-faced Sophie stood perched in the bath glaring at him.

"You couldn't have got rid of him sooner?"

Enzo shrugged helplessly. "I tried Sophie."

"Not very hard." She spoke through clenched teeth as she stepped out of the bath. "Seemed to me you were more interested in scoffing that damned mirabelle." She sniffed the air. "I can even smell it off you." As she strode out into the sitting room Enzo followed. "Next time someone knocks on the door when I'm here, let's just pretend you're asleep, huh?"

She opened the door a crack and peered out into the hallway before opening it a little wider. Then she turned back and lowered her voice.

"And don't think I've forgotten about you and brother Jack. I want that story, papa. The whole, unexpurgated truth."

And then she was gone, slipping off into the darkness, pulling the door softly shut behind her.

Chapter Twelve

Enzo wandered into the bathroom to wash his face and brush his teeth. He felt tired, slightly heady from the mirabelle, and still heavy with the emotion of unburdening himself to Sophie about Jack. It was something he had never intended to do, and yet now it was out in the open, he wondered how on earth he had been able to keep it from her for so long.

He thought, too, about Marc Fraysse. How, in some ways, they had a lot in common. The dominating elder brother, the early lack of ambition or direction in life.

But while Marc had found his *raison d'être* in a career-long quest for *les trois étoiles de Michelin*, Enzo had found his motivation in a more negative way. The overweening desire to do better than his brother. To prove himself superior in everything he did. School grades, university degree, career, marriage. It had taken a long time, and Jack's complete indifference, to make him realize that measuring yourself against others was a futile pursuit. But some lessons come too late in life to be able to undo the mistakes you make in learning them.

He went through to the bedroom and undressed before slipping between the cool sheets of his bed. Despite his fatigue he lay for a long time unable to sleep, turning on to one side, then the other, before lying finally on his back and staring wide-eyed at the ceiling. He cursed the restless thoughts that filled his mind and held sleep at bay, before throwing back the covers and padding through to the sitting room again to retrieve his laptop.

He carried it to the bed, propping the pillows at his back so that he could sit up with the computer balanced on his thighs. The screen cast a strange blue light around the bedroom, and he felt the glare of it illuminating his face. He reopened the file of Marc Fraysse's fragmented memories and scrolled through them in the dark, searching for... what? He had no idea.

Then something caught his attention, and he brought his cursor to a stop on the scrollbar. It was the name 'Elisabeth' which had registered on his consciousness, and as he sped read through the first few sentences at the top of the screen, he realized it was Marc's account of their first meeting.

It was one of those secret meals that Elisabeth had told Enzo about, which the apprentices from the Lyon d'Or had cooked for the trainee nurses in the lakeside boathouse. A first rendezvous organised by one of the older apprentices, co-opting the assistance of the others to partake in a night-time raid on the kitchen, borrowing pots and pans and stealing food from the larder.

I remember the first time I saw her, Marc wrote. *There in the boat house as we all sat around the fire. Her face was caught in the light of the flames. A soft, warm, flickering yellow light. And I thought she was the most beautiful thing I had ever seen. I had no idea then how that chance meeting would drive a wedge between Guy and me, a war of hatred and attrition that would last for the next twenty years.*

Enzo sat up, startled by the unexpected revelation. There had been no hint in anything the family had told him so far of any kind of a feud between Marc and Guy. He spent the following ten minutes scrolling back and forth through the notes and anecdotes. But there was nothing to explain exactly how, or why, Elisabeth had caused this rift between them.

He closed the lid of the laptop, and slid it down on to the floor, lying back again in the dark, feeling the warm arms of sleep enticing him into their soft embrace. And as he slipped, at last, into a restless, dream-filled slumber, he was conscious of a final thought flitting through his mind: that here was yet another parallel between him and Marc. It had been a woman who had deepened the rift between Enzo and Jack. But while somehow the brothers Fraysse had found resolution and closure, the brothers Macleod never had.

Chapter Thirteen

An ice cold wind blew across the Massif, down from the northwest, blowing leaves and litter through the narrows streets of Thiers beneath a leaden sky heavy with the portent of winter. There was even a smell of snow in the air, although it was still too early in the season.

Enzo and Dominique sat behind the glass frontage of the Café Central on the corner next to the gendarmerie, and watched the traffic roll past. Buses, lorries, private cars, and pedestrians huddled in coats and scarves scurrying across the *terrasse*, tilting against the wind. Beyond, the shadow of the volcanic crags that rose above the town dwarfed the pale pastel houses that clung perilously to their slopes.

Dominique was off-duty, transformed somehow by her lack of uniform into the merest slip of a woman. Petite, elegant, with her hair tumbling luxuriantly across narrow shoulders, she was suffused with a femininity that the dark, gendarme blue, had contrived to conceal. Her lips and eyes were made-up in a way that would have been frowned on in uniform. But it was not overdone, being just enough to emphasise the fullness of her lips and the warmth of her eyes. She wore tight-fitting jeans with knee-high suede boots, and a warm, knitted sweater with a high, fold-over collar that swaddled her neck. Enzo noticed how small her hands were, folded together in front of her on the table, and how carefully she kept short nails painted the faintest pearl pink. Her yellow anorak hung over the back of her chair, and she sipped her coffee, listening attentively and with wide-eyed curiosity as Enzo told her about the revealing notes he had found in Marc Fraysse's computer.

"Did you know about a feud between the Fraysse brothers?"

She shook her head. "No, I didn't. Of course, Guy only returned to the area after Marc got his third star. He'd been in Paris before that. But there was no hint of any animosity between them. Nothing apparent, anyway. And nothing said about it during the investigation."

Enzo nodded. "What do you know about Marc's gambling habit?"

"I know that he was accustomed to coming into town most mornings, when he wasn't dashing off for interviews. He would buy the racing paper at the Maison de la Presse, and sit in here studying the form while he had a coffee, before heading off to the PMU to place his bets."

Enzo frowned. In his experience the giant French betting franchise, Pari Mutuel Urbain, was invariably found in cafés and bars. "Where's the PMU in Thiers?"

"In Le Sulky, a bar just down the road."

"Why didn't he take his coffee there?"

She shrugged. "Who knows? Some people like to separate business and pleasure."

"Can we go and take a look at it?"

"Sure." She pushed back her chair and got to her feet, pulling on her anorak. Enzo left some coins on the table to pay for their coffees.

Outside, the wind stung their faces, and she kept close to him, as if seeking to steal his warmth as they bowed their heads into the icy blast that blew up the Rue François Mitterand. They hurried past cutlery shops with lit windows full of Thiers and Laguiole knives.

Le Sulky stood next to yet another kitchen shop on the corner of a narrow street that zig-zagged up into the labyrinthine center of the old historic town. It had the seedy air of most PMU establishments, so often frequented by drinkers and gamblers. In days gone by, the bar would have been lost in a fugg of cigarette smoke. Now the smokers were forced to stand outside in the cold to pursue their habit, and the lack of smoke inside allowed the smell of stale alcohol and coffee grounds to predominate.

A man with almost shoulder-length, dark hair swept back from a lean, nervous, smoker's face stood behind the bar. It was early yet, and business was slow. A television screen flickered on the wall behind him, but the sound was turned down. He recognised Dominique immediately, and was on his guard. A gendarme, even off-duty, was never a welcome customer. He found a smile from somewhere to greet them, but it stopped short of his eyes.

"*Salut*, Fred," Dominique said, as if she knew him well.

But Fred was much more formal in reply. "*Bonjour Mademoiselle. Monsieur.* What can I get for you?"

Dominique smiled. "A little information." And Fred's smile slowly dissipated. He glanced nervously toward the few faces in the bar that were turning toward them now in curiosity.

"I don't sell information, Mlle Chazal, you know that. Beer, liquor, coffee, and I'll put your money on a horse for you. But information?" He shook his head. "Not my business."

"I'm not buying, Fred. I'm asking. And I can ask you here, or I can ask you at the gendarmerie."

Fred paled visibly. Anxious eyes darted toward Enzo and back again. "What do you want to know?"

"We want you to tell us about Marc Fraysse's gambling habits."

Fred frowned. Whatever he might have been expecting, it wasn't that. He seemed to relax a little. "Is that case not long dead?"

"No. Marc Fraysse is long dead. The case is still very much alive." Dominique glanced at Enzo, his cue to ask what he wanted to know.

Enzo said, "Fraysse was in here most mornings, is that right?"

"Sure."

"To place bets on horses."

"That's what people usually come here for."

"He never took a coffee, or a beer?"

Fred let a little burst of air escape from between his lips. "Not his kind of place, monsieur. I mean, nice guy and all, but he came here to put money on horses, not drink coffee."

"How many bets would he place in a day?"

Fred shrugged. "I dunno. Varied. Three or four. Sometimes he went for a triple."

"And what sort of money did he put on?"

Fred hesitated. "I don't remember."

"Oh, come on," Dominique said, her tone sharp.

"Hey." Fred laid his palms open on the bar in front of him. "The guy's been dead, what, seven years? I get hundreds of people in here every week. How the hell am I supposed to remember what kind of money Fraysse put on his horses?"

Enzo spoke calmly and evenly. "The same way you remembered that he placed three or four bets a day, and sometimes a triple."

Dominique said, "I can get the auditors in here, Fred. We can go back through every entry in your books for the last ten years, if that's the way you want to play it."

Fred's pallor had a tinge of grey about it now. He shrugged again. "I dunno, fifty, a hundred euros a horse?"

"Are you asking us or telling us?" Dominique was getting impatient, and Enzo could see that Fred was starting to shut down. Whatever he knew, he didn't want to say, especially not in front of Dominique.

"Well, thanks very much," Enzo said, and he felt Dominique turn toward him in surprise. "That's been very helpful." He turned to Dominique. "Why don't you head on up to the Café Central and get a couple of coffees on the table for us. I'm just going to have a little flutter here myself." And he reached into his satchel for his wallet.

The skin around Dominique's eyes darkened, and he saw the anger in them. He was getting rid of her, and she knew it. But whatever thoughts went through her mind she kept them to herself. "Okay," was all she said. She nodded to Fred and left.

Enzo waited until the door had closed behind her before sliding a hundred euro note across the bar. "Whatever you tell me, Fred, is between us." He raised his eyebrows. "Okay?"

Fred looked at the note, Enzo's fingertips still on it, pinning it to the counter, then glanced up to search the Scotsman's eyes for some kind of illumination. None was forthcoming, but his hesitation did not last long. He lowered his voice. "Not here. Not now."

"Where then, and when?"

"Tonight. About seven, after I get away from here. I'll meet you outside the gates of the old Château Puymule on the road to Saint-Pierre. You know it?"

Enzo nodded. He had passed it several times on the road, sitting off to the right on the way up to Chez Fraysse. An impressive, historic building open every day to the public during the tourist season. But shut now. Fred's eyes turned down toward the note on the counter, and Enzo lifted his fingers.

One blink and it was gone.

He saw her through the glass, sitting alone, her hands on the table in front of her, fingers intertwined. The café was empty, and she cut a lonely figure sitting there under the harsh fluorescent light. She looked up as the door opened, and her face darkened. There were no coffees on the table.

He sat down opposite her, and for a moment she refused to meet his eyes. Then, when she did, he saw that all the warmth had left hers. "Don't ever do that to me again." Her voice was low and controlled.

He felt the stab of her anger, and his own face colored. "He wasn't going to say anything with you there."

"Then you should have gone back later. I have to live here, Enzo. And you completely undermined me in front of him. Stripped me of all my power and authority. Turned me into some silly woman who can be brushed aside."

Enzo drew a deep breath. "I'm sure he didn't see it like that."

"I'm sure he did."

Enzo reached out to take her hand. "I'm sorry."

She withdrew it quickly. "Don't make it worse. I'm not some silly woman, and you can't just appease me with a squeeze of the hand and a patronising apology."

Enzo withdrew his own hands and pushed them into his pocket. "Ok. Then let me put it another way. I'm here to investigate a murder, Dominique. I have a few days at the most. They're closing the hotel next week and everyone will be gone. I'm not going to pussyfoot around fragile sensibilities and risk losing any of the little time I have." They glared at each other for a moment. Then Enzo sighed. "I'm genuinely sorry if I stepped on your toes. I didn't mean to, and it won't happen again."

Her voice remained steady. "No, it won't." The tension between them almost crackled in the air, like electricity. Before suddenly she seemed to relent, and it dissipated. "What did he tell you?"

"Nothing. Yet."

She searched his face. "I've been straight with you, Enzo. Shared everything I have."

"And I'll be straight with you, too. He didn't want to talk in there. I'm meeting him tonight. And whatever he shares with me, I'll share with you."

"You told him that?"

"No, I told him that whatever he told me was between him and me." He grinned. "But I gave him a hundred euros, so I figured that bought me the right to lie a little."

A reluctant smile pushed its way on to Dominique's lips and a little of the warmth returned to her eyes.

Enzo said, "Listen, what are you doing for lunch?"

She shrugged. "Don't know. Probably open a tin of soup or something. I'll get some bread at the *boulangerie* on the way back to the apartment."

"No one to cook for you?"

A sadness dulled her smile. "Or to cook for."

Enzo shook his head. "That seems incredible to me. An attractive woman like you."

She caught his glance at her ring hand. "Oh, I used to be married. He was a *fonctionnaire* at the *mairie*. We had a little apartment away from the gendarmerie. Both employees of the state, but our hours never quite matched up. In the end he found someone else to share his time off with." She shook her head and made herself smile. "And the kind of hours I work, I'm not going to find someone else in a hurry."

Enzo gazed at her thoughtfully for some moments.

She said. "Don't pity me. I don't feel sorry for myself."

Enzo shook his head. "I wasn't feeling sorry for you. I was just thinking what a waste it was." He hesitated. "Maybe I can offer you something better for lunch than a tin of soup and a *baguette*."

She laughed. "Don't tell me you cook, too."

"I do actually. But that's not what I meant. I'm having lunch at Chez Fraysse today. Why don't you join me, since it's your day off?"

Her mouth fell open just a little, before she became aware of it and snapped it shut.

"After all, you did tell me you'd never eaten there. And maybe at last you can say you've met a man who would be happy to spend that kind of money on you."

She stared at him for some moments, almost in disbelief, before her face broke into a grin. "Oh, my God! What am I going to wear?"

Chapter Fourteen

The staff ate in a long recreational shed out back, behind the kitchen. Canteen style tables and chairs were laid out in two rows to feed the twenty kitchen staff and other employees of the hotel. The toilets and locker rooms stood at one end.

Morning service for the staff was at eleven, and lasted no longer than thirty minutes, so that the kitchen was geared up and ready for lunch service in the restaurant by midday. Most of the chefs had been in preparing for the day's services since eight, and were more than ready to eat.

As Enzo wandered in, the shed was filling up. Big pots of steaming food were being placed along the two lines of tables: Andouillette sausage, bowls of pasta, salad, potatoes, several huge containers of hot brown lentils in a thick onion gravy. Bottles of water and cheap *vin de pays* stood at intervals along the tables. But no one was drinking the rough, red wine. Cutlery was grabbed from piles at the ends of the tables, but Enzo noticed that most of the cooking staff had their own Laguiole or Thiers knives that they unfolded from pockets and used for eating.

He noticed, too, the men he had seen putting in snow poles along the road the day he arrived. The big man with the dark haunted expression who had caught his eye then, caught it again now. He was unshaven, his hair long and greasy, hanging over his collar. Enzo nodded and smiled. But the man gazed back at him from behind unfathomable dark eyes, and made no acknowledgement whatsoever. He wore thick, workmen's overalls and a fluorescent yellow vest. The treads of his green Wellington boots were caked with mud. His eyes dipped back to his food which he shovelled unceremoniously into his mouth with big, dirty hands.

Enzo squeezed past and scanned the faces of all those taking seats along the length of the two rows of tables. He saw Sophie, assiduously avoiding his eye. She was sitting amongst a group of young kitchen staff, obviously *stagiaires*, who were laughing and joking as they passed the food along and snatched chunks of rough cut bread from one of the many baskets.

And then his eyes fell on the person he was looking for.

Georges Crozes sat at the end of the far row, on his own. There were several empty chairs between him and the other staff, as if he either discouraged mealtime company, or the others were simply reluctant to sit beside the boss.

Enzo pushed along to the end of the row and sat himself in the seat opposite. He waved aside the offer of a plate from one of the *chefs de partie*, two seats away. He wasn't here to eat. Georges Crozes raised his eyes to look at him, as if Enzo had just invaded his private space. Which he probably had.

"You don't mind chatting for a few minutes while you have lunch, do you?"

Crozes shrugged. "Do I have any choice?"

"It's up to you."

Crozes ripped open a piece of sausage with his pearl-handled Laguiole, allowing its stuffing of pig's intestine to burst out of it. The smell almost turned Enzo's stomach. So this was how a three-star Michelin chef ate at lunchtime. "What do you want to *chat* about?"

"Marc Fraysse."

"What about him?"

"How long had you worked for him before his death?"

"I was with Marc from the time he got his second star."

"So that was about… seven years before he was killed?"

"I guess so."

"You must have been pretty close."

Crozes glanced up as if he suspected Enzo of loading the question in some way. "Professionally, yes. Personally, no."

"But you must have spent, what, ten, twelve hours a day with him?"

"I must have done."

"You spend that much time with someone every day over seven years, you must get to know them pretty well."

Crozes sighed, and a mouthful of sausage was followed by a forkful of lentils. "The man was a genius. I never worked with anyone like him. His attention to detail was extraordinary, and he brought me to realize just how important those details were. He made me, Monsieur Macleod. He moulded me in his image. And I knew the only reason he did that was because he saw himself in me. He saw what I could be. And he made damn sure I fulfilled my potential."

"You liked him, then?"

Crozes shook his head. "No. I didn't like him. I loved him, monsieur. He was father, brother, mentor, friend, all rolled into one. But only in the kitchen. It was the only place we ever spent time together. I didn't know the first thing about his private life. Nor he about mine. That was beside the point. The only thing that mattered was what we put on the plate."

Enzo found it hard to imagine how such an intense professional friendship could fail to spill over into a personal one. And yet something in Crozes' tone, and his choice of words, led Enzo to believe him. And he supposed that outside of the kitchen, neither man really had much of a personal life anyway. Which brought him to the question which had been burning through the facade of patience he had been at pains to build around himself. He glanced along the table, and saw the glowering face of a young man turned in his direction. The youth, in his chef's whites, immediately averted his gaze when he saw that Enzo had seen him. But something in his eyes had left Enzo feeling distinctly uncomfortable.

Enzo turned back to Crozes, lowering his voice. "I heard a rumor that Marc Fraysse and your wife were having an affair." He watched carefully for a reaction.

Crozes jabbed a forkful of sausage into his long, lean face and chewed in silence, still staring down at his plate. Then slowly he raised his eyes again to meet Enzo's. "You repeat that to anyone, monsieur, and I will personally beat the crap out of you." There was no doubting his sincerity, and given his ten year advantage over Enzo, there was a distinct possibility he could keep his promise.

"Does that mean it's true?"

Anger fired in his eyes. "No, it does not. I don't know where it came from all those years ago, and I don't know who's repeating it to you now, but it's a lie. It always was." He leaned forward, his voice low and threatening. "You're eating in the restaurant today, I hear."

Enzo nodded apprehensively.

"Then take care, monsieur. You shouldn't upset the chef before dining. You never know what you might find in your food."

He wiped the blade of his Laguiole on his sleeve and folded it up, standing suddenly, his meal unfinished in front of him, and pushed his way brusquely past the other diners to make his exit.

A hush fell over the shed, and Enzo felt eyes turning toward him. There couldn't have been anyone at the two rows of tables who wasn't aware that something fractious had passed between *le patron* and the Scotsman. He waited for a few minutes, until mealtime conversations had resumed, albeit, tentatively, before rising from his seat and making his way outside.

He could almost feel the buzz of speculative chatter that started up at his back.

◇◇◇

Enzo entered the empty west dining room from the garden terrace. Tables were set. Crisp, fresh white table linen laid out with simple but elegant bone-handled silver cutlery made in Thiers. Condiment dispensers were fashioned from the horns of Auvergnat cattle. Serving staff were administering the final touches to the presentation. The hotel, Enzo knew, was full. Both dining rooms were fully booked, lunch and evening, as they were every day. Seventy-five *couverts*, with diners asked to make their menu choice while still in the lounge, sampling their *amuse-bouches* and quaffing their *aperitifs*, to provide the kitchen with maximum advance notice of the numbers ordering from the two set menus, and any unusual orders from the *carte*.

Enzo attracted one or two glances as he made his way from the dining room, through the lounge and into the reception area. He caught a glimpse of the large figure of Guy Fraysse emerging from the *cave*, and he hurried after him.

"Guy…" The big man stopped and turned, and his face broke into an infectious smile when he saw Enzo. He pumped Enzo's hand.

"How are you today, my man? The mirabelle help you sleep?"

"I'm not sure if it was the mirabelle, or the rarified air up here on the plateau, or maybe a mix of the two, but I slept like a log, thanks."

"Excellent. Worked up a good appetite for your lunch?"

"I have." Enzo hesitated. "About lunch… I wanted to ask if I could bring a guest." And he added hurriedly, "I'll pay, of course."

Guy nodded. "Well, since I've set up a table specially for you, it'll be no problem to add another place."

"Great."

"Who's your guest?"

"It's Dominique Chazal. The gendarme from Thiers."

Guy raised his eyebrows in surprise. "Ah. Well, in that case, she will be my guest, too."

"Oh, I couldn't possibly accept that," Enzo said.

Guy grinned and placed a big hand on Enzo's shoulder. "I'm not asking you to. Just telling you… there'll be no charge. I'm the boss. It's my prerogative."

Enzo shook his head. "That's incredibly generous of you."

But Guy waved his hand dismissively in the air. "A few vegetables, a couple of pieces of meat or fish… I don't think that'll break the bank."

Enzo found himself momentarily distracted by the appearance at the reception desk of Georges Crozes' wife, Anne. She came from the hotel shop beyond, and was starting to shuffle through files in a mahogany cabinet when she looked up and caught his eye. He could have sworn that her face colored.

Guy put a friendly arm around his shoulder and steered him away toward the sliding glass doors to the kitchen. He leaned in, confidentially, lowering his voice a little theatrically. "So tell me, Enzo… what would induce a chap like yourself to spend the kind of money it costs to eat here on a young female gendarme he's just met? Eh? Do I detect the perfume of testosterone in the air?"

Enzo was not at all sure how to respond. And for a moment he wondered why he *had* asked her to lunch. Had he felt sorry for her? Or was he simply trying to atone for undermining her authority at the PMU? Or was Guy right? Was he, as so often had been the case in the past, a victim of his own libido? In the end, he just grinned in response, and let Guy take from it what he would. And Guy's lecherous return grin provided a fairly good indicator of just what that might be.

He unpeeled his arm from around Enzo's shoulder as the doors ahead of them slid open. "I might join you for a glass or two during lunch, if that's alright. Meantime, I have some unpaid suppliers to appease. I'll see you later." And he vanished off into the kitchen.

Enzo turned and hurried back into reception. But Anne Crozes was gone. He heard a car starting up in the car park and went outside in time to see her turning her Renault Scenic into the driveway to head off down the hill.

Enzo stared after her as her car rounded the bend and disappeared among the trees. He wanted to talk to her, in spite of her husband's warning. But it seemed possible that she might have anticipated his interest, and was trying to avoid him. He would catch up with her, he knew, at some point. Though perhaps, in the light of Georges Crozes' advice about not upsetting the chef before eating, it was just as well that lunch would come first.

Chapter Fifteen

Dominique's transformation from the almost plain young gendarme whom he had first met, to the beautiful young lady who sat opposite him in the lounge was quite extraordinary. Eating at Chez Fraysse would be, for her, a once-in-a-lifetime experience, and she had clearly spent most of the time since Enzo had left her preparing for it.

She wore a simple, white silk blouse with pleated chocolate brown pants and elegant tan shoes with medium heels. A pale pink chiffon scarf was held loosely at her neck by a pearl brooch, and her chestnut brown hair, tonged to gentle, lustrous curls, tumbled extravagantly over her shoulders. The hints of pink and brown around her eyes emphasised their depth, the cherry red of her lips contrasting with the white of beautifully even teeth made a radiant smile dazzling. And she could hardly keep the smile from her face.

Even although Enzo had donned fresh shirt and pants, he felt positively shabby by comparison. He was pleased that he had, at least, taken the time to shave. "I hope you're hungry," he said.

"I'm famished!" She paused. "I don't know how I can ever thank you for this."

Enzo smiled. "Don't thank me. Thank Guy. When I told him I was bringing you to lunch, he insisted that you were to be his guest. We both are."

"Oh." Her smiled faded a little. "Is that wise?"

"I have never felt compromised by accepting someone's hospitality, Dominique. I live by that old adage, never look a gift horse in the mouth. Particularly if it's a three-star gift horse."

She laughed.

"What would you like for *aperitif*?"

But before she could answer, a server all in black arrived with a silver platter and two glasses of champagne. "Compliments of Monsieur Fraysse," he said, placing the glasses in front of them. He opened two leather-bound menus, handing one to each in turn. "Monsieur Fraysse will take your orders himself."

They lifted their glasses and touched them together across the table with a resonant chime of crystal. "*A votre*," Dominique said.

"*Santé.*"

And they sipped the gloriously lemony, yeasty champagne, the finest of bubbles exploding softly around their lips.

"Mmmh, wonderful." Dominique sat back in her chair, caressed and seduced by its soft leather. "If only all investigations were like this." She glanced at the menu. "Which one should we go for? When someone's treating me I always feel I have to order the cheapest."

"Well, we won't tolerate that here."

They both turned as Guy approached their table.

"No, don't get up." He stooped to kiss Dominique on each cheek. "I insist you go for the two hundred. And if you allow me to choose for you, then I can guarantee one hundred percent satisfaction."

Enzo said, "We are entirely in your hands."

Guy pulled up a chair and joined them, taking away their menus to close on his lap. "What do you think of the champagne?"

"Delicious," Dominique said.

Guy grinned. "What do you taste in it, Enzo?"

Enzo took another sip and focused on the flavours that filled his mouth. "Vanilla. Ginger. Nutmeg. Citrus…"

"Bravo!" Guy clapped his hands like an excited little boy. "It's a 1992 Krug brut, *blanc de blanc*, Clos de Mesnil."

Enzo almost choked. The 1992 Clos de Mesnil was one of *the* best vintages, and would cost, he knew, around a thousand euros a bottle to buy in a store. Double that in a restaurant. Guy was watching him closely.

Enzo tipped his head in appreciation. "Extraordinary, Guy."

"Excellent." He rubbed his hands together. "Then I hope you will allow me to choose the wines to go with your meal."

Enzo laughed. "I don't think either of us is going to argue with you over that."

Dominique's eyes sparkled with anticipation. "What are you going to recommend us to eat?"

Guy smiled a secret smile and waggled his finger. "One course at a time, *mademoiselle. Une surprise à chaque plat.* But for your entrées I would suggest the frogs' legs."

Enzo detected a flicker of disappointment in Dominique's smile, but Guy just shook his head knowingly. "These are no ordinary frogs' legs," he said. "This is essentially a dish created by the incomparable Bernard Loiseau. Marc borrowed the concept and added his own twist to it. Of course, only the plumpest and juiciest of Burgundy thighs are used, served with *purées* of baby spinach and garlic. Loiseau followed tradition and used flat parsley, but Marc found that a little astringent. He did, however, employ Loiseau's technique of boiling the garlic cloves, changing the water several times in the process, to remove the impurities and mellow their attack. The *purée* is thinned with a little milk. And, of course, with this dish, presentation is extremely important. You will see why later." He stood up. "I'll catch up with you in the dining room."

When he had gone their *amuse-bouches* arrived, eggshells in pewter eggcups, the tops removed to leave a perfect, unbroken ring. Inside they contained a concoction of hollandaise, balsamic vinegar, and herbs, to be soaked up by fingers of bread which had been drizzled with olive oil before being toasted.

Dominique's face dissolved into wreaths of ecstasy with the first mouthful. "Oh, my God, it's wonderful."

Enzo had to agree. The toast was crisp, but melted in the mouth, carrying with it the delicate flavours of the mixture from the egg. They ate in silence, savouring every mouthful, until the appetiser was finished, and their appetite for the meal ahead fully whetted.

Enzo cleansed his palate with more champagne. He glanced around and lowered his voice to make sure they were not over-heard. The buzz of conversation that filled the lounge made discretion a little easier. "I've been meaning to ask you what you know about Anne Crozes."

Dominique tilted her head, clearly surprised. "The chef's wife?"

"Yes."

"Not much. Except that they've been married for years and live somewhere just outside Saint-Pierre. She's a receptionist here, isn't she?"

"She is." Enzo hesitated. "You didn't pick up any chatter during the investigation about a possible relationship between her and Marc Fraysse?"

This time her eyebrows shot up in astonishment. "No, I didn't." She paused. "Was there?"

"It's what I've heard."

Dominique frowned, spoiling the radiance of her face. "Where would you 'hear' something like that?"

Enzo allowed himself a tiny shrug of the shoulders. "Let's just say I have access to a little inside information."

She stared at him for a moment. Very still. "I thought we were sharing everything."

"We are, and I am. Haven't I just told you what I heard?"

"Yes. But not who told you."

"That's a source I'm not prepared to reveal just yet. But I will, in time." He leaned forward. "The point is, if you had known that Marc Fraysse and Anne Crozes were having an affair, how much would that have influenced your investigation?"

Dominique blew air through pursed lips. "Enormously. It would have had the immediate effect of creating three potential suspects."

"Elisabeth, Georges, and Anne herself."

"Exactly."

"And you never had a single suspect, did you?"

She shook her head. "No we didn't. No motive, no suspect." Her eyes darted cautiously around the room, and she leaned, if anything, a little closer. "But were they? Having an affair, I mean. Marc and Anne."

Enzo sighed. "I don't know. I confronted Georges with it this morning, and he reacted pretty fiercely. He denied it absolutely, of course, and threatened me with violence if I were to repeat it."

Dominique looked thoughtful. "And Anne?"

"Haven't spoken to her yet. Although I do get the feeling that she might be trying to avoid me."

"But there is no evidence that they *were* having an affair?"

"None at all."

"So it's just some gossip passed on to you by your 'source'."

"Clichés become clichés, Dominique, because they are oft repeated universal truths. And here's one that I always pay attention to. No smoke without fire." He drained his champagne glass. "A hotel-restaurant like this is a particularly tight, insular world. I can't imagine that there's much goes on around here that pretty well everyone doesn't get to hear about. If Marc and Anne really were having an affair, how could it possibly have been anything other than an open secret?"

"An open secret that nobody chose to tell the police about."

"Why would they? The police are outsiders. And unless somebody thought that it had anything to do with Marc's murder, I can see how everyone would just close ranks."

Their server arrived to remove their plates and glasses, passing the debris tray to an assistant. "Your table is ready whenever you are," he said.

Dominique nodded, and they both stood.

"Follow me, please." The server led them from the lounge to the south-facing conservatory, and Enzo was disappointed to see that the flat quality of the light spawned by a pewtery sky overhead had stolen the depth from the view that was spread out below them. Its detail was smudged and lost in the grey yellow of the early afternoon.

White linen napkins were draped on their laps, and the *sommelier* arrived to open a bottle of 2005 Domaine de la Pépière, Muscadet Granite de Clisson, which he placed in an ice bucket on a stand by their table. "Monsieur Fraysse will be with you in a moment."

And true to his word, Guy arrived smiling at their table after less than a minute. He lifted the bottle from the ice, wiped it down, and poured half an inch into Enzo's glass. "Now, this," he said, "is much more modestly priced than the Krug. But you can rest assured that I wouldn't serve it to you if I didn't think it was a bit special. The winemaker is a lovely, biblical character called Marc Olivier. He has recently gone organic, the *terroir* is granitic, and this particular vintage was left to age for two years on the lees. It's not a classic Muscadet, but it's a classic Loire white. Creamy, aromatic, herbaceous, with wonderful complex acidity. It will go superbly well with the frogs' legs."

He waited with excited anticipation for Enzo to taste the wine. Enzo rolled it slowly around his mouth. "Wow! Honey and cream. Wet stone. Lime, tarragon. A hint of smoke, and pepper."

Guy's eyes lit up with delight. "My God, man, you really do have a good palate." He filled both their glasses and put the bottle back on ice as their starters arrived.

They came on large, round, white plates. Circular pools of puréed spinach, with smaller ponds of creamy white garlic at their center. The frogs' legs, crisply fried in the lightest of batters, were arranged all around the edges of the plates, fanning out from the middle.

"You eat these by hand," Guy said. "The calves have been removed, leaving the bone to act as a stick for you to hold them by. Just dip them in the spinach, and then the garlic, and eat. Like savoury lollipops." He beamed broadly. "*Bon appetit.*"

Enzo and Dominique glanced at each other across the table, and shared a moment of smiling anticipation before commencing their journey into three-star heaven. Enzo closed his eyes as his palate was suffused with the flavours of his plate. The soft, meaty thighs all but dissolved on his tongue. The spinach was sweet and sharp, the garlic creamy and mild. The combination of flavours was exquisite. He lifted his glass and washed the residue over with the delicious Loire *blanc*, and savoured its after-taste for thirty seconds or more, before its long, long finish finally began to fade. He opened his eyes to find Dominique's shining back at him. He raised a single eyebrow, in search of her opinion.

But all she did was laugh. "Do I really need to say?"

He returned the laugh and shook his head. "No." And they lapsed once more into silence as they succumbed to the inheritance of a dead man's genius.

Enzo mopped up the last of his spinach and garlic purée with soft, crisp-crusted bread fresh-baked in the kitchen, and washed it over with another mouthful of wine. An attentive wine waiter quickly replenished their glasses. "So…" Enzo said. "Are you Thiers born and bred, Dominique?"

"I am. A real country girl, actually. Probably not very sophisticated by your standards, and certainly not accustomed to eating in a three-star restaurant." She ran a slender finger around the rim of her glass. "My dad was a farmer. We ate wholesome French country cuisine that my mom prepared in a kitchen that would probably seem mediaeval to you. Certainly to the Fraysse brothers."

Enzo shook his head. "Don't do yourself down, Dominique. The Fraysse brothers were just country kids, too, learning to cook at their mother's apron in a cramped little kitchen. And the family relied on their dad's income as a travelling shoe salesman to pay the bills." He took another sip of wine. "As for me, I came from a working class family in the east end of Glasgow. No silver spoon in my mouth. I've never considered myself better than anyone, or thought anyone better than me. We're all cast from the same mould."

Pursed lips concealed her amusement. "Sounds like socialism to me."

"It's not really. I take my inspiration from a Scottish poet called Robert Burns. A marvellous poem called *A Man's a Man For a' That.*"

"Meaning?"

"Well, let me quote the last two lines of the first verse: *The rank is but the guinea's stamp, The man's the gowd for a' that.*"

Dominique laughed. "I'm afraid I'm not any the wiser."

Enzo smiled. "A guinea was a gold coin worth one pound and one shilling. What Burns meant was that the design stamped on the gold coin might denote its value, but it's real worth was in the gold. And that by implication, regardless of a man's office, or reputation, or ancestry, his real value is in himself. Or not."

Dominique thought about it for a moment, then slowly nodded. "I like that." She looked at Enzo. "I didn't know you were Scottish. The newspapers just call you *Britannique*. Is Enzo a Scottish name?"

"No, it's Italian. Short for Lorenzo. My mother was Italian."

She raised her hand to her forehead and flicked it back over her head. "And the stripe. Is that an... affectation?"

He grinned. "No, it's a syndrome."

"Oh. Nothing serious, I hope."

"Well, I haven't died from it yet." It was his standard response.

Her smile was a little perfunctory, as if she didn't quite get his flippancy. "You used to be a forensics expert."

"Yes."

"Why did you quit?"

"I fell in love with a French woman."

"Oh."

He wondered if he detected some disappointment in that. "And the two are not mutually compatible?"

He laughed. "When I first came to France my French wasn't good enough to pursue my career in forensic science. So I ended up teaching biology at Paul Sabatier University in Toulouse."

"Where you've opened a department of forensic science." It wasn't a question. She had done her homework on him.

"That's right. The publicity I get from solving these cases encourages sponsorship from both the state and the private sector."

"And your wife… I take it you married her?"

"I did."

"Is she also involved in forensics?"

"She was."

"And now?"

Enzo hesitated for just a moment. "She's dead."

Dominique flushed. "Oh. I'm so sorry."

"Don't be. She died a long time ago. Giving birth to my daughter, Sophie, who's now twenty-four."

"And you never re-married?"

"I never did."

"And no one special in your life?"

Again he hesitated. "Well… yes, and no. Someone special, yes. But not in my life any more."

"You're a man of many sadnesses."

Enzo thought about all the regrets of his life. "I suppose I am. But I'm trying to keep cheerful. And good food and wine helps. Especially in the company of a beautiful woman."

Dominique blushed. "Are all Scots such flatterers?"

"Yes. It's our genetic inheritance. The three Fs. Flattery, flirting, and flippancy." He grinned. "What made you become a gendarme?"

She shrugged. "Unemployment. When there are no jobs around, military service seems like a good option, and I didn't fancy the infantry. I certainly wasn't cut out for academia, and at eighteen marriage seemed like a very distant prospect." A reluctant smile turned up the corners of her mouth. "It wasn't what you might describe as a calling. But I've enjoyed it well enough."

"What age were you when you married?"

"Twenty-five. I should have waited, though. They say you know better at thirty. And I did. By that time I was older, wiser, and divorced."

"And no one special on the horizon now?"

"Only my dog, Tasha. And Tasha's a she. So, no men in my life at all."

"And no children?"

"No, thank God! What a complication that would have been."

"Yes. Children endlessly complicate your life." Enzo's heartfelt observation caused her to cast him a glance of curiosity.

"You have more than one?"

A little gasp, half laughter, half exasperation, burst from his lips. "I have too many and not enough."

Her interest piqued, Dominique was about to ask him what he meant when she was interrupted by the arrival at their table again of Guy Fraysse. He tipped his head toward them, raising an enquiring eyebrow. "How was it?"

"Absolutely wonderful, Monsieur Fraysse," Dominique said. "I have eaten *cuisses de grenouille* many times, but they never tasted like this."

"Excellent." He beamed his delight and placed a bottle of red wine on the table, which he began to open very carefully. "This is a Burgundy, as you can see. Domaine Michel Gros. Aux Brulées, 2005." He turned toward Enzo. "Which, as you will know, is being hailed as the vintage of the century. And I still find it hard to see past the *pinot noir*. I'm just going to leave this to breathe for a while. It's to have with your veal. But more of that later." He checked how much of the Muscadet was left. "Good. I'm happy to leave you this to finish with your fish." He raised a finger. "Although, you may wish to forego wine with this dish altogether. It is served in a sauce of red wine."

Enzo couldn't conceal his amazement. "Fish in a red wine sauce?"

"Another nod to the incomparable Monsieur Loiseau. He liked to serve *sandre* with his red wine reduction. Marc served it with *filets de rouget* lightly sautéd with rondelles of steamed leak. The sauce itself is quite extraordinary. Seven litres of strong, raisiny, southern wine reduced to one, thickened to the consistency of blood, and finished off with a nob of butter."

The tiny *rouget* fillets, three each, were served on white china, the skin side crisped to an almost caramel finish. The sauce was, indeed, the consistency of blood, startlingly dark red against the white, and delivered in a swirl with what seemed like an artistic flourish. Both fillets and sauce were sprinkled with the delicate rondelles of leek and half a dozen soft green peppercorns.

As recommended by Guy, they abandoned the wine to focus on the delicate flesh of the soft, moist fish, the burnt crunch of the skin, the mellow flavour of the sauce, all offset by the bite of the leek and the occasion burst of spicy pepper. Conversation, again, took second place to appreciation of the food, and it wasn't until they had mopped their plates clean that Dominique returned to the subject that had so intrigued her before Guy's interruption.

"So how many children do you actually have?"

Enzo dabbed his mouth with his napkin and wondered just how much of himself he should reveal. Finally he said, "I have three children. A daughter by my first marriage. My daughter by my French wife." He hesitated. "And a son I have never seen."

Dominique's eyes opened wide. "How old is your son?"

"About six months."

She sat back in her chair and looked at him in amazement. "And you've never seen him?"

"I don't even know his name."

"You're kidding!"

"His mother didn't want me to have anything to do with him. Doesn't even want him to know who his father is."

"That's not fair. On him or you."

Enzo gazed at his empty plate. "That was the deal."

"What deal?"

He looked up. "When she found out she was pregnant she delivered an ultimatum. She would have the child aborted unless I would agree to stay out of their lives. What was I going to do? I couldn't let her kill my son."

Dominique shook her head, her eyes filled with the horror she felt. "Why on earth did she even tell you she was pregnant?"

"I guess, because she knew I would find out."

"Who is she?"

"Her name's Charlotte. She's a forensic psychologist. Lives in Paris. I met her during my investigation into the first case in Roger Raffin's book. She was Raffin's ex-lover."

"My God, what a complicated life you lead! Did you know Raffin?"

"Not before I started investigating his cold cases. And I only got involved in that because of a stupid bet with the police chief in Cahors and the Préfet of the Lot." He turned his dessert spoon around in his fingers, watching its polished silver catching light reflections from around the dining room. "Now Raffin and my elder daughter are involved."

Dominique frowned. "Involved? You mean they have a relationship?"

"They sleep together." Just saying it was painful.

"You sound like you don't approve."

"I don't. I don't like Raffin. I never did. At first I felt sorry for him. He was only motivated to write his book of cold cases because of the unsolved murder of his own wife. But I found him cold, slightly reptilian, and never felt easy in his company." He sighed and put his spoon firmly back in its place. "But Kirsty is her own master. She is over thirty now. She does what she wants."

Dominique put her elbow on the table and leaned her chin in the upturned palm of her hand, gazing at him, awed by what she clearly saw as his complex and exotic existence. "Do you have any other family? Brothers, sisters?"

Again Enzo hesitated. But this time he lied. "No. My parents are both dead." And he was anxious now to switch the focus of the conversation away from himself. "How about you?"

"Oh, I have a brother and two sisters. All older, and all living in other parts of France now. We only see each other at Christmas. My mom's still alive, but she went back to be with her family in the north-west after dad died."

"So you're all alone here."

She smiled. "All alone. Just me and Tasha. It's a good thing I have a job that takes up most of my life."

Guy returned to let Enzo taste the red. "It's a Vosne Romanée *premier cru*," he said. "Tell me what you think."

Enzo sipped the rich red wine and his brow furrowed with pleasure. "Spice. Coffee. Pure, concentrated cherry." He shook his head. "An amazing wine, Guy. Really amazing."

"Good. Because you need an amazing wine to go with your humble veal chop. Marc always cut the chop from the ribs himself. A beautiful, thick slab of meat on the bone. And he perfected a process he called double deglazing to produce the most concentrated and wonderful *jus* to go with it, thickened with *foie gras*." He paused. "Oh, and in case you are in any way squeamish, all our veal calves are raised in the open and feed from their mothers. Marc always insisted on that. He believed that the animals we eat should be respected in every way."

The veal, when it came, was beyond doubt the best veal chop that Enzo had ever tasted. While it looked no different on the plate from any he'd had before, the flavour was so rich, and the meat so tender, that it was hard to believe that it was not the mythological food of the Greek gods. And if the veal was the ambrosia, then the wine was the nectar. It was as if the gods themselves had designed them to be eaten and drunk in concert. He finished his plate, and looked up to see in Dominique's expression the regret that he felt himself in bringing the experience to a conclusion.

They drank the last of the wine with a selection of delicious local mountain cheeses, and completed their meal with a delicate tart of tender pumpkin on a chocolate-coffee sauce, served with hazelnut flavoured ice-cream.

Dominique sat back, flushed from the wine, her eyes shining. "I have never eaten a meal like that," she said. "And I probably never will again. Thank you for the experience, Enzo. It was truly wonderful." She laughed. "I will now go on a diet for the next month. And after all that wine, it's a good thing I came up by taxi."

Chapter Sixteen

After coffee and *petits fours* in the lounge, Enzo and Dominique wandered through the lobby to the main entrance. Enzo noticed that there was still no one at reception, and no sign of Anne Crozes.

As the revolving door ushered them out into the cold wind coming off the mountains, Dominique slipped her arm unself-consciously through Enzo's. Much to his surprise. He didn't react, but Dominique did. Suddenly aware of what she had done she quickly withdrew it.

"Oh, I'm so sorry!" Her face flushed even more darkly. "Must be the wine. I'm forgetting who I'm with."

Enzo smiled. "You can put your arm through mine any time you like, Dominique."

She looked at him speculatively. "I'm probably not that much older than your eldest daughter."

He laughed. "You're not."

"And you probably think I'm far too young and unsophisti-cated for a man like you."

Almost unthinking, he reached out to brush away the hair that the wind was blowing in her eyes. "Neither of these, Dominique. You're smart, attractive, and single. And all of those things make you very appealing." He grinned. "Especially to an old guy like me." He chuckled. "The only observation I would make is that I am far too old for you. You want a young man with a future ahead of him."

"I want a man I feel something for. It doesn't matter to me what age he is." Her eyes met his very directly. And the smile on her face was replaced by something a little more intense. He felt his tummy flip over. "I'd like to cook for you sometime." And she laughed, breaking the tension. "Not that I can offer you anything like we've had today. But it would be nice. Just the two of us."

"And Tasha."

She laughed unrestrainedly. "Yes. And Tasha."

"I'd like that," he said.

They turned at the sound of a car horn, as Dominique's taxi pulled up in the turning circle in front of the hotel. She leaned forward quickly, pushing herself up on her tip-toes, to kiss him briefly on the lips. And then she was gone, down the steps, and pulling in the tail of her coat as she closed the rear door of the taxi. The car revved and coughed diesel fumes into the wind and was gone with a crunching of tires over gravel.

Enzo was suddenly aware of a presence at his shoulder, and he turned to find Guy there.

"Attractive woman," Guy said thoughtfully. "I've only seen her in uniform, so I had no real impression of her before."

Enzo shook his head sadly. "And far too young for me."

Guy nodded. "Me too. A young woman like that? She'd drive you to an early grave." And he laughed. "Anyway, I hope you enjoyed lunch."

"We did, very much. It was an extraordinary experience, Guy."

Guy scratched his chin. "You probably feel like going and sleeping it off right now. But I was going to suggest that you might like to go for a walk this afternoon. I'll take you down to see the kitchen garden, and then up on the hill to stretch your legs. Better for you to walk it off than sleep it off."

"I'd like that," Enzo said. "It would give us a chance to talk. There are some things I have been meaning to ask you."

The sound of a car coming up the hill drew his attention away from the elder Fraysse brother. He saw Anne Crozes' Renault Scenic emerging from the pine trees as it rounded the bend in the road. She accelerated past them, and up into the car park beneath the plane trees.

Enzo turned back to Guy. "I'll catch you in about half an hour, then." And he headed off around the east side of the hotel toward the car park.

◇◇◇

Anne Crozes saw him approaching as she slammed the driver's door shut. She looked around for a moment, almost in a panic, as if seeking an escape. But there was only one way to exit the car park, and she couldn't do that without passing him. He saw the resignation in the slump of her shoulders as he approached, and he looked at her this time with different eyes.

When he had first encountered her at the reception desk, he'd had an impression of a woman in her early forties, slim, attractive. But out here, in the unforgiving fall light of late October on the plateau, the cold pinching skin and draining color from her face, he saw that she looked older. That she had been attractive when younger was clear. And it was the impression she still gave at first glance. But shoulder-length auburn hair cut in an old-fashioned pageboy style was surely dyed now, and the lines around her eyes and mouth, and the thinness of her face, gave it a certain meanness on closer inspection. Enzo had the sense of a woman worn down by life, disillusioned, bitterness revealed in the thin line of her lips.

"Madame Crozes. Could I have word?"

Nervous grey eyes gave him a cold look. "I have to get back to work." She tried to step around him, but he moved to the side to block her.

"It won't take a moment."

"A moment to what? Ruin my life?"

"I would say there's a good chance that's already happened."

A look like pain flashed across her eyes, to be replaced almost immediately by anger. "And what would you know about it?"

"That's what I am hoping you'll tell me."

Her jaw set itself in a jut of determination. "I don't want to talk to you, Monsieur Macleod."

"Or you don't want to be *seen* talking to me." Again that flash of pain. "The fact is, madame, you can talk to me here, and now. Or we can do it at the gendarmerie."

She sighed and folded her arms across her chest. "What do you want?"

"I want to know if you were having an affair with Marc Fraysse."

She stared at him, eyes unflinching. "Yes."

Which took Enzo completely by surprise. He was momentarily discomposed. She saw it in his face, and something like a smile stretched her lips.

"No point in lying to you about it. Everyone knew at the time anyway."

"Even Madame Fraysse?"

"Of course."

"And Georges?"

"It was an open secret, monsieur." And Enzo was struck by her use of the same phrase he had employed with Dominique earlier. He had guessed it just right. "Open in that everyone knew. Secret in that nobody acknowledged it. But the relationship died with Marc, and those of us who were left behind just had to get on with it."

"Get on with what?"

"Life. Work."

Enzo frowned and shook his head in puzzlement. "I'm surprised that Madame Fraysse would have kept you on, in the circumstances. Why didn't she just sack you?"

"Because she needed Georges. He was the only chef on the staff capable of keeping the three stars that Marc had got them."

"And he would have gone if you'd been fired?"

"If Madame Fraysse had lifted one finger against me, it would have been admitting to the secret, Monsieur Macleod. As long as we all maintained the facade of ignorance, nobody lost face. Elisabeth Fraysse may still be my employer, but she hasn't spoken to me in seven years."

"And Georges?"

"Georges is a weak and spineless man. Marc was his lord and master in every sense. Georges would have done anything for him, including sacrificing his marriage. Which shows you just how much he thought of me." Anger curled her mouth. "He turned a blind eye at the time, and has never referred to it since." She glanced at her watch. "Now, if you don't mind, I'm late. I don't want to give Madame Fraysse an excuse to fire me after all this time."

She side-stepped the big frame of the Scotsman and hurried off through the plane trees toward the hotel. Enzo turned to watch her go. She seemed a slight, almost frail figure as she rounded the corner of the east extension and disappeared from view.

Chapter Seventeen

Marc Fraysse's kitchen garden was vast, spread over an acre of south-facing hillside below the *auberge*, and protected by a high stone wall. It was built on terraces linked by stone steps covered in lichens and mosses. Parts of it were shaded by fruit trees: apple, pear, cherry, and plum. Extensive rock gardens provided haven for many of the herbs and wild flowers that the chef had used to flavour his dishes. And a huge greenhouse ran along the top end of the *potager* where it would catch most sunlight for germinating seeds and cultivating bedding plants that would be transferred to the great outdoors in the late spring.

Now, however, large parts of it were being dug over in preparation for winter, with clear polythene sheeting stretched over ribbing to protect the winter vegetables. Along the far wall, huge orange pumpkins sat among fleshy green leaves in soft earth.

As Guy opened the gate to let them in, Enzo saw the dark-haired man with the haunted face who had been putting in snow poles on the road, and who had cast such dead eyes in his direction in the staff canteen that morning. He wore a cloth cap now, and was wielding a long-pronged fork to turn over rich earth near the bottom of the garden.

"Of course, the garden alone can't supply all our needs," Guy was saying. "We buy fresh vegetables at the market in Clermont three days a week, and we get a lot of produce from the local farmers." He chuckled. "They generally turn up at the kitchen door with stuff they've just dug out of the ground. Marc always sent the *sous-chef* to check out the quality and haggle for a price. But we paid them well. Marc believed in supporting the locals. Most of our employees were born within ten kilometres of the *auberge*."

He started off down the steps and Enzo followed him.

"But almost all of our herbs and wild flowers come from the garden. Marc laid out these terraces himself, you know. A labour of love. That was in the early days. But when success came, he no longer had the time, and so he asked Lucqui to look after it full time for him."

The man turning over the earth looked up as they approached.

"Enzo meet Lucqui. Lucqui meet Enzo."

Lucqui glowered at Enzo from beneath abundant eyebrows and thrust out a big hand to crush Enzo's and leave it cold and muddy. Enzo tried not to wince, and nodded solemnly. Lucqui's eyes never left his.

Guy said, "There's not enough in the garden to keep Lucqui occupied all year round, so he does other odd jobs around the estate, and also acts as gamekeeper and water bailiff."

"Ah," Enzo said. "Looks after the flora in the summer and the fauna in the winter."

Guy smiled, Lucqui didn't. Guy said, "There's some good fishing in the river, and we have deer and wild boar in the woods. We also have poachers. A problem which has kept Lucqui out of his bed for quite a few nights recently." He looked at the gardener. "Still no luck, I take it?"

Lucqui shook his head.

Guy turned to survey the fallow *potager* at its end of season. "Marc and Lucqui spent a lot of time together here in the old days. God knows what it was they talked about all those hours in the garden. I always figured Lucqui knew Marc better than me." He turned a grin on Lucqui. "That right, Lucqui?"

Lucqui pushed out his jaw in an unspoken acknowledgement.

Guy slapped Enzo's shoulder. "Anyway, we should head up the hill before the light starts to go." And Lucqui returned to forking the earth as Guy and Enzo climbed mossy steps back up to the gate.

"Talkative sort," Enzo said.

Guy glanced at him. "What?"

"Lucqui. He never spoke a single word." ˋ

Guy laughed. "That's just Lucqui. Loquacious Lucqui I used to call him. But Marc always said there was nothing he didn't know about what makes things grow. A real man of the soil. He never seemed to be short of words in conversation with my brother, but he's pretty much kept his own counsel these past seven years."

Enzo glanced back down over the terraces, and saw that Lucqui had dismissed them from his mind already, focused instead on the dark volcanic soil that he turned over and broke up with his fork.

By the time they reached the top of the hill the wind was strong enough to almost knock them over, whistling through clumps of already dead mountain grass. They had taken a path north from the *auberge* across the treeless, west-facing slope, and now it felt like they were scraping the sky. It really did seem like the top of the world up here.

Far off, Enzo could see the peaks of mountains pushing up out of the Auvergne, reaching much higher than where they stood now, but dwarfed somehow by the distance. The landscape formed an irregular mosaic of green and brown, land divided and sub-divided by generations of fractured French inheritance. Looking south toward the lower plateau, they could just see the old ruined *buron* where Marc's body had been discovered.

Enzo's ponytail whipped and blew about his neck and face, and Guy had to hold his *béret* to stop it blowing away. He said, "You know, in the whole history of mankind, only a handful of people will have stood on this spot, and seen what we see now. That gives me a sense of being very privileged. A privilege that goes beyond money or position."

Enzo gazed around the panorama of the world laid out at their feet and knew what he meant. He turned suddenly to the surviving Fraysse brother and said, "What did you and Marc fall out about?" It was an interrogation technique he had learned long ago. Always open with a question to which you knew the answer.

But it was a question out of left field, and it clearly took the big man by surprise. "How did you find out about that? There's not many people know."

Enzo just shrugged. "It's my job. The way I understand it, you barely spoke for nearly twenty years."

Much of Guy's joviality left his face. "Yes." He was lost for a moment in his own thoughts. "It was a woman, of course."

"Elisabeth?"

He nodded and half-smiled. A touch of sadness in it. "Yes."

"What happened?"

"We met her at the same time. While we were still working as apprentices for the brothers Blanc. And I guess we both fell for her that very first day. But it was Marc who asked her out first. God knows where he found the courage, because he was a shy boy in those days. I was the one who knew how to chat up the girls. But he beat me to it, and I could have kicked his skinny ass." He pushed his hands deep in his pockets and bent his head into the wind to set them walking south along the ridge. Enzo followed, straining to catch his words above the whine of the wind.

"They went out a few times, and then she seemed to lose interest. At least, that's how I saw it. It wasn't a regular *copain, copine* thing. I knew she had knocked him back on a couple of dates, so I asked her out. And she said yes. I didn't see any point in telling Marc. I mean, he never discussed her with me anyway. I started seeing her quite regularly. She told me she wasn't seeing Marc anymore, but I think they still went out from time to time."

He took a deep breath and stopped, turning to face Enzo, and the wind caught his *béret* and whipped it away on its edge. Guy flailed at it with a futile hand in an attempt to catch it. But it was gone, and what was left of his hair stood almost straight up, waving in the current of air like a sea anemone. "Damn!" Then he grinned unexpectedly. "Probably Marc's ghost getting his own back."

And whatever animosity there had been between them at one time, Enzo could see that Guy still had genuine fondness in the memory of his brother. "So what happened?"

"He was out one night, playing *pétanque* at the *boulodrome*. He loved that, you know. And he was good at it. Used to gamble half his wages on his ability to drop those balls right on the jack." He shook a smiling head at the memory. "Anyway, I knew he wouldn't be back for some hours and persuaded Elisabeth to come to the Lion d'Or. I figured I could smuggle her in through the back door. And the only way I was going to have sex with her was by providing some privacy and a bed." He ran a hand back across his head in a vain attempt to tame his hair. "Anyway, Marc had a bad night at the *boules*, and he came home early. Found us in bed." He pulled in his mouth, lips pressed together in regret. "And that was it."

"That was what?"

"The end of our relationship. Me and Marc, I mean. He went crazy. Wouldn't talk to me, refused to share a room with me. Managed to make all the other apprentices see me as some kind of traitor. Did everything he could to make an idiot of me in the kitchen. So I quit. Fuck it! I was never cut out for it anyway. And I fell straight into the first course that would take me." He laughed. "Accountancy! I'd never have seen that coming in a million years. But you know what? Turned out I was good at it. A head for figures I never knew I had."

"And Elisabeth?"

"Oh, I kept seeing her. And when she finished her training we got a little apartment together. She was earning, I had a summer job. We had a little money, and it was bliss. At first. Eating for next to nothing in all those cheap little bistros, walking together in the park, making love whenever we felt like it. Sleeping all day when she was on the night-shift. I thought I had discovered heaven on earth."

"But?"

His smile was tinged with sadness. "Yes. There's always a but, isn't there? In this case, the but was that it didn't last. By the time I was going into my second year in college, it was over. Whatever the magic was, we'd used it all up. Spent it. Gone. Just like Elisabeth. And all I was left with was a brother who thought I'd betrayed him. A brother who wouldn't talk to me for… yes, you're right… nearly twenty years."

They started walking again, the ridge dipping ahead of them, carrying them down toward the southern treeline and the old ruined *buron*.

"I went to Paris when I finished my studies and learned a few years later that he and Elisabeth had got together again. Of course I was never invited to the wedding. The only contact we had was when our folks were killed in a car accident and we had to settle the issue of inheritance.

"Marc wanted to continue to run the *auberge* as a hotel and try to make his name with the restaurant. I didn't see why not. So the lawyers put together a deal whereby he paid me rental on my half of the property, and I let him get on with it. I tried to speak to him at that time, but he still wouldn't have it. And so my lawyer spoke to his lawyer, and his accountant spoke to me." He sighed. "Sad, really."

"What brought about the change?"

"Marc did. Quite out of the blue. I'd been following his progress at a distance. The early critiques of the restaurant. The first Michelin star. The second. He was becoming a star himself. You know, it's funny Enzo, there was a time when chefs were servants employed by the wealthy, or hired by restauranteurs or hoteliers. Now the top chefs are celebrities in their own right and the people who once employed them bow and scrape at their feet." He laughed. "I love the irony in that."

They clambered over some rocks, then, and across a wet stretch of bogland that sucked at their feet.

"Anyway, I got a call from him one day. I couldn't believe it when I heard his voice on the phone. I could hear other voices in the background, like there was some kind of party going on, and he might have had too much to drink. He'd just heard that day that he was getting his third star. It still wasn't public knowledge. It made me think of the day the Blanc brothers got theirs, and even the apprentices got to drink champagne. He said he needed more than a silent partner now. He needed someone who would know how to run a three-star business. And if I was prepared to put the past behind us, then so was he."

Enzo searched his face as they came to a halt by the tumble-down *buron*. "And how did you feel about that?"

"I was rotting in Paris, Enzo. Gazing into a grey future. I jumped at the chance. And, you know, it made sense. In this business you don't employ outsiders. They'll steal from you. Marc needed someone. I was family. So we buried the hatchet and built the multi-million-euro Fraysse empire together. A brand that has survived everything." He cast solemn blue eyes in the direction of the *buron*. "Even if Marc didn't."

"And you and Elisabeth?"

Guy threw him a quick look. "What about us?"

"Well, wasn't it a little bit difficult, given your history?"

Guy just shook his head sadly. "What we had, way back, was special, I think. Intense. But the light that burns twice as bright burns half as long, Enzo. We were burnt out so long before I came back to Saint-Pierre that we were like strangers, really. And in many ways still are. We might run the business together, but our private lives, such as they are, never cross."

Chapter Eighteen

A fourteenth century *monument historique,* Château de Puymule sat up on a rocky mound above a tiny collection of mediaeval houses in a bend on the road about two kilometres below Saint-Pierre. The turreted roofs at each corner of this tall, square stone edifice gave it a Disneyesque appearance that was not quite real. Trees and rock gardens climbed the slopes all around it behind high iron railings. A path wound up from the gate to an arched entrance beneath a square tower with a steeply pointed roof.

When Enzo pulled up on the road below, the light was failing. It was not yet dark enough to trigger the floodlights that would illuminate it against a black sky once night had fallen, but it was the kind of twilight that robbed the world of clarity and created uncertainty in the shadows.

There were no lights in any of the houses, and only the distant sound of a barking dog and the smell of woodsmoke in the air gave any indication that there was life nearby.

Enzo checked his watch. He had overestimated how long it would take him to get here, so he was a little early for his meeting with Fred. He walked up a rough, cobbled track to the gate and saw that the padlock which would normally secure it was open, its chain dangling from one of the spikes. The right-hand gate itself stood slightly ajar.

Enzo was surprised. A plaque on the gate announced daily visits between 2.30pm and 5.30pm from May till September.

The château was closed to the public from October till April. He strained to see through the gloom toward the dark shadow of the castle and wondered if, perhaps, anyone still lived there. Many historic monuments were privately owned and only open to the public to raise funds for restoration.

The wind whistled through autumn trees around the building, detaching the last stubborn leaves and rattling branches. Enzo pulled his jacket more tightly around him and stamped his feet. It was damned cold. On an impulse, rather than stand around waiting, he pushed the gate open and started up the curve of the path toward the main entrance, drawn by curiosity and impatience.

Lichen-covered stone walls bounded what had once been a moat, lined now with grass and shrubs and saplings of mountain ash. Enzo crossed the stone bridge that spanned it to the tall wooden doors that arched beneath the tower. A heavy, black-painted iron ring hung from the right-hand door. Enzo lifted it with both hands and tried to move it. To his amazement, it turned clockwise, lifting some ancient, heavy latch on the other side, and releasing the door to swing inwards. He heard the sound of it echoing away into darkness. There had to be someone here.

"Hello?" Only the echo of his own voice replied before it was smothered by the night.

He moved forward cautiously over centuries-old flagstone, feeling the cold rising from them through his feet. Somewhere ahead was the faintest glimmer of light. Enough, at least, to allow him to distinguish his way forward through the shadows. He was in a vast entrance hall, with stone steps spiralling away to his right. Ahead, another tall, arched door stood ajar, and he could see an orange-yellow light flickering beyond it.

"Hello," he called out again. Still no response. He pushed the door wide enough to reveal a long banqueting room awash with the light of dancing flames in an enormous open fireplace, its chimney rising up to the rafters, clad in decorated oak panelling.

A long table was set with, perhaps, twenty places, as if for a mediaeval banquet. Damp air was warmed by the flames and felt clammy on his skin. There was nobody here. But the scrape of a shoe on stone flags somewhere out in the entrance hall stilled his heart. He was going to feel more than a little foolish, and certainly embarrassed, if he had walked into someone's private home.

He moved back out into the hall and felt the soft, damp darkness slip over him like a glove. A movement caught the peripheral vision of his right eye and made him turn in time to see a fist coming at him out of the dark. White knuckles, the glint of a ring. Instinctively he pulled back, ducking away, and was struck only a glancing blow. Still, it hurt like hell, filling his head with light, and dropping him to one knee. He heard, and felt, more than saw, his attacker coming at him again. And he pushed off, with his standing leg, dipping his head low and leading with his shoulder, a technique he had learned on the rugby fields of Hutchie Grammar. He made contact with soft flesh and hard bone. Rank garlic breath exploded in his face. A loud grunt filled his ears. With his weight for leverage, Enzo pushed the attacker back against the wall, and heard the crack of a skull against stone, almost like a bullet shot.

This time the man cried out in pain. Enzo had a handful of jacket in his right hand, and lashed out with his left fist. He felt it strike the hard, unyielding, protective shield of the man's rib cage. Bone against bone, and pain went spiking up his arm. The man tore himself free of Enzo's grasp and Enzo heard the rasp of his leather soles on the stone as he staggered away toward the main door. Enzo went after him, damned if he was going to let him get away. Out on to the old drawbridge, awash now with sudden moonlight. He saw his attacker just ahead of him. Tall, dark-haired, wearing a short fleece jacket and jeans. Now the moon was gone, the man reduced to the merest shadow. But Enzo could see the fugitive had hurt himself and was not moving freely. He almost hurled himself across the bridge, gasping to draw breath into protesting lungs, and lunged at the man's back. A classic rugby tackle. They both went down, Enzo on top, and the air was expelled from the man beneath him like air from a bellows.

Enzo scrambled to his knees and straddled the man, grabbing him by the shoulder and pulling him over, just as the moon emerged once more from a fractured sky. He was shocked to see the face of the young chef whom he'd seen glaring at him in the staff canteen that morning. There was blood streaming from a gash in his forehead.

"What the hell do you think you're doing?" Enzo shouted.

To his surprise the young man shouted back. "Just stay away from her!"

Enzo grabbed his lapels. "What are you talking about?"

"You're just some dirty old man who can't keep his filthy hands to himself!"

"What?" Enzo glared at him, filled with anger and incomprehension.

"She's *my* girl, okay?"

"Who?"

"Sophie!"

There was a moment's hiatus before rage tore through Enzo like a storm, and he lifted the young man's shoulders by the lapels and then slammed them down again. Hard. "You stupid little shit! Philippe, that's your name, isn't it? She told me about you." He sucked air into his lungs. "I don't know what Sophie is to you, and I don't care. But she's *my* daughter!"

Philippe's face froze in an expression of incredulity. Confusion filled flickering, troubled eyes as he tried to process the information.

"It was you spying on us in the hall outside my room the other night, wasn't it?"

"I... I... I didn't know. I didn't realize..."

"No, of course you didn't. And you didn't stop to think, or ask." Enzo let go his lapels and got stiffly to his feet, brushing mud and moss stains from his trousers and his sleeves. He ran a hand over the side of his face and felt a swelling on his cheekbone. Philippe pulled himself on to one elbow and looked up at the figure of Enzo looming over him. Enzo stabbed a finger at him. "You stay away from my daughter, you hear? And keep your mouth shut about me and Sophie, sonny. Or I might just tell her real boyfriend that some scrawny chef's been sniffing around her like a dog in heat. Bertrand's a body-builder, jealous as hell, and got a temper to go with it. I wouldn't like to be in your shoes if he comes looking for you."

The young man got to his feet with difficulty, holding his ribs where Enzo's knuckles had made contact, bruising them, maybe even cracking one. He turned and limped off into the darkness. Enzo stood breathing hard, and was filled with a momentary sense of elation. He had done not badly for an old guy. The young chef was certainly less than half his age, but Enzo had still seen him off.

If the thought briefly puffed him up, then sudden floodlights illuminating the *château* and a gruff voice shouting at him from across the moat deflated him just as fast.

"What the hell do you think you're doing here?"

He turned to see a large man in workman's overalls and shirt sleeves rolled up over muscled forearms striding toward him. He was caught in the full glare of the floodlamps on Enzo's side of the moat, casting a giant shadow behind him on the castle wall.

"I'm sorry," Enzo said. "Are you the owner?"

"I'm the caretaker. Who are you?" He stopped and glared at the intruder, a definite sense of threat in all of his body language.

Enzo's confident facade faltered a little. "I just saw that the gate was unlocked, and wondered if the *château* was still open for viewing."

"Are you blind? There's a notice on the gate. We've been shut for a month. Now clear off before I call the gendarmes and have you arrested for trespass!"

Enzo raised a hand in peace. "Okay, okay, I'm going. Keep your shirt on." He had no illusions about being able to see this man off if it turned physical. And he headed down the path, through the trees, feeling bruised and stiff, and thinking how ridiculous it was for a man of his age still to be getting into fights.

He pulled the gate closed behind him and saw a car sitting at the foot of the path, next to his own, engine idling, headlights cutting across the road and absorbed into the darkness beyond. As he reached the passenger side, he peered in to see Fred sitting impatiently behind the wheel. He opened the door and slid into the passenger seat. Fred cast him a wary look. "You're late."

"Actually, I was early. I got distracted."

"You alone?"

"Yes, why?"

"I saw some guy running down the track and then heading up the road on a motorbike."

"Nothing to do with me." Enzo felt himself blush as he lied. But he wasn't about to even try to explain.

Fred's eyes narrowed a little as they wandered over Enzo's face, and then down over his dirt-stained jacket and pants. "You look like you've been in a fight."

"I fell," Enzo said too hurriedly, and it was clear that Fred didn't believe him. "Anyway, we're not here to talk about my adventures in the dark. You were going to tell me about Marc Fraysse's gambling habit."

Forced to refocus on the purpose of their meeting, Fred retreated again into a self-protective shell. "How do I know you won't go repeating this?"

"You don't. But if the choice is between an official audit and an off-the-record chat with me, I know which I'd choose." Enzo breathed deeply and smelled the alcohol on Fred's breath, along with the unpleasant perfume of stale cigarette smoke. "Come on, Fred! What are you hiding?"

"We had an unofficial arrangement, Marc and me." He flicked a nervous glance at Enzo, then held the steering wheel in front of him with both hands and stared off through the windscreen into darkness. "There were the bets he laid off officially, through the PMU. And then there was the money I put on for him unofficially through... well, let's just say through people I knew."

"Illegal gambling."

He saw Fred's knuckles whiten on the wheel. "Just a little freelance betting."

"Of which you took a percentage?"

"I'm not a charity."

"What sort of money are we talking about?"

Fred hesitated. "A lot."

"What's a lot?"

Fred shrugged. "I don't know exactly."

"Oh, come on!"

"Over the piece… maybe two or three hundred thousand."

Enzo was stunned. "You mean that's what he bet?"

"No, that's what he lost. He bet a lot more. Sometimes he won."

"Jesus." Suddenly Enzo saw Marc Fraysse in a whole new light. And he recalled his brother's words of just a few hours before. Marc's predilection for gambling on games of *boules* during their days in Clermont Ferrand. *Used to gamble half his wages on his ability to drop those balls right on the jack,* Guy had told him.

"It was an obsession, monsieur," Fred said. "I mean, at first I saw it as a way of making a bit of extra cash. But it got out of hand, know what I mean. And I couldn't get out of it. He just didn't want to stop."

Enzo reached into an inside pocket and produced the printouts he had taken from Marc Fraysse's email folder. He had brought them with him on a hunch, more than an instinct, if not quite an educated guess. He handed them across the car. Fred dropped them into his lap, rolled down the window, and lit a cigarette, before reaching up to switch on the courtesy light. Enzo saw the nicotine stains on his fingers as he pulled smoke into his mouth.

Fred lifted the sheets into the light. "What's this?"

"You tell me."

He peered at them myopically for a moment before his eyes widened and he turned to look at Enzo. "Jesus Christ! I didn't know he was into this, too."

"Tell me."

Fred stabbed a finger at the email address. "Jean Ransou. Bookmaker to the stars."

Enzo frowned. "Legal or not?"

"Oh, definitely not. Gambling turns over nearly thirty billion a year in this country, monsieur, and the government takes twenty-five percent. So that gives you an idea of the margins for making money on the black. If you're a movie star, or a pop singer, or a celebrity chef… even a big wheel in the underworld… and you want to bet big money without sharing your winnings, or paying taxes, then you go to Jean Ransou."

"Who takes his own cut, of course."

"Sure he does."

"And the authorities don't know about him?"

Fred laughed. "Oh, you can bet they do. They've just never caught him. Or maybe they don't want to. I mean, who knows how many politicians and judges and high-ranking cops use his services? I don't know how he does it. Money gets laundered through the system somehow. He's got plenty of legit operations. Whether they make money, or it's just a cover, I wouldn't know. But he's the man."

"Was it you who introduced Fraysse to Ransou?"

Fred's laugh was derisive this time. "Hell no! A guy like me wouldn't get within spitting distance of a guy like Ransou."

Enzo waved a hand at the emails. "So what does all this mean?"

"Just dates, and races, and horses, and the amounts he wanted to bet. Take this line, for example…" He pointed to the top sheet, first line: *PV: 18/12: 3e: 14: 150; 7e: 4: 130; 9e: 5,9,10: 200.* "PV is the *hippodrome* at Paris Vincennes. 18/12 is the date. Third race, horse number fourteen. One hundred and fifty euros. And so on."

"So the initial letters always indicate the racecourse?"

"Sure. Paris Vincennes, Deauville, Longchamp, Paris d'Auteuil, Marseilles Borely. There's a lot of racecourses in France."

Enzo did some quick calculations based on the emails he had looked at. "So Fraysse was putting upwards of a thousand euros a day on these horses."

Fred nodded. "Looks like it. And that's in addition to what he was putting on with me, above and below the table."

Enzo exhaled through pursed lips. "He was a seriously addicted gambler, then."

"He was."

And on the basis of the figures Fred had already quoted him, Enzo realized that Fraysse's losses must have been enormous.

Chapter Nineteen

Evening service was in full flow in the dining rooms when Enzo got back to the *auberge*. There was no one at reception, but as the *sommelier* emerged from the *cave* with a bottle of Beaune he gave him a very odd look. Enzo caught a glimpse of himself reflected in the window, and realized just what a state he was in. His ponytail was a shambles, with stray strands of hair hanging down over his shoulders. His jacket and trousers were covered in dried mud, and stained green in patches by moss. No wonder Fred had looked at him so strangely. He hurried up the stairs before anyone else would see him.

In his room he changed back into his shirt and cargos, washed his hands and face, and sorted his hair. He examined his face in the mirror. There was quite a swelling on his right cheek that was already beginning to show signs of bruising. He cursed Philippe. And Sophie for encouraging him. She was, no doubt, flattered by the attention.

He went through to the living room and picked up the phone, dialling Elisabeth's room, and waiting while it rang, and rang, unanswered. Finally he hung up and slipped out into the hallway. The door to Marc's old study was just three doors along. He hurried past the others and hesitated in front of the study, listening for a moment in the stillness of the house. He could only distantly hear the chatter of guests downstairs, and the chorus of voices delivering and acknowledging orders in the kitchen. Half-fearing that he would find the door now locked, he tried the handle. But to his surprise and relief it turned and opened. He stepped quickly inside and closed it behind him. The room was in darkness, and he knew he would have no option but to turn on the light.

It had been embarrassing to be caught here yesterday. If he were found again today, it would be more than that. It was likely that he would be asked to leave. Elisabeth had made it clear she expected him to ask for anything he wanted to see. But he didn't want to alert anyone to this new focus of his interest.

Almost holding his breath, he flicked the light switch down and bathed the dead man's study in cold yellow light. He moved silently across the room to roll back the lid of the desk and open up the laptop. The start-up chorus reverberated around the room, and the operating system seemed to take forever to load. At last the desktop appeared on the screen, and he opened the mailer and quickly navigated his way to the archive folders. He stared at the screen with incomprehension, before scrolling up and down the row of folders. But there was no doubt. The *Cheval* folder was gone. Erased. All evidence of Marc Fraysse's gambling relationship with Jean Ransou lost forever, along with any record of exactly how much he had placed in bets. All that remained were the two printouts he still had in his pocket.

He had always known that it would be possible for any computer-savvy person to retrace his steps through Marc Fraysse's laptop to see exactly what he had looked at the day before. Erasing those files would have been a simple matter.

And it seemed to Enzo that the only possible person who could have done that was Elisabeth Fraysse.

Back in his room he stripped off, leaving a trail of clothes behind him as he headed for the bathroom and turned on the shower. Hot water cascaded over his face and shoulders, down his back and over his belly, warming his thighs. He stood for several minutes feeling the healing heat of the water relax muscles tight with tension and stiff from unaccustomed exertion.

He rubbed himself with a big, soft bath towel, and dried his hair vigorously before slipping into the soft silk of his black embroidered dressing gown and padding back into the living room. There he poured himself a large single malt from the fridge, diluted it with a little water, and sank into the seductive softness of the settee.

He lifted his laptop on to his knees and checked his email, then opened the *moi.dssr* file and scrolled through it until he found the passage he was looking for. He had sped-read through it previously, but wanted to go back now and read it more carefully, to be certain that the impression he had come away with from that first scanning had been accurate. If so, then there was a puzzling inconsistency between what he'd been told and what he had read.

Chapter Twenty

Saint-Pierre, France, February 1998

It had been a long, miserable winter. Like so many winters up here on the plateau, there had been snow, which kept people away. Certainly from Paris, and further afield. There were always a few regulars from Clermont, but local and passing business was never going to be enough. The dining room (I closed the west conservatory during the winter months) had remained stubbornly empty on some days, and on others only two or three tables were occupied. It was soul-destroying. I had two Michelin stars, and on some days fewer than two customers.

Elisabeth, as always, tried to persuade me that we should close for the winter. We would save on staff and heating, she said. And people wouldn't forget about us. As soon as the spring came they would return, like the geese. But I always told her: how can we expect Michelin to give us a third star if we are only part-timers? I was convinced we had to stay open, regardless, if that third star was ever to come our way.

I had watched all through the winter months for the Michelin inspector. Every lone customer, man or woman, who came and sat in a quiet corner was a potential spy for the Guide. And yet I was never sure why I was so obsessed with the notion. Would I have treated him, or her, any differently? No. And, of course, I knew there was no point in trying to open a discussion on the subject. That would only have worked against me.

I just wanted to know. That Michelin had been, and seen, and eaten, and that there was at least the chance that my rating would be reconsidered before the publication of the next Guide. I had spent a lifetime in the kitchen working for that. The first two stars had come quickly, it seemed. The third was infuriatingly slow to arrive, and I was beginning to fear that it never would. The low cloud, bruised and dark, that hung over us that February, spitting sleet in our faces from the teeth of a bitter north wind, reflected my mood in more ways than one.

It was a miserable day late in the month when the call came. I can remember, we'd had three bookings for lunch and five for dinner, not enough to cover the cost of even one chef. The rain was driving in across the Massif from the north-west. It was Georges who answered the phone in the office and came running through the hotel to find me. There was a Monsieur Bernard Naegellen on the phone to speak to me, he said. And, of course, both of us knew that Monsieur Naegellen was the Director of Michelin's Red Guides. I almost broke my neck to get to the kitchen, and then had to stand with my hand over the mouthpiece for almost a minute while I tried to control my breathing. When I spoke, finally, you would never have guessed how my heart was racing beneath my chef's white blouse. *"Bonjour Monsieur Naegellen. Comment allez-vous?"*

But he didn't beat about the bush. There were no niceties to be observed in the matter of Michelin stars. "Monsieur Fraysse," he said. "As you know the 1998 edition of the *Guide Michelin* will be published next month. I am just calling to let you know that you will have a rating of three stars in the new Guide."

I suppose it must have given great pleasure to successive directors of the Guide to deliver such news, and I have no doubt they were on the receiving end of many different reactions. I was so tense, I think that all I said was, "Oh? That's good." I could hardly have understated more the emotions that were bubbling up inside me.

He told me that, of course, this was not yet public knowledge, and that I was to keep it to myself until publication. But he must have known, even as he spoke, that there was not a cat in hell's chance of that happening.

When I came off the phone, I realized that the entire kitchen staff was crowded into my office. Someone had told Elisabeth about the call, and she was there, too, pink-faced and wide-eyed. Everyone, it seems, was holding his breath. But it took me a moment to find my voice. "Ladies and gentlemen," I said. "Welcome to Chez Fraysse. Saint-Pierre's first and only three-star restaurant."

The place exploded. I have never seen, nor felt, such unrestrained joy. If you work in this business, be you dishwasher or head chef, it feels like the crowning moment of your life. I remembered so well those celebrations in the kitchen of the Blanc Brothers all those years before, how the champagne had flowed, and how it seemed like my life had just begun in that moment. The moment when I knew, beyond any shadow of a doubt, that this was what I wanted. That this was what my life would be all about.

Beyond that, I remember very little. Except that I cried a lot, and drank a lot. Everyone who had reserved to eat in the restaurant that day, I declared, would dine on the house, the very first customers of the three-star Chez Fraysse.

It wasn't until that night, when the dust had settled and the last customer been served, that I managed to find some time and space to myself. I went to my study and closed the door and sat at my writing bureau. There were unfinished and unresolved issues in my life. Regrets and sorrows. It had been in my mind for some time that if ever I won my third star I would put these things right. So I did it there and then, without pausing to think, or to remember the pain.

Still intoxicated by my news, I wrote a long and rambling letter to my estranged brother, Guy. It was time, I told him, that we put the past behind us and together built a future for the place our parents had left us. Something that would honour their memory. Something that would have made them proud. I knew that my life was about to change irrevocably, and that

I would no longer be able to run the kitchen *and* the business. Who better to take over the business side than my own brother? I posted that letter the next day.

Before the end of the week he called me. It was the oddest feeling to hear his voice again after all those years.

"I received your letter," he said. "And I have only one thing to say." I remember holding my breath, thinking that he was going to turn me down. And then he said, simply, "Yes." And somehow my life felt whole again.

Guy arrived from Paris the very next day with a crate of champagne. We hugged and cried and got drunk together, and I realized what folly it had been to have wasted so many years locked in such bitter enmity.

Chapter Twenty-one

Enzo closed the laptop and allowed himself to sink back into the settee. Two entirely different accounts of the same moment. Guy had told him that Marc had called him the day he received the news. That there had been a party going on in the background.

According to Marc, that telephone conversation had taken place several days later, after Marc had sent him him a letter.

In essence, both accounts conveyed the same information, and the same emotions. Only the detail was at variance. But Enzo knew that memory often plays tricks. That a series of moments can be condensed in recollection into a single event. Several conversations into one. Guy's account of hearing celebrations in the background of their phone call rang true, somehow. It didn't seem like the kind of detail you would invent. Perhaps there had been some more formal celebrations going at the time of his call, and that's what he remembered. At any event, there seemed no reason to doubt Marc's account of the writing of the letter, the return call, and the tearful reunion.

In fact, there seemed no reason to doubt either account, and Enzo decided that he should focus his thinking on Marc's gambling, which seemed like a more fruitful line of investigation.

A soft knocking at the door startled him. He glanced at his watch. It was after eleven. If it was Guy again with more mirabelle he would have to find some diplomatic way of putting him off. He eased himself stiffly out of the settee and crossed to the door, opening it just a crack. In the light that spilled out into the gloom of the hallway, he saw Sophie's anxious face, and quickly opened the door wide to let her in.

She breezed into the room, dragging the usual cold air behind her, and turned to face him with shining eyes. Excitement was bubbling out of her like champagne overflowing from a glass poured too quickly.

"Papa, I've got news."

"Good." Enzo strode past her to recover his whisky from the table. He was not feeling particularly well-disposed toward his daughter since his encounter with Philippe.

"Well, don't you want to hear it?"

"Sure." He took a sip of his whisky and she glowered. "Don't I get a drink?"

He nodded toward the fridge. "Help yourself."

And she did, opening a fresh bottle of Chablis and pouring herself a glass, before rediscovering the enthusiasm which had propelled her into his room in the first place. "You'll never guess," she said, turning to face him.

"Not if you don't tell me."

"Everyone knew Marc and Anne Crozes were having an affair, right?"

"So it seems."

"But what isn't common knowledge is that they broke up very shortly before his death." She beamed triumphantly.

Enzo frowned. "How do you know this?"

Her smile contained an element of smugness. "I've been cultivating the *Maitre 'd.*"

"Patrick?"

"Yes." She twinkled. "He's got a little fancy for me, I think."

Enzo pressed his lips together in disapproval. "It seems it's not safe to let you out these days."

But she just laughed. "Anyway, I managed to wheedle it out of him after lunch today. He likes a drink, does Patrick. And he'd had one or two more than he should have."

"With your encouragement, no doubt."

She grinned. "Apparently he found Anne Crozes in tears one day in the locker room out back. Just about a week before Marc Fraysse was murdered. She told Patrick that Marc had dumped her, and that she didn't know how she was going to be able to carry on. Really distressed, Patrick said she was."

"Did she tell him why Marc had broken it off?"

Sophie shook her head. "No. Just that it had come out of the blue. A complete surprise."

Enzo absorbed Sophie's news in thoughtful silence and swilled some whisky around his mouth. Why would he have split up with her? Had he been under pressure from Elisabeth, who clearly knew about the affair? Or had he simply felt that the relationship had run its course? If Elisabeth knew that it had come to an end, then that would surely have taken away any motive she might have had for killing him. Anne Crozes, on the other hand, might have been motivated by grief, or revenge, to do just that.

"You don't seem very pleased."

Enzo smiled. "No, I am. It's valuable information, Sophie. Sadly, I'm not sure it does anything more than muddy the waters. What I lack is any kind of real evidence… of anything."

She frowned suddenly, taking a sip of wine and approaching to touch his cheek with her fingertips. "What happened to your face?"

Some of his anger from earlier returned. "Your boyfriend is what happened to my face."

She frowned her confusion.

"Philippe." He took another comforting mouthful of whisky. "I had a rendezvous with a contact at the Château de Puymule earlier this evening. Your little puppy dog must have followed me down there. He jumped me in the dark."

Disbelief exploded from her lips. "You're kidding!"

"I wish I was." Enzo rubbed his cheek ruefully. "The little shit thought I was some kind of dirty old man having an affair with you. Warned me to stay away."

Sophie's eyes opened wide in astonishment. "What did you say?"

"I told him I was your father, and that if he didn't quit bothering you I'd set Bertrand on him."

If possible, her eyes opened even wider, embarrassment verging on humiliation coloring her cheeks. "You didn't!"

"I did. And sent him away with a flea in his ear, and maybe a couple of cracked ribs for his trouble."

Fear now drained the earlier rush of blood to her face. "Oh, papa, he'll tell. My cover'll be blown."

But Enzo just shook his head. "I don't think so. I warned him what would happen to him if he did."

Now anger colored her face again, as she thought about it. "The stupid idiot! What did he think he was doing? He doesn't own me. He's not even my *copain!*"

"He seems to think he is."

"I'll kill him!"

"No you won't, Sophie." Enzo's voice carried a threat in it that she knew well from childhood, and it stopped her in her tracks. "My advice is to stay away from him whenever possible. I've warned him off, but there's no telling what he might do if you start laying into him. We can't afford for people to find out who you really are."

She was barely mollified and cast sulky eyes over her father's bruised face. "He had no right."

"No, he didn't. But let's just leave it at that for the moment." Enzo crossed to the fridge to replenish his glass. He poured slightly more whisky into it this time.

She was briefly silent, turning it over in her mind. Then, "Okay," she said. "I will let it go for the moment. On one condition. You tell me about you and Uncle Jack."

"Oh, for heaven's sake, Sophie! You don't have an Uncle Jack!"

"Yes, I do. If he's your brother…"

"Half brother."

"Half brother… He's still my uncle. And I want to know why you and he haven't been on speaking terms for thirty years."

"I told you, it's a long story. And I'm not at all sure I want to tell it."

"Well, I'm not leaving until you do." She planked herself down in the settee, curling her legs up beneath her, and poured another glass of wine. "I'm listening."

"Damn you, Sophie!"

"Don't damn me, just tell me." She sipped calmly on her Chablis, while Enzo turned away, emptying his glass and refilling it again. When he looked up he caught his own reflection in the black of the window. For a moment, it was like a window on his past, and he saw himself as he had been all those years before. A gauche young man in search of his place in the world, and trying to find a way through it.

"I was still at primary school when Jack went to university," he said. "Still a child, while he was a young man. But a young man who'd been educated in the sexually enclosed world of an all-boys school. Like so many of his peers, he had no idea how to relate to the opposite sex."

"Didn't they have school dances?"

"Sure. Once a year. They bussed in the opposite sex from Hutchie Girls, and they were just as inexperienced as the boys."

He recalled his own exposure to those annual events where adolescent hormones were released to pulse frustratingly through the bodies of hopelessly ill-prepared teenage boys and girls who stood eyeing each other up across the breadth of the school hall, without the first idea of how to conduct themselves.

"Back then, and probably still, all the female roles in the school play had to be performed by boys." He smiled. "An early introduction to the idea of cross-dressing."

Sophie laughed. "Did you ever have to do that, papa?"

In spite of himself Enzo blushed. "Once, yes. I was dressed up as a geisha to play one of the little maids in the school production of The Mikado."

Sophie sat up, her face shining. "Oh. My. God. You don't have any photographs, do you?"

Enzo laughed. "Even if I did, I wouldn't let *you* see them. I'd never hear the end of it, and you'd have them all over the internet before I could say Gilbert and Sullivan."

Sophie's smile was wicked. "Note to self. Must search through papa's family photos for incriminating evidence."

Enzo cast her a dangerous look.

"Anyway. So Uncle Jack went to university knowing nothing about women…" Sophie offered him a cue to take up where he'd left off.

Enzo nodded, and a flood of memories broke over him. "He got himself into big trouble. Awash with testosterone and no idea how to handle it, he stumbled from one disastrous relationship to another. In fact, I figure he was probably still a virgin even by the time he went into his second year. Which is when he got himself into really deep doodoo."

"What happened?"

He wasn't quite sure now where all the details had come from. Things he had heard Jack say. Gossip among his peers. Conversations between his parents, conducted in hushed tones and overhead through half-shut doors. "One of his friends was having a New Year's party at his house. One of those big red sandstone terraced houses off Highburgh Road in the west end. The father was some big wheel lawyer, but the parents had recently got divorced and the father had moved out. The mother, Rita, was this…" he hesitated, searching for the right word, "…diaphanous sort of creature. Almost winged. Beautiful and breathless. Delicate, like an Arthur Rackham illustration. She was lonely and sad, but sexually experienced. And she took a fancy to Jack. In fact, took him to bed that very night, from all accounts, and probably took his virginity, too."

Sophie was rapt. Eyes fixed on her father, wide with wonder, and trying to picture the moment.

Enzo shook his head. "A chance encounter, really, and it changed his life. He fell for her. Completely, unreservedly, insanely."

"What was wrong with that?"

"Rita was almost thirty years older than him. Nearly fifty."

"So? An experienced woman, an inexperienced young man. Why shouldn't they enjoy the moment?"

"They didn't just enjoy the moment, Sophie. Rita took up almost every moment of his life from that day on. He dropped out of university before the end of the spring term, and they were married within six months."

"Oh."

"Yeah. Oh." He paused. It had been a period of great turmoil in the Macleod household, with Enzo little more than a fascinated spectator. "My parents did everything they could to dissuade him. Of course, he never listened to my mum anyway, but dad couldn't talk him out of it either. No one could. I suppose if I'd been older, I might have tried. But I was just a kid, way in the background somewhere, kind of aware of all the rows and tension in the house, but not really a part of it."

"Did you go to the wedding?"

"Of course. We all did. A pretty lavish affair it was, too. Rita paid for it herself. Her divorce settlement had left her financially independent and she owned that big terraced house in the west end. As much for his own self-respect as anything else, Jack felt he had to work, having quit his studies. He got a job in the civil service, way below the level he'd have gone in at if he'd finished his degree. We hardly saw him for two years."

"What happened?"

"Rita hated him being out of the house. Hated being left alone. She was lonely and depressed, and increasingly hypochondriac. It was clear to my parents, on the few occasions they saw him, that it wasn't going well. He never brought her to the house. And any time they visited him she was 'indisposed'. Not feeling well, and taken herself off to bed."

"That must have been awful for him. Embarrassing."

"It was worse than any of us knew. We didn't find out the whole truth till later. It seems she had started drinking and took to her bed full-time, spending her life in a darkened room with the curtains drawn. Jack remained faithful and dedicated, doing everything for her. Bringing her meals to her room, organising a maid to come in three days a week, and learning to do the laundry himself.

"But increasingly she saw him as errant and absent. Finding fault with everything he did. Arguing over every little thing, flying off the handle at the slightest excuse."

He paused, catching sight of his reflection again in the window, recognising that in retrospect he felt much more sympathy for Jack than he ever had at the time. Then, he had believed his elder half-brother to be foolish and selfish. But looking back, he could see now what a living hell it must have been for him. It was strange the way that time and experience changed how you saw things, lending an insight you'd never had in the moment.

"Anyway, one day he came home from work to find her dangling at the end of a rope in the stairwell. She'd left a note for him, full of self-obsession and self-pity, but somehow she had managed to spill a bottle of perfume over it and the ink had run, obliterating most of her words. So he never really understood why she had done it. Except that she had been a deeply troubled soul. He blamed himself, of course, even though he had been dedicated to her and done everything for her that he could. There was no consoling him."

"I can imagine." Sophie finished the last of her wine and filled the glass again. It was clear that her father's story was not yet over.

"After the funeral everything got messy. Jack should have inherited the house, but there was no will. And Rita's ex, who had paid for it in the first place, didn't see why he should get it, so contested it in court. Of course, being a lawyer himself, it *was* no contest. Jack lost everything and came back home to live with us."

"Hah," Sophie said. "You must have loved that."

Enzo remained silent for a long moment. "There were only two bedrooms in our flat. My parents had one, and when I was wee, Jack had the other. I slept in a recess off the kitchen that they drew curtains over at night. When Jack left home, I got his room."

"And when he came back, you got tossed out and into the recess again?"

Enzo nodded. "It was like the cuckoo had returned to the nest." He paused. "Actually, more like the prodigal son. He was welcomed back with open arms, the total focus of my parents' attention. My father did all but kill the fatted calf."

"And you resented that?"

"At the time yes, I did. I was in my teens by then. Not an easy age at the best of times. The kitchen was where the family cooked and ate and lived. There was a big, black range along one wall with a coal-burning stove that heated the hotplates and the oven. The sitting room was only ever used when we had visitors. The kitchen was the warmest room in the house and there was always someone in it. So I lost all my privacy. And at that age, when you're only really beginning to discover yourself, privacy is important."

"How long did he stay?"

"Right up until I was eighteen."

"And he never got involved with anyone else?"

"Not during my school years, no." Enzo was silent for some moments, still choking on the memory. "I stayed on for a sixth year at secondary school and got a place at Glasgow University. My folks said I could have a party at the flat, to celebrate. And I asked a whole bunch of my school friends. Including the girl I'd met at the fifth year dance the year before. Fiona. We'd been going steady for the whole of sixth year, and I was head over heels for her, Sophie. Completely besotted. She was tall and willowy and dark and sultry, and had me totally wrapped around her little finger."

"Uh-oh." Sophie had already seen it coming. "And Jack came to the party, too?"

"He was in the house, so it was hard for him not to be a part of it. And I suppose he cut a kind of glamorous figure for all my friends. The older man. Experienced, but still young. And good-looking, too. Jack had always been a good-looking boy."

Enzo sighed and sipped contemplatively on his whisky.

"It was another six months before I discovered that Jack and Fiona were having a relationship behind my back."

"After meeting at the party?"

"Yes." He broke off to collect himself, wondering how it could possibly still hurt after all these years. "It was a double betrayal, Sophie. My girlfriend and my brother."

"Your half-brother," Sophie corrected him, and he flicked her a glance. "So what happened?"

"I had a furious row with Jack. It felt like he'd been fucking me up all my life. And this was the final straw. Stealing the first and only girl I'd ever been in love with."

"You can't steal people, papa, you know that. My mother didn't steal you, did she?"

Enzo turned on her angrily. "That was different!"

"Was it?"

"Yes, it was. It wasn't what Jack and Fiona felt for one another that hurt. People can't help their feelings, I do know that. It was the betrayal. They lied to me, Sophie. And connived, and hid their relationship from me. Fiona could just have ended it with me. It would have broken my heart. But it would have been clean, and honest. Instead, she continued with the charade for a whole six months. They both did. I wasn't just hurt, I was humiliated."

"So you never forgave them? Either of them?"

He sighed in exasperation, partly from his recollection of events, and partly with himself. "You get locked into these things, Sophie. I was young, I was angry, I was humiliated. Jack and I had the most awful falling out. I couldn't bear to be in the same house as him. Couldn't get out of the family home fast enough. I was starting university in the fall, and got involved in a flat-sharing arrangement with some friends, including the girl that would become Kirsty's mum. That's how I met her, really, although I'd been vaguely aware of her for a couple of years. We kind of fell into a relationship, me on the rebound. It was all far too fast, of course. We were married before I had time to realize what a mistake it would be."

"What happened to Jack and Fiona?"

Enzo drew a long, slow breath, wondering why it should still hurt after all these years. "They got married, had kids, and as far as I know went on to live happily ever after. The last time I saw or heard anything of Jack was at dad's funeral. And that was thirty years ago."

Enzo woke up, startled, in the dark. For a long, disorientating moment he had no idea where he was, before remembering Marc Fraysse and the unsolved murder at the tumbledown *buron*. In the dim light of the digital bedside clock, his bedroom slowly took shadowed shape around him. He glanced at the time. It was three o'clock. Sophie had left not long after midnight, and he had spent some time on his own sitting in the dark, drinking more whisky than was good for him, going over again and again in his mind memories that he had purposely put aside for most of his adult life.

He could only have been asleep for an hour or two, and already his head was starting to hurt from too much whisky. Something had wakened him. Some bleak, disturbing nightmare that had vanished with his sleep, like smoke in the wind.

He found himself thinking again about Jack, trying to put features to the memory of him. In his mind, he remembered him clearly, but his mind's eye could no longer furnish him with the physical details. And from nowhere, he suddenly recalled an incident that he had not thought about for close on forty-five years. A moment overlooked, buried under an avalanche of other memories.

He had been nine years old, still in his first year at Hutchie, while Jack was in his last. The threats over keeping his mouth shut and the incident at the pond were things that had long retreated into the dark lockers of unwanted memory. In truth, beyond that first day, he'd had little or no contact with Jack or any of his friends.

There was a group of boys in fourth year at secondary, who had been going around terrorising the younger kids. Just bullies, forcing boys much younger than themselves to hand over food from the tuck shop, or toys, or cigarettes, or anything that took their fancy.

It was a day toward the end of the summer term when Enzo fell foul of them for the first time. It was just after his birthday, and he'd been given money by an aunt. He'd decided to spend it in the tuck shop, buying packs of chips and bubble gum and candy bars, and sharing them among his friends. Which was making him very popular.

It also attracted the bully boys like flies to the dung. They pushed their way through Enzo's circle of admirers to demand that he hand over the goodies. It was Enzo's first lesson in the meaning of fair weather friends. Within a matter of seconds, they had all melted away, leaving him to confront the big boys on his own.

He hadn't yet acquired the silver stripe that streaked his dark hair, but he had a stubborn streak that ran through him, a character flaw rather than a physical one. He refused to hand over his stuff, and the older boys quickly lost patience. One of them, the ringleader, a boy called Andy, grabbed Enzo by his collar and slammed him up against the school wall. His goodies from the tuck shop spilled all over the playground. And a single, sharp voice cut through the mêlée. "Leave him alone!"

Andy and his mob turned around to see who'd had the temerity to interfere in what was clearly none of his business. And as the boys parted, Enzo saw Jack standing there. "What's it to you?" Andy demanded.

Jack hesitated a long time. "He's my wee brother. So just take your hands off him, okay?"

Enzo could hardly believe his ears. Andy looked at him in disbelief, then laughed. "What? The *wop*'s your brother?"

Enzo saw Jack flinch, and his voice carried an edge of anger almost too fierce in its denial. "He's not a *wop*! And I'll kick your fucking head in if you say it again."

Andy's face contorted into an ugly sneer. "You and who's fucking army?"

Although a year younger than Jack, they were big boys all the same. From the fourth year first-fifteen scrum. And Jack was on his own. But he didn't flinch. He said to Enzo, "Get your stuff and go."

Enzo had hesitated, then, but Jack was insistent.

"Go! GO!"

And Enzo stooped to quickly gather his spilled comestibles, and scurry off toward the far classrooms without looking back. No one made a move to stop him. All the focus had turned toward Jack.

It was with a sharp sense of guilt and regret, that Enzo remembered now how Jack had returned home that night, bruised and bloodied. He'd gone straight to his room, retiring like a wounded animal, and told their parents that he'd been hurt playing rugby.

That he had taken a beating for Enzo was without question. But neither had spoken of it, and it had never been referred to again.

And for some unaccountable reason, lying there in his bed in the dark, with whisky on his breath, and a head full of memories, Enzo felt tears fill his eyes.

Chapter Twenty-two

Madame Fraysse seemed a little shadowed around the eyes this morning, as if perhaps she had not slept. But in response to Enzo's enquiry, she professed to have slept the sleep of the dead. She took her seat opposite him at the breakfast table and her smile seemed very slightly forced.

She had her back to the view, as if all these years of exposure had made her immune to it. But Enzo could hardly take his eyes off it. The weather had changed again. The wind was coming straight down from the north, and it had blown away all those leaden rainclouds that swept into western Europe across three thousand miles of Atlantic Ocean. The cloud cover was high, and broken, allowing sunlight to flit across the plateau in ever shifting patterns of gold and green and brown. It was the constantly changing and unpredictable nature of it that was so compelling, perhaps like Madame Fraysse herself, although it was her Delphic quality that intrigued Enzo most.

He watched her pour her infusion of *tisane* into an elegant china cup, and sip gingerly on it through pale lips. Steam rose in wreaths around her mouth. He said, "You told me the day I arrived that Marc would make frequent trips up to Paris to record radio or television interviews."

"That's correct."

"And he drove all the way back down in time for lunch?"

"Sometimes, yes."

"That's quite a drive, Madame Fraysse. About four hours, according to Google maps."

"I suppose that would be right. Although Marc liked fast cars, and pushed them to their limits, Monsieur Macleod. I'm sure he probably cut thirty to forty minutes off that."

"Even, so… a round trip of seven hours or so before lunch… When would he find time to record the interviews?"

She cast him a curious look, as if she thought he might doubt her. "He sometimes went up the night before. He would see service underway then head off. He was a regular on the *Télé Matin* morning show on France 2. And that goes out live. They would slot him in anywhere between seven and eight. And then he would be on the road home. Very occasionally he would leave for Paris late afternoon, for an appearance on one of the late night round tables. And as for recording… well, he was a big enough name that the broadcasters would accommodate him. I've seen him set the alarm for two, to get up to Paris for six, and then be back by *midi*."

"Why did he feel compelled to do these broadcasts?"

"If you are wondering if it was ego, then I would have to say yes. To an extent it was. But there was also a very practical purpose in them, monsieur. Marc understood that if you were going to draw customers to a restaurant tucked away in a remote corner of the Massif Central, then you would have to keep it in constant view. If you own a restaurant in Paris, it is not hard to fill it, especially if you have three stars. But out here…" She glanced out at the view. "If you are stuck away out here, then you have to persuade the mountain to come to you."

Enzo nodded and refilled his coffee cup, before reaching for another *croissant*. "What else did Marc do in Paris, Madame Fraysse?"

She pushed up her eyebrows, but he could see in her eyes that her surprise was not genuine. "What do you mean?"

"I understand that Marc was fond of putting money on horses. In fact, more than fond of it. It was a daily ritual."

Whatever warmth the chef's widow might have shown Enzo when he first arrived vanished now, along with the sun as it slipped behind a passing cloud. Her tone was frosty. "I'm not sure that I understand the point you are trying to make."

"I was just wondering if he ever went racing when he was up in Paris."

"I have no idea where you heard that. But it is absolutely untrue."

"I didn't hear anything, Madame Fraysse. I'm just asking."

Her face had become quite flushed, and she was containing her anger with some difficulty. Whether it was real or feigned, Enzo couldn't tell. But he noticed that the dark smudges below her eyes had grown penumbrous. "Yes, he enjoyed the odd flutter." Her voice was brittle but controlled. "Everyone knew that. But there was no question of his having a problem. None at all." She pushed her cup away and rose stiffly. "Now, if you'll excuse me, I have a very busy morning ahead of me."

Enzo watched her stride away across the dining room, then turned back, compelled by the view to gaze out over the kaleidoscope of color that characterised the plateau. And he wondered about her use of the word "problem". The thought may have been in his head, but while he had not actually given voice to it, she had.

Chapter Twenty-three

Enzo found Guy in the *cave*. At the north-west corner of the cellar he had a small office, and Enzo saw the light burning in it, reflecting on the rows of precious bottles that lined the floor-to-ceiling racks. His footsteps echoed back from bedrock as he made his way to the far side of the *cave,* a sense of culture and wealth and history pressing all around him, dark liquid gold in darker, dusty bottles.

Guy looked up from his computer as Enzo's bulk filled the open doorway. His face lit up in a smile. "Good morning, Enzo. Slept well, I hope."

Enzo put a rueful hand to his forehead and pulled a face. "Too much whisky."

"Damnit, man! Solitary drinking's not good for you. You should have given me a shout. I'd have helped you with the bottle." He grinned and waved a hand at his computer. "Updating my inventory. Had a delivery this morning of some rather excellent 2005 Bordeaux. I'm very tempted to open a bottle to let you try it. Very frustrating, but the inventory comes first, I'm afraid." He looked out over his unique collection of wines. "Wine, wine everywhere, and not a drop to drink."

Enzo tipped his head in smiling acknowledgement. "You know your English poets, then."

Guy raised his jaw theatrically and quoted from memory. "And every tongue, through utter drought,

Was withered at the root:
We could not speak, no more than if
We had been choked with soot."
Enzo grinned. "*The Ancient Mariner.*"

"Imagine, Enzo, you're dying of thirst, and surrounded by water you cannot drink. I just thank the Lord I'm not an alcoholic." He chuckled. "I'd hate to be the owner of such a *cave* and unable to drink any of it."

Enzo shook his head. "Well, as it is, Guy, even if you lived to be a hundred you could only drink a fraction of it."

"Ah, but I can choose any fraction of it that I want. There's the rub. And that's the pleasure in it." He swivelled round in his chair. "Listen, how would you like to come to market with me one day? Marc used to go to the markets in Clermont Ferrand three days a week. And I still do it. I may not be a three-star chef, but I know about quality in the produce, and I don't want to leave that to anyone else."

"I'd like that."

"Good. Day after tomorrow, then." Guy paused and gave Enzo a quizzical look. "Did you want me for something special?"

Enzo leaned against the architrave of the door. "I wanted to ask you about Jean-Pierre Graulet."

"The food critic?"

"Elisabeth told me there was a history of enmity between Marc and Graulet. Just wondered if you could tell me why."

Guy roared with laughter and slapped his thighs. "Oh, Enzo, I can. I certainly can. It's one of my favourite Marc stories." He looked at his watch. "Goddamn, I don't care if it's early. This is a story that merits cracking open a bottle. Grab a seat."

And he vanished off into the gloom of the *cave* as Enzo eased himself into a hard chair and groaned inwardly. His head was still delicate from last night's whisky. Guy returned with a bottle of 2005 Château Margaux. As he went through the ritual of uncorking it, he said, "Only eight percent Merlot in this, and eight-five percent Cabernet Sauvignon. The Merlot was harvested at more than fourteen percent alcohol. Too rich for the Margaux. So most of it went into the château's second wine, the Pavillon Rouge." He poured them each a small glass.

"Oh, well, I suppose a hair of the dog will either kill me or cure me."

Guy frowned. "A hair of the dog?"

Enzo laughed. "Celts have built a whole culture around the need to find a cure for hangovers. In the case of having a hair of the dog that bit you, the cure is more of the same."

"Ah. Worth a try, then." Guy breathed in the wine, swirled it, breathed again and then took a small mouthful to wash around his gums. "Oh," he said, a look of ecstasy washing over his face. "Try it, tell me what you think."

Enzo sucked oxygen into his mouth along with the wine. He felt the flavours fill his head. "Sensational," he said. "Wonderful harmony."

"Yes, first reports suggested it might be overly tannic, but it's ageing nicely. I'll not tell you what it cost." Guy filled both their glasses and sipped pensively at his own. "Yes… Graulet." And he laughed again. "A pompous ass of a man. Freelance critic. Writes for several of the Paris papers, and has a couple of online blogs of his own. Self-appointed judge of good cuisine on behalf of us poor, ignorant plebs. He sneaks around the top restaurants in various disguises, taking clandestine photographs, and sometimes video, for his blog. He believes that Michelin stands for everything that is dull and old-fashioned in French cuisine and just loves to target their three-star darlings with his most virulent criticism."

"I thought he was renowned for 'discovering' his own restaurants of distinction."

"Oh he is. He adores finding the undiscovered genius working in the kitchen of some obscure *bistro* tucked away in a hidden corner of Paris and revealing him to the world." Guy chortled. "I've tried a few of them myself, and can't say I have ever been particularly impressed."

"So how did he and Marc come to cross swords?" Enzo let more wine slip back over his tongue, and felt the soothing warmth of the alcohol ease the ache in his head.

Guy perched himself on the edge of his desk. "Not long after Marc got his third star, Graulet came to sample the *style Fraysse* for himself. Made no secret of his presence, and despite everyone bending over backwards to please him, he was really quite objectionable. Marc had never been a target of his criticism before, and so was quite prepared to give him the benefit of the doubt. Until, that is, his column appeared the following week, panning Marc for his over-priced, over-rated, under-cooked, unimaginative cuisine."

"How did Marc react?"

"At first he was furious. And then hurt. And then depressed. It sent him into a black funk for nearly a month. Nothing that anyone could say could snap him out of it. But as luck would have it, the following month he had to go to Paris to kneel at the feet of the Michelin gods."

Enzo frowned. "What do you mean?"

Guy sipped some more of his nectar. "Every year, a procession of three-star chefs present themselves before the headmaster for a kind of end-of-term report. All trooping one by one into the eight-story edifice at No. 46 avenue de Breteuil. No one is above making the pilgrimage. Not even the great Paul Bocuse himself.

"It was the first time Marc had been asked to go and genuflect before the Director himself. But it wasn't the same Director who had awarded him his third star. Naegellen had been replaced that year by one Derek Brown. An Englishman, for God's sake! Can you imagine? Some damned *rosbif* telling us *frogs* what constitutes good French cuisine!" He laughed. "Actually, he was a good man, Brown. But don't let on I told you that."

Enzo grinned.

"Anyway, while in Paris, Marc met up with a few of his three-star compatriots. A couple in particular who had also been on the receiving end of Graulet's vitriol. They let Marc into a little plot they were hatching, and he was only too happy to participate.

"A young chef who had worked as a *second* to one of them had just opened a little *bistro* in Clichy, right on the outskirts of Paris. Graulet was being set up. A strategically placed tip-off had alerted him to the fact that this particular *bistro* might be an excellent 'find' for his blog. And so he had booked a table, and in one of his ridiculous disguises turned up incognito with a group of friends. What he didn't know was that the food he had ordered was being prepared for him in the kitchen by the very three-star chefs whose talents he had so recently derided." Guy topped up their glasses and laughed again at the memory.

"Of course, his meal was 'sublime'. And he wrote as much in his blog, praising this talented young chef that he had 'discovered' to the rafters. The following day, the three musketeers as they came to be known, announced to the media that they had in fact cooked Graulet's meal that night."

Enzo laughed. "Which must have made Graulet feel like a bit of an idiot."

"Complete and utter humiliation." Guy's face positively glowed with delight at the recollection of the moment. "It took Graulet a long time to get over it. For some reason he got it into his head that Marc had been the ringleader. But he didn't dare criticise him again. In fact, as far as I'm aware, he never ever mentioned Marc again in his columns or his blogs." His face darkened. "Until, of course, he became the first to print the rumor that Marc Fraysse was on the verge of being downgraded to two stars." He gazed thoughtfully into the dark red liquid in his glass. "Which I have no doubt gave him the greatest of pleasure."

Chapter Twenty-four

Dominique's apartment was on the third floor of a six-story block built into the hillside below the mediaeval center of Thiers. French windows opened on to small balconies with commanding views of the rest of the town spread out below, and the great curvature of the valley beyond.

It had been dark when Enzo arrived, the twinkling lights of human habitation down in the valley creating an inverse firmament. Tasha had leapt on him on his arrival, excited and breathless, and desperate to make friends. She was a beautiful, sleek-coated, golden labrador retriever, and it hadn't taken long for Enzo to wrestle her to the floor, engaging in mock battle, and trying to avoid the flapping pink tongue that Tasha seemed determined to lick all over his face.

Dominique stood helpless with laughter. "I think she likes you."

"I think she does," Enzo said, gasping to catch his breath. "I have this fatal attraction for women. They can't resist me." He managed to turn the dog over on to her back and rub her belly. Almost immediately, Tasha relaxed, paws in the air, folded over at the joints. "See what I mean?"

"As long as you don't try that with me!"

Enzo grinned. "Spoilsport!" Tasha's muzzle showed slight signs of greying around the whiskers. "She's not young. You must have had her for a long time."

"She's ten, but I've only had her for a year. She was a police sniffer dog for most of her life. They always try to find good homes for the dogs when they retire them. I was in the right place at the right time and needed a friend."

"She's a beauty." Enzo stretched himself out beside the dog, leaning on one elbow and gently stroking her chest and belly."

Dominique smiled at him fondly. "I wouldn't have put you down for a pet lover."

"I've always loved dogs. But living in the town like I do, and being away a lot, I never felt it was right to have one."

Dominique recovered a disarranged bouquet of flowers from the floor where they had fallen at Tasha's first assault. "I take it these were meant for me?"

"No, they're for Tasha. There's a bottle of wine for you on the coat stand."

Dominique laughed unrestrainedly. "You're a funny man, Monsieur Macleod."

"Enzo." He got to his feet and Tasha immediately got to hers, ready to continue the game. But Dominique raised a finger and gave a sharp warning blast of air through her front teeth. A real pack leader. Tasha stopped and looked up at her with lugubrious eyes which grew wide and excited when her mistress held up a black rubber ball about the size of a tennis ball.

"Bed!" Dominique said. And Tasha immediately trotted across the living room to where a large dog basket made soft with blankets was pushed against the wall. Dominique followed her and gave her the ball, which Tasha was delighted to grab between her front paws and chew at with an almost frenzied relish. "She loves her ball. I can get her to do almost anything by giving her the ball as a reward."

Enzo brushed himself down and straightened his ponytail. "That's her training."

Dominique gave him a quizzical look. "How do you mean?"

"It's how they train sniffer dogs. On the principle of reward. And it's very rarely food. Almost always a favourite toy." He followed Dominique through to the kitchen where she filled a vase with water to set and arrange his flowers. "Dogs have no interest at all in finding drugs or guns or whatever it is they're trained to sniff out. It's the reward that motivates them. It's the game they love, with the toy as the reward. Some of them get obsessed with it. And the more obsessed, the better the dog at doing its job."

Dominique turned from her flower arranging. "I didn't know that. You're a veritable font of information, aren't you?"

He laughed. "I did some work with dogs during my forensics training in London." He sniffed the air. "Something smells good."

"It'll be ready in a minute. Just lasagne, I'm afraid. Nothing fancy. We're eating *en famille* tonight."

"Pasta's perfect for a guy called Enzo."

She grinned. "You could open that bottle of wine you brought and pour us a couple of glasses. They're on the dining table by the window through there." And she nodded toward a tiny dining room off the kitchen where flickering candlelight sent shadows dancing around the walls.

Enzo fetched the bottle and took it through to the dining room. The small round table was set in the window recess. He guessed that in summer you could dine almost al fresco with the French windows open, taking your coffee and *digestifs* on the tiny balcony afterwards. The town seemed to fall away sheer beneath it. The windows faced west, so the sunsets would be spectacular.

He cast his eyes over the fresh, white linen tablecloth, the pink cloth napkins in onyx rings. Three candles burned in chunky onyx holders, throwing a pale orange glow across the table with its circular gold chargers. Polished Thiers cutlery was laid out with meticulous care at facing place settings. She had strewn a small handful of crisp, curling yellow and red leaves across the table, giving it an autumnal effect, and he was both touched and aroused by the care with which she had prepared it for him.

And for just a moment he had the sense of a very lonely person, hungry for company, deprived of love and warmth and intimacy, and it filled him with tenderness.

"Poured that wine yet?" Her voice startled him, and he turned with bottle in hand to find her standing in the doorway watching him.

"Just about to." He filled both their glasses. "Come and taste."

He handed her a glass and they sipped the soft fruity red of the Côtes de Rhone in silent appreciation.

"It's lovely," she said.

He put his glass down and took hers away from her, placing it on the table next to his. And he took both of her hands. He registered the surprise on her face. "I just wanted to say thank you."

She laughed. "What for?"

He tipped his head toward the table. "This."

She smiled, and her hands felt very small in his. And almost before he knew what was happening, he had drawn her into his arms, holding her there, feeling how she slipped her arms around him, too, tightening their hold. He brushed her hair back from her forehead with the backs of his fingers, and she turned doe eyes up to meet his. Then suddenly she laughed again and said, "Better not speak too soon. You haven't tasted my lasagne yet." They stood for a moment, both self-conscious, till she sniffed the air and added, "I think I smell burning."

He released her to hurry off into the kitchen. Of course, he knew it wasn't burning at all. It was just her way of extricating them both from the moment, but in a way he would have been happy for the moment never to end. Maybe he was as lonely as she was.

They had a starter of foie-gras and toasts, and she had thought to sprinkle the plate with *fleur de sel* and garnish with tiny *boules* of *confit de figues*. She had also opened a bottle of sweet white *Monbazillac* which complimented the savoury, salty flavour of the liver perfectly. "That," she said, "is as high as my *haute cuisine* goes. And I didn't cook any of it. Oh, except for grilling the toasts. I went on an eight-week course to learn how to do that."

"Yes." Enzo nodded solemnly. "It's one of the most difficult skills to master. I frequently burn mine." He enjoyed her laughter, which came easily. As he looked up, he trapped her in his gaze and held her there for a moment. "I'd love to cook for *you* sometime."

"Mmmmh," she said. "Burnt toast. Definitely the way to a woman's heart."

"Yes, I've always found that."

She took away their empty plates and retreated to the kitchen to remove their lasagne from the oven. He smelled the beef and the melted cheese, the tomatoes and herbs, and was for a moment transported back to his childhood, to the bolognese and lasagne dishes his mother would prepare And simple spaghetti, with her home-made tomato sauce. He had never tasted anything quite so good since. He wondered what recollections Jack had of those days, or if he even thought about them. Jack had disliked Enzo's mother with a fervor that was almost racist.

"Penny for them."

He looked up from his trance as Dominique brought through a piping hot casserole dish to place on a mat next to a couple of plates and a serving spoon. "Just thinking about the food my mother used to cook for us when we were kids."

"We? I thought you didn't have any brothers or sisters."

His heart jumped. How easy it was to be caught in a lie. "Just the family, I meant."

She served them each large portions of steaming lasagne and brought a bowl of salad through from the kitchen. "Help yourself." And she watched as Enzo spooned a couple of helpings of salad over his lasagne. "I've been thinking…"

Enzo looked up, grinning. "That can be dangerous."

But she didn't return his smile. "About you and Charlotte." And his smile faded, too. "It's not fair Enzo. She has no right to deny you access to your son."

He shrugged, not at all certain that he wanted to get into a discussion about this. "That was the deal."

"To hell with the deal!" He was startled by her passion. "She threatened to take the life of your unborn child if you didn't agree to stay away. That was cruel and unfair, and you had no choice. But she can't threaten you with the life of the child now.

And that changes everything. You have every justification for claiming your rights as a father. You have to go to her, Enzo, and demand that she let you see your son."

Her outburst left him momentarily speechless.

But she wasn't finished. "It's been on my mind ever since you told me about it. I've hardly been able to sleep for thinking about it. It's just not right!"

Her obvious outrage and concern on his behalf touched him deeply. He reached across the table to take her hand and squeeze it gently. "You sound like my daughter."

"Which one?"

"Well, both of them, actually. They never let me hear the end of it."

"And neither they should. He's not just your son, he's their brother. They have a stake in it, too."

Enzo nodded slowly. It was the first time he had looked at it that way. The girls had never expressed the thought, just their outrage on his behalf. He managed a smile. "We'll see." He dug his fork into his lasagne, and its seductive aromas rose from his plate with the steam. They ate in silence for some minutes, then.

"I'm sorry," she said at length. "I just had to get it off my chest."

"Don't be. I appreciate your concern. I really do."

"I didn't mean to spoil the evening."

"You haven't." He took another forkful from his plate. "The lasagne's great."

She forced a laugh. "As good as your mother's?"

Enzo waggled a finger at her. "You can't ask a man a question like that, Dominique. It's not fair to make him choose between his mother and another woman."

This time her laugh came more freely. "I guess not."

"Suffice to say that my father would probably have fallen for you in a heartbeat."

"And his son?" Her face colored immediately. She had surprised herself, perhaps, by her own directness.

He smiled. "His son is far too old for you." And he remembered with a tiny stab, how Charlotte had used the age argument on behalf of her unborn son. Enzo, she had said, was old enough to be the boy's grandfather, and that was not what she wanted for him.

"We've had this conversation before."

He found himself locked in the gaze of dark eyes shining in candlelight. "We have." He lifted his wine to wash over a mouthful of lasagne. "I've been thinking, Dominique, about the pouch that Marc Fraysse carried on the belt around his waist."

"Ah." Dominique sat back with a slightly sad smile and lifted her glass to her lips. "Subtle, or not so subtle, change of subject."

"No." He returned her smile. "Just something that's been on my mind since I got here."

"Oh? Why?"

"Tasha."

Dominique frowned. "I don't understand."

"Your superiors used the missing pouch to posit the idea that the motive for Fraysse's murder could have been robbery, right?"

"Yes."

"But someone out running is hardly likely to be carrying valuables. Even if his killer had been trying to rob Marc, one look in the pouch would have told him there was nothing of value in it. I mean, if he'd wanted the phone he would just have taken it."

"I suppose he would."

"So why did he take the pouch?"

Dominique turned it over in her mind for a moment. "To make it *look* like a robbery?"

"Exactly."

"Maybe the killer just took the bag and didn't look in it till he got clear of the crime scene."

"In which case he would probably just take the phone and throw the bag away. He certainly wouldn't want to be caught with it."

"So where's this leading?"

"You told me you searched the area."

"Yes. Officers from the *police scientifique*. They didn't find anything."

"What was Tasha trained to sniff for?"

Dominique shrugged. "I don't know. Anything they gave her the scent of, I guess."

"So if we gave her something of Marc Fraysse's to smell and let her loose up by the *buron*, the chances are she would pick up anything around there that still carried his scent?"

"After seven years? That's pretty unlikely, isn't it?"

"Any tracks, of course, would have been washed away at the time. But scent can cling to objects for years. Anything up there belonging to Fraysse might still carry his smell on it."

Dominique nodded in doubtful agreement. "Might be worth a try, I suppose." She finished her wine and he refilled her glass. "I remember inheriting an aunt's scarf when I was a child, and it had the scent of her on it for years afterwards. No matter how often I wore it."

"So we'll take Tasha up first thing tomorrow?"

"Sure."

"And don't forget to take her ball. That's the game, remember?" He finished his lasagne and mopped the plate clean with some moist, yeasty bread. "That was delicious. My mother would have hated you."

◇◇◇

Dessert was fresh mango slices and vanilla ice-cream. Afterwards, they adjourned to the sitting room, sitting together on the settee by the light of dying embers in an open hearth. There, under the watchful gaze of Tasha, they drank coffee and Armagnac. Dominique sat side on, one leg tucked in beneath her, the other folded up under her chin, arms wrapped around her shin, and she watched him as he talked about the training which had led him to become an expert on serious serial crime analysis, specialising in blood pattern interpretation at major crime scenes.

He laughed. "Great topic of conversation to round off a romantic evening. Blood spatter and hair analysis."

She shook her head. "What on earth made you give it all up."

He shrugged and said simply, "Love."

"She must have been very special."

"She was."

"Do you still miss her?"

"There's not a day goes by that I don't think about her. And I see her in our daughter every time I look at Sophie."

"Would you ever think of having a serious relationship with someone else?"

"I did. With Charlotte. At least, it was serious for me. But not for her, as it turned out. She valued her independence too much."

"Independent can sometimes just be another word for lonely."

Enzo turned his head to look at her. She looked lovely in the dying glow of the fire. Tight jeans, a man's white shirt out over her hips, long sleeves rolled up to the elbows, bare feet. "Are you lonely, Dominique?"

She hesitated for a long moment. "Very."

He reached out and touched her cheek with his fingertips, and she unfolded herself to move across the settee, taking his head in her hands. Their faces were very close. He felt her breath on his skin. Their lips touched, without any sense that either had initiated it. A soft, sweet kiss full of tenderness. She drew back a little. "You can stay if you want."

He felt butterflies in conflict in his stomach, and a deep desire burgeoning in his loins. "I want."

Chapter Twenty-five

The wind had dropped, and there was an odd, chill stillness in the air as he drove up from Thiers to Saint-Pierre at first light. He wanted to be back, and in his room, before anyone became aware that he had spent the night elsewhere. He also had another reason for being back before breakfast.

He parked beneath the naked branches of the plane trees and walked, ankle-deep, through fallen leaves around to the front door. There was still a warm, fuzzy glow somewhere deep inside him. The taste of Dominique lingered on his lips, as did the sense of her wrapped in his arms, as she had been all night, head resting on his shoulder, purring gently.

Enzo himself had slept very little, but he didn't feel tired. The comfort of intimacy had made him more relaxed than he had been in a very long time. He had savored it through all the dark hours of the night, dozing intermittently, vaguely erotic dreams washing over him, to be lost from grasp or memory on surfacing once more to consciousness. In some ways he had not wanted to sleep, as if in doing so he might have missed it all; the feel of her skin on his; the closeness and warmth of another human being.

Anne Crozes was behind the reception desk as he came through the revolving door into the lobby, bringing the cold air of the early morning with him. He glanced at her, and saw a faintly inquiring look cross her face, as if she was wondering what he might be doing out at this time. But she wasn't going to ask, and he wasn't about to offer any explanation. He nodded and turned immediately toward the staircase, following it up to the first landing.

Back in his suite, he showered quickly and got dressed, all the time keeping half an eye on the clock. For the past few mornings, Elisabeth had gone down to breakfast at eight sharp. He did not want to miss her descent to the dining room today.

By 7.55 he was standing with his back to the wall next to the door of his room, listening. There were a couple of false alarms; another guest heading down for breakfast; a maid delivering a breakfast tray to a room further along the hall. Each time he heard a movement, he opened the door a crack to see who it was.

Finally, a little later than on previous mornings, he heard a door opening along the hall, and brisk footsteps softened by the deep pile of the runner. He eased his door open just after they passed, and saw Elisabeth heading for the staircase.

He allowed her several minutes to get herself ensconced in the dining room before slipping out into the hallway and hurrying along toward her apartment. At the door to Marc Fraysse's study he stopped and tried the handle. To his dismay it was locked. And he wondered if somehow Elisabeth had found out about his foray into it the other night. But he dismissed the idea. This was a classic case of shutting the barn door after the horse had bolted. Only now, the horse had returned, and couldn't get back in.

He cursed under his breath. This was going to make things a little more difficult. He moved quickly along the hall toward the double doors leading to Elisabeth's suite. With hope more than expectation, he tried the handle, and almost to his surprise discovered that it was not locked. He stepped quickly inside and closed the door behind him.

He could hear the blood pulsing through his head. Now he really had crossed a boundary. And there was no way back from here if caught.

He slipped like a ghost through the sterile stillness of her living room, and into the bedroom. It was warm in here, with the smell of bedsheets and bodies. Tangled covers were thrown carelessly aside, a pink nightdress lying in a heap on the floor. Presumably such things were attended to by the staff.

The clothes which Marc Fraysse had once worn still hung from the rail in the wardrobe. Neat rows of laundered shirts, jackets, trousers. Not much chance of his scent surviving the washing machine, or a trip to the dry-cleaners. His shoes, perhaps. Enzo's eyes ran along the neat row of shoes lined up beneath the hanging clothes. But concealing a shoe as he tried to leave the hotel might prove more difficult in practise than in theory. Shelves rose one above the other at the far end of the *armoir*, beyond the rail. Underwear. Underpants and undershirts. Socks. All crisply laundered. And then above them, a pile of neatly folded winter scarves. He remembered Dominique's story of her aunt's inherited scarf, and the smell of her it had retained for years beyond her death. In general, scarves were things that people wore and put away, wore and put away. How often, if ever, were they washed or laundered?

He reached up and took down a folded Paisley patterned silk scarf lined with camel-colored cashmere. As he opened it up he immediately saw the dead man's hairs still clinging in places to the wool. He lifted it to his face and breathed it in. There was a faintly damp smell, like something you might find in the cellar. A hint of something perfumed. Aftershave perhaps. And something else with a slightly sour note, like stale body odour. This was, he felt certain, the best example he was likely to find of something that still bore the dead man's scent.

The sound of the door opening into Elisabeth Fraysse's living room caused his heart to freeze. His face stinging with shock, he stood stock still, listening, almost paralysed. He heard her clearing her throat and knew that he was trapped. His mind went into superdrive, computing every possible alternative open to him. There weren't many, so it didn't take long.

He closed the wardrobe door and moved toward the door to Marc's study with all the care of a man walking barefoot on glass. If it was locked, the game was up. To his enormous relief the handle turned in his fingers and the door opened with the faintest creak of its hinges. In his head it sounded like a saw cutting through steel. He moved quickly from one room to the next and pulled the door shut, just as he heard the bedroom door opening from the living room.

He looked around in a panic. There was nowhere to hide. And then he saw the key in the door leading the hall. Three long, soft, strides took him to the door. He turned the key and pushed down the handle, and was out into the hall, even as he heard the door to the study opening from the bedroom.

He almost ran along the hallway, fumbling for his keycard to let himself into his rooms, shutting the door behind him and leaning back against it, hearing and feeling the thump of his heart as it hammered against his ribs. If anyone tried the study door, he or she would know it had been unlocked from the inside. But nobody had seen him, and he had left no traces. There was nothing to point to him. Any member of the housekeeping staff might have unlocked it for access and forgotten to re-lock it.

He looked down at the scarf still clutched in his hand. This was, perhaps, the longest shot that he had ever taken. But he needed evidence, hard evidence. A place to start. Without it, he knew, there was little or no chance of ever finding out who had killed the most famous chef in France.

Chapter Twenty-six

Enzo met Dominique in the parking area at the foot of the track which led up through the woods to the old *buron*. He parked his 2CV beside the dark blue gendarme van and was greeted by an affectionate assault from an excited Tasha, who danced and leapt around him like a demented dervish.

There was a moment of strangeness between him and Dominique. Her uniform created a distance between them, and neither was sure if a kiss was appropriate. All the intimacy of the night before had vanished, it seemed, like snow melting on water. Some unspoken agreement that somehow passed between them put business ahead of personal pleasure. They were, after all, investigating a man's murder.

"Did you get something?"

He nodded and patted a bulge beneath the zip of his anorak. "A scarf. It still has some of his hair on it."

"Good. Let's go."

And they started up through the trees. Rain drifted down through the unaccustomed stillness around them, like a mist, soaking everything it touched. Tasha ran on ahead, barking at shadows, picking up the scent of rabbits or deer, and zig-zagging away through the dripping pines on fruitless tangents.

When, finally, they broke cover of the trees, Enzo felt the rain seeping into his soul. His pants were sodden, the collar of his shirt beneath his waterproof was wet, his hair plastered to his head. Even his feet felt damp. Dominique's face was pink and shining wet as she turned to wait for him to catch her up. Tasha was already bounding away through the dead grasses of the hillside, ignoring the track, revelling in her freedom.

Enzo and Dominique, however, followed the track to where it doubled back on itself and climbed steeply up toward the plateau. The wet stone shadow of the ruined *buron* appeared on the horizon above them like a ghost. By the time they reached it, Enzo was short of breath, and they stood inside sheltering from the rain until he recovered.

Dominique called Tasha and the dog came leaping and bounding inside to join them. The gendarme made her sit. Enzo took out Marc Fraysse's scarf to let her sniff it. Tasha buried her nose in the wool, snuffling with interest at these new and unexpected smells, millions of tiny receptors in her nose registering and translating them into coded messages to be sent and stored in her brain.

Dominique watched her absorb the scent left in this world by a dead man more than seven years before. "It's amazing. As if her sense of smell is even more important than her sight."

"It is," Enzo said, "Smells, for a dog, create a kind of architecture of the world around them that their brains translate into a mental picture. Tasha's sense of smell is a thousand times better than ours. She has around two hundred million nasal olfactory receptors, and can detect odours at concentrations nearly one hundred million times lower than us. If we asked her to, she could detect one drop of blood in five liters of water."

She glanced at him, her eyes wide with wonder. "You know your stuff."

He grinned. "I do."

Dominique reached into her pocket and produced the black ball that was the object of Tasha's obsession. It excited her interest immediately, causing her to abandon the scarf, but Dominique instantly withdrew the ball to hold it behind her back and reintroduce the scarf.

Tasha's training kicked in. She remembered the game, and her eyes shone with excitement. She barked, then, as Dominique held the ball out of reach and pointed at the door.

"*Allez! Allez!*" she shouted, and Tasha went bounding out into the rain. Enzo and Dominique went after her, struggling to keep up as Tasha went running left and right, her nose to the ground, absolutely focused on finding the scent that she knew would bring the reward of her ball. For a while she followed the path above the treeline, then went haring off among the rocks on the plateau, lifting her head occasionally to sniff the air, sampling the scents it carried.

After fifteen minutes, her obsession was driving her further and further from the *buron*, without success. Enzo and Dominique were finding it hard to keep up, and something about the vast open space of the plateau and the density of the hillside forest brought it home to Enzo just how hopeless this was. The words needle and haystack came to his mind, but even they seemed inadequate to measure the enormity of the task they had set the dog, and the odds against her finding something that might not even be there.

Dominique stood with her hands on her hips. "Looks like a waste of time," she said and called out Tasha's name. Her voice rang across the hillside before being soaked up by the rain. But Tasha's fixation was making her deaf, or at least impervious, to her mistress' call. She was two or three hundred meters away, and disappeared down into the trees. Dominique sighed and looked up into the low cloud that hung, it seemed, just above their heads. The rain was more than a mist now, and Enzo could hear it beating a tattoo on their waterproofs. "I guess she'll give up in time. We should get back to the shelter of the *buron*. She'll know where to find us."

They trudged wearily back across the plateau to the old ruined shelter and squeezed into the damp and dark beneath the *lauzes*, to peer out miserably into the gloom. The valley below them had been swallowed up by cloud and rain. The chill in the air was raw, and Enzo was not sure if he had ever felt quite so cold.

Dominique reached up to lean against the cracked stone lintel above the door, her face set in grim acceptance of failure. "What will you do when this is all over here?"

"Go back to Cahors, the university in Toulouse. In a few months I'll start looking at case number six."

She nodded, knowing that this man who had come so unexpectedly into her life would leave again just as suddenly. In twenty-four hours, everything had changed, and yet nothing had changed. "Will this be your first failure?"

Enzo allowed himself a wry smile. "I haven't given up yet."

"But you have no real evidence. Nothing to work with. And that's what you need, isn't it? I mean, what do you know that you didn't know before?"

"I know a lot more about Fraysse himself. I know that he and his brother had a feud that lasted nearly twenty years, and that the falling out between them was over Elisabeth. I know that Marc Fraysse had a gambling problem. Elisabeth's word, not mine, although she used it in denial. But he had an addiction, that is certain, and owed somebody a lot of money. I know that he'd been having an affair with the wife of his *second*. An affair that he ended abruptly just days before he was murdered."

He had been over it all with her the previous night, but condensing it now, like this, made him realize just how little he really had to go on. And he saw in her eyes that she knew it, too.

Somewhere in the far distance they heard Tasha barking. A bark that echoed dully among the trees, absorbed by the stillness and the wet, but which was repeated and persistent.

Dominique looked alarmed. "Oh, my god, I hope she's alright. I know that there have been poachers up here recently. I suppose they could have set traps. I never thought about that." Even as she spoke, Tasha's distant bark seemed to turn hoarse, almost into a whine. Dominique rushed out on to the hillside, and Enzo followed, filled with a dread sense of guilt, knowing that he wouldn't be able to forgive himself if anything had happened to her dog.

They followed the track, Enzo struggling to keep up, to the point where they had seen Tasha disappearing among the trees. The barking was much closer now, and if anything, more frantic. Dominique thrashed through the undergrowth, finding herself eventually on a deer track that cut through the woods. Both she and Enzo found rain-laden webs bursting on their faces as they broke through virgin territory where spiders had labored in the dark the night before.

They saw Tasha in a small clearing below them, an area of fern beaten down by gathering animals, probably deer. Moss-covered rocks had been exposed in the slope at some point by tiny mud slides. A fallen tree lay across the track. Enzo scrambled after the young gendarme as she climbed over it, and they found Tasha digging frantically at the foot of one of the rocks. Barking and whining, excited, almost frenzied.

Dominique crouched beside her, to be greeted by a flapping pink tongue in her face and muddy feet scrabbling at her thighs. She produced the black ball. Tasha snatched it from her hand, moving away then, chewing it and growling, dropping it and snatching it. Job done. Obsession rewarded.

Enzo crouched down beside Dominique. "What did she find?"

"I don't know. Something buried here beneath the stone, maybe."

Enzo took a pair of latex gloves from his pocket and snapped them on before starting to move away the earth and pebbles disturbed by the dog. He reached a slab of flat stone a matter of inches below the surface, and dug away the earth with his fingers until he found its edge, then pulled it up.

There, in a shallow hollow beneath the stone, lay a discolored purple waterproof fanny bag still attached to its belt.

The Scotsman and the gendarme exchanged looks. "Marc Fraysse's missing bag." He allowed himself a tiny smile. He had played very, very long odds, and won. Fraysse himself would have approved.

Enzo ripped off his soiled and torn latex gloves and replaced them with a fresh pair. Carefully, he removed the pouch from its seven-year resting place, and with almost trembling fingers unzipped it. Both he and Dominique peered inside.

"My god," she whispered. "The phone and the knife are still there."

The Thiers knife, a Nokia cellphone, and the bag that Marc Fraysse had once worn around his waist lay on Dominique's desk in clear plastic evidence bags. All three items would be dusted for prints and subjected to minute forensic examination. But Enzo was only too acutely aware of the fact that while he had been responsible for their discovery, he had no claim over them whatsoever. On finding them, they had immediately become official evidence in a murder enquiry that could no longer be considered 'cold'.

Dominique slumped into her chair, her waterproofs still dripping on the coat stand. "I'll have them couriered to the *police scientifique* labs in Clermont Ferrand. We should have results back in a few days."

Enzo gazed at the dead man's possessions recovered from the hill, frustrated, eaten up by impatience. "How about holding off on that for twenty-four hours?"

She looked at him in surprise. "Why?"

He shrugged. "They may, or may not, turn up something interesting. But on balance, I figure probably not."

"What difference would it make to wait twenty-four hours?"

"Maybe all the difference in the world. And what's one day after seven years?"

She narrowed her eyes and cocked her head to one side. "So what are you proposing?"

"You can dust the phone for prints here, right?"

She nodded. "I could, yes."

"Well, why don't you do that, and then let me borrow it? Just until tomorrow."

She frowned, and then laughed. "Why? I mean, you can hardly make calls with it. The battery's been dead for years."

"I'm figuring there are some decent-sized cellphone shops down in Clermont."

"Sure. All the major providers. SFR, Bouygues, Orange… I know it was in a waterproof bag, Enzo, but surely you don't think they could get it working?"

"No." He sat down opposite her. "But the sim card is intact. And it should be a fairly simple matter to access the information on it. Addresses, phone numbers. Calls made. Calls received. We know now for certain that theft wasn't the motive for the murder. The sim card should be able to tell us out who was the last person he spoke to on that phone. And that could be crucial." He tilted his head and gave her his most appealing smile. "Is that not worth a one-day wait? I'm going down to Clermont with Guy Fraysse early tomorrow. We could know by lunchtime."

She drew a deep breath. "You're taking advantage of me."

"Of course."

"It could cost me my job."

He shook his head. "I won't tell if you don't."

Chapter Twenty-seven

Guy's bright yellow Renault Trafic wound down the hill in the dark toward the *autoroute*. Empty crates rattled and clattered about in the back. Enzo held on with white knuckles to the handle on the passenger door, but refrained from expressing the opinion that Guy was driving far too fast on wet roads. He had obviously done it many times over the years, in all weathers, and was still here to tell the tale. Presumably he knew the road as well as the map of broken veins he saw on his face each morning as he shaved. And that he had found time to shave before leaving this morning was evinced by the powerfully pungent smell of aftershave that filled the cab.

He had been oddly quiet when they met up in the car park just after five, and they had driven in silence over to Thiers and then down into the valley to connect with the motorway. It wasn't until a curling slip road took them on to the A72 west, and the lights of vehicles heading toward the city became a dazzle in the rearview mirror, that Enzo broke the silence. In fact, he did more than break it. He dropped a bomb into it.

"Did you know about your brother's gambling problem, Guy?"

Whatever thoughts had occupied him until now, Enzo's question startled them away. He flicked a frown toward the Scotsman. "Marc liked to put a few euros on the horses, sure. But a problem? Where did you hear that?"

"His wife."

Guy's head snapped around again. "Elisabeth told you Marc had a gambling problem?" He seemed incredulous.

"No, she denied that he had. Unprompted. Which, in my experience means that he did."

"Well…" Guy seemed to be focusing his attention on the road again. "He loved a wager, I'll give you that. All his life. But when he bet his wages on a game of *pétanque* all those years ago, he was gambling on his own ability."

"Maybe he thought he knew a thing or two about horses."

Guy laughed, but it was a laugh without humour. "Marc? I don't think so. Nobody wins putting money on horses, Enzo." He paused, and Enzo thought he saw the slightest curl of contempt at the corner of Guy's mouth. "Except the bookies."

◇◇◇

Guy backed his Trafic up to the tradesman's entrance of the St. Pierre indoor market in the old town. The market itself was housed in an ugly modern building of blue and yellow that stood in the shadow of the twin spires of the cathedral. The contrast with an age of elegance, in which aesthetics had once counted for something, could hardly have been more stark. Graffiti covered the doors and shutters, but the real vandalism lay in the building itself. It defaced this otherwise charming square overlooked by the wrought-iron balconies of gracious eighteenth century apartments, and lined with speciality food and flower shops.

Enzo followed Guy inside where traders were setting out fresh produce straight from the surrounding farms of the Massif. A bewildering display of fruit and vegetables, meat, and cheeses. Raised voices echoed among the rafters in the cold as the *commerçants* called out early morning greetings and cracked jokes, fingerless gloves on chilled fingers, feet stamping on hard concrete for warmth. Breath misted and swirled around their heads like smoke, while the freshly hosed floor reflected overhead lights as if it had just been painted and not yet dried.

Guy strode among the stands, shaking hands and calling out greetings. Everyone knew him and called him *Monsieur Fraysse.*

And although they used the familiar *tu*, there was a sense of respect in the way they addressed him. He was one of them, but had somehow risen above them. And that, it seemed, was worthy of their deference. A country boy made good.

He glanced back at Enzo. "I won't buy any vegetables here. I like to get them straight from the farmer, but my butcher is incomparable." He stopped at the Boucherie Clermontoise and shook hands with the *boucher*. They bantered for some minutes before getting down to the serious question of what was available, what was best quality, and how much it was going to cost. The butcher was a ruddy-faced man with hardly any hair and cracked, blood-red hands. He displayed several cuts of meat, still on the bone, the butchered carcasses of sheep and pigs, great dark mounds of liver. Guy inspected the quality of the meat and the duck, the *poules* and the *poulets*. Whatever he ordered it was going to be in bulk, enough at least to feed several hundred mouths over several days, and they haggled keenly over the price, almost coming to blows apparently, before finally shaking hands, smiling and winking as if it had all been a game. Which it probably was.

Guy turned to Enzo as they headed back toward the exit. "He'll package it all up for me and I'll come and pick it up later. We'll head out to the warehouse at Brézet now and choose the vegetables. Then on to the fish market."

"Could I meet you back here? There's some business I'd like to attend to while I'm in Clermont."

Guy seemed surprised, a little disappointed. "Sure." They went down the ramp into the square, where Guy had left the van's engine running to keep the cab warm. "Anything I can help you with?"

"I need to find a phone shop," Enzo said. "I've got a problem with my cellphone."

"Who are you with?"

"SFR."

"Oh, well, no problem, then. I think there's one just around the corner there in the Rue des Gras." He waved a hand vaguely toward the far side of the square, then nodded toward the Coq Argente next to the cheese shop. "Why don't I meet you in the café in about an hour or so, and we can have breakfast?"

◇◇◇

The SFR store was at the foot of the steep and narrow, pedestrianized Rue des Gras. At the top of the street the cathedral gazed down on to the city below, tasking the faithful with the punishing climb up the hill to pray and confess and show their penitence. There was no forgiveness without pain.

Enzo had to wait for some time, stamping his feet in the cold, till the store opened. Eventually, sliding glass doors in a stone arch admitted him to its help counter where a young man with long, nimble fingers and hair gelled into spikes examined Marc Fraysse's old cellphone with a dismissive shrug.

"Almost a museum-piece," he said. Such was the pace of technology. "What exactly do you want me to do with it?"

"I was wondering if it would be possible to transfer the data from the sim card into one which I could use in my present phone." And Enzo laid his own, much more recent model of cellphone, on the counter top.

The young man took a quick look at Enzo's phone, and Enzo was certain that he detected a faint sneer in the pursing of his lips. Enzo's cell was at least two generations old. No touch screen, no built in video or satellite navigation, no chipful of apps. Just a simple phone, with a camera that Enzo hadn't even wanted. "Sure. You're an existing client, right?"

"Yes."

"No problem, then. Have to charge you for the sim card, though."

"That's fine."

"Wanna keep your old one?"

"Yes please."

"Okay." His long, bony fingers opened up Marc Fraysse's cellphone with amazing speed and dexterity and slid out the sim card. He took it away to snap into some kind of data reader and download its contents to a computer. Then he inserted a new sim and transferred the information back again. It took less than two minutes. He slapped the fresh sim card down on the counter. "There you go."

With a growing sense of anticipation, Enzo made his way back along the Rue St. Barthelemy to the Place St. Pierre, and pushed through more glass doors out of the cold and into the steamy warmth of the Coq Argente. There he slipped into a black, tubular chair behind an orange-topped table opposite the bar, and in response to the raised eyebrows of the barman, ordered a *petit café*. He placed both phones on the table in front of him, and carefully snapped the fresh sim free of its holder card. With considerably less dexterity than the young man in the phone store, he opened up his own phone and slid out the sim card. Careful not to touch the patterned gold of the chip, he took the new card and clipped it into place. He closed up the phone, turning it around to press the red button.

The tiny screen flickered, delivered an annoying little melody, then booted up its welcome: a silvered graphic of cogs and wheels, a three-bar indicator that showed the battery was full, and a signal index that registered an almost full-strength signal. Using the up-down, left-right arrow keys on a control wheel beneath the screen, he navigated his way through the menu, finally finding and bringing up the calls register. It showed the telephone numbers of the last calls made, and received. There had been calls to and from both Elisabeth and Guy, and one from Georges Crozes. There were other names and numbers that meant nothing to Enzo. It could take some time to track down who was who, and who owned the numbers without names attached to them.

The last call registered had been at 2.15pm on the day he died. It was a call made to a number not in his address book, because there was no name appended. But it must have been made shortly before he set off on the run from which he would never return. Enzo felt unaccountably disappointed, as if he had thought the phone might somehow replay the conversations and share its secrets. And then it occurred to him that perhaps there might still be messages held by his answering service.

He dialled 123 and listened to it ring until a mechanical voice told him that there were no new messages. He followed the option to listen to archived messages, but was disappointed to be told that there were none. Perhaps they were only held for a limited length of time. Marc Fraysse's actual account must have lapsed in the first year after his death.

He went back to the menu and selected *Messaging*. Any text messages sent or received would not be held by the server, but saved in the memory of the sim card.

There were over sixty messages in the *Sent* box. Enzo flicked through them. Many of them were cryptic SMS texts sent to a number he recognised from the scribbles on the blotter in the dead man's study. Jean Ransou. Bookie to the stars, as Fred had described him.

The most recent had been sent to the same number he had called on the day of his murder, but twenty-four hours earlier. It said simply, *Please forgive me*. Like a dying man's last words.

Enzo opened up the *In* box. It contained fifteen messages. The final text had been received on the actual morning of his murder, and it had come from the same number he had texted the previous day and called after lunch. It read, *Meet me at the old buron at three*. Enzo felt all the hair standing up on the back of his neck. There was a very good chance that this rendezvous had been requested by his killer.

He sipped on the coffee which had gone cold as he searched through the dead man's phone history and wondered what it all meant. Marc had texted someone the day before his death with his request for forgiveness. The same person had responded the following morning, asking for a meeting at the ruined *buron* that afternoon. Shortly after lunch, he had made his final telephone call to the same number. Had it been a call to confirm the requested rendezvous? If so, whoever had asked for it was likely to have been the last person to have seen him alive? Which would also make that person his killer. Enzo knew that if could find out whose number it was, there was a good chance it would lead him to the murderer.

"How did it go? They fix your phone?"

Enzo looked up, startled, to see Guy approaching him across the café. He slipped his phone into his pocket, realizing only at the last moment that Marc's old cell was still lying on the table. He snatched it quickly away, uncertain whether or not Guy could have registered that it was Marc's, or if indeed he had even noticed it. He managed a smile. "Yeah, they gave me a new sim. Seems to have sorted out the problem."

Guy dropped into a seat opposite and waved a hand at the barman. "Bring us a basket of croissants, Jacques. And I'll have a *grande crème*." He cast an enquiring look at Enzo.

"Same for me," Enzo said. "Get everything you wanted?"

Guy grinned. "Several kilos of *rouget*, flash frozen on the quayside as it was landed off the boat at Sète, and a good selection of fresh autumn vegetables. Just got to pick up the meat and cheese after breakfast, and that should see us through till we close next week."

But Enzo wasn't listening. He was a million miles away, replaying text messages and telephone calls in his head.

Chapter Twenty-eight

Enzo stood by the window gazing out through the cold, damp air at the mist that lay in strands across the hillside, partially masking the houses that climbed its terraces to the volcanic crags that dominated the town. He could hear Dominique's voice as she spoke on the phone, but he wasn't really listening. He was picking through the complex web of relationships that Marc Fraysse had spun around his life, trying to determine which, if any of them, had led to his murder.

Dominique hung up on her call, and he heard her gasp of frustration. "Nothing is ever simple, is it?"

He turned from the window. "What did they say?"

"The number that he called, that he sent and received the texts from, is out of use. Has been for years. And the phone company that originally serviced it no longer exists. It was taken over by France Telecom and eventually subsumed into Orange. It's going to take some time to track down who the original owner of that number was."

Enzo nodded thoughtfully. "By 'some time', how long do you mean?"

"Two, three days… who knows?"

"In that case I think I'll go to Paris for a couple of days."

"Why?" The disappointment in her voice was patent.

"I have some personal things to attend to."

"Charlotte?"

He shrugged. He was still undecided on that issue. "Maybe. I'll see Raffin and my daughter. My *other* daughter, Kirsty."

"And that's the only reason you have for going to Paris?"

"No. There are some people I'd like to talk to about Fraysse."

"Like?"

"Like someone at Michelin. I'd like to know if the rumor that Fraysse was about to lose his third star was true or not." He turned to gaze out of the window again. "And Jean-Louis Graulet."

"The food critic?"

He nodded. "Marc and a couple of other three-star chefs pulled a pretty humiliating stunt on him. If we're looking for motive, then Graulet has plenty, even if Elisabeth did say he was in Paris at the time." He turned around to find her looking at him intently. "Was that something you checked out during your investigation?"

She shook her head. "I didn't even know there *was* bad feeling between Marc and Graulet."

He nodded again. "Then there's the whole gambling issue and his relationship with Jean Ransou. He's a man I definitely need to talk to."

Dominique frowned. "Be careful, Enzo. I did some checking on Ransou after you told me about him. A very dangerous man from all accounts. Well connected on both sides of the legal divide. He's been suspected of complicity in several murders, but always manages to get himself off the hook."

"All the more reason to speak to him, then."

As he turned once more toward the window, he saw that the light was fading. Somehow the day had just vanished. The sim card had been a breakthrough, but the defunct cellphone number had stalled it again. One step forward, two frustrating steps back. It was time to dot the i's and cross the t's on all the other threads of the investigation. Or was he just looking for an excuse to go to Paris? Dominique's impassioned plea for Enzo to confront Charlotte over the issue of their son had forced back to the surface the deep sense of grievance he had been trying to keep buried.

He suddenly became aware of Dominique standing very close to him at the window. He could feel the heat of her body, hear her breathing. Beyond the door of her office, he was conscious of the chatter of keyboards, the voices of other gendarmes, phones ringing.

"Come and eat with me again tonight." Her voice was little more than a whisper.

He turned to find her face upturned toward his, and something in her dark eyes made his stomach flip over. He took her face in his hands and softly kissed her lips as her arms slid up under his jacket, around his back, pulling herself into his chest.

"I don't want you to go to Paris. I just found you. I don't want to lose you."

He wrapped his arms around her and held her close. And he knew that whatever turn of fate had made their paths cross, it was almost certain to bring them back to divergence, sooner rather than later. He said: "It's not lasagne again, is it?" And she laughed.

"Tasha and I had the leftovers yesterday. I was thinking more… take-away pizza?"

He grinned. "Another fine Italian dish. How could I resist?"

Chapter Twenty-nine

The temptation had been to stay over. But Enzo was concerned that he had not seen Sophie for a couple of days. Not since the night that her aspiring boyfriend had attacked him at the *château*. And he wanted to be around if she needed him. So it had been with some difficulty that he had managed to tear himself free of Dominique's arms and get dressed again for the drive back up to the hotel.

It was almost midnight, and the road was deserted. The cloud was low over the hills, the air made opaque by the damp delineating his headlamps in misted white beams that raked across hectares of thick pine forest as he navigated the winding road up the hill.

Finally he reached the turn-off and took a left, accelerating up into the private road that cut through the trees toward the auberge. The dark seemed particularly impenetrable here, and the two horsepower engine of his old *deux chevaux* strained as he pulled back into third and pushed the accelerator to the floor. He passed the beaten parking area at the foot of the track that led up to the *buron*, following the curve of the road past the point where he had seen the men putting in snow poles the day he arrived. The red-and-white striped poles reflected the light of his headlamps now. With the road falling away, first on the right, then on the left, he could see why they would be vital for keeping a vehicle on the road in heavy snow.

With the warm air powering out of the heating vent below the dash, Enzo felt a wave of fatigue wash over him, and he remembered the taste and scent and touch of the woman he had been lying in bed with just half an hour before.

He rounded a bend, and a dark shape loomed up at him suddenly out of the night. He jammed on his brakes and skidded to a halt centimetres before making contact with the tree that lay directly across the road blocking his path. Cursing his luck, he got out of the car to take a look, his body cutting through the beam of his headlights and casting a long shadow ahead of him into the night.

The old pine tree was half-rotten and must have been on the verge of falling for some time. Pine needles stabbed him through his pants as he clambered over the trunk to see if there was any way it could be rolled aside. But it was completely immovable. It would take a mechanical digger to shift it.

It was only then that he became aware of the light around him fading, and he looked up to see the headlights of his car receding as the vehicle started rolling backwards down the hill.

"Hey!" he shouted. As if it might somehow hear him and stop. He clambered back over the trunk, feeling branches tearing at his clothes, and started running after it. For a moment he seemed to be catching it, but with the steepness of the descent it was rapidly picking up pace, and he realized it was hopeless. Still he ran, arms windmilling now as he too started losing control, stopping himself from falling at the last moment only by jarring his feet against the pitch of the incline. He brought himself to a shuddering halt just as his car disappeared silently from view, tipping backwards down the slope at the bend in the road, its headlights tilted suddenly upwards, like spotlights searching the sky.

Enzo ran on to the bend and stood at the edge of a steep precipice, looking down at his car half buried in bracken at the foot of the slope. It was cradled by a mesh of sapling branches and undergrowth in an impossible position, its headlamps still pointed straight up, the engine racing.

Enzo was almost tempted to go down after it, but it was a treacherous, crumbling scree, and in the dark he risked a fall that could break his neck. And to what end? There was no way he could get the car out of there. All he could have done was extinguish the engine and the lights and plunged himself into complete darkness.

So he stood, breathing hard, his heart pounding, wondering how in God's name it could have happened. He had secured the handbrake before leaving the car. Either the brakes had failed or the cable had snapped.

He turned and peered back up the hill through a darkness so dense he could almost touch it. Mist and cloud cover effectively blacked out any light from the sky. He could only see his hands in front of him because of the reflected light from his car's headlamps in the gully behind him. But as he started up the hill that quickly faded, and he felt the night wrapping its blindness around him. Very soon he could see nothing ahead of him at all, and almost fell, stumbling as he blundered into the fallen tree. Needles and branches scratched and tore at him and he clambered clumsily to the other side of it.

He had no option but to try to follow the road up through the trees until he could see the lights of the auberge. But strain as he might through the veil of darkness that lay all around, he could discern no sign of them. Not even a distant glow in the sky. For the first time in his life he experienced how it must feel to be blind. Only his feet beneath him would tell him that he was still on the paved road, his outstretched hands preventing a collision with some unseen obstacle. He had rarely felt so helpless.

Progress was painfully slow as he took one careful step at a time, only too conscious of how the land dropped away to his left. After several minutes, the sound of the waterfall that he had seen many times as he drove up the road began to impinge more powerfully on his consciousness. What had begun as a background ambience had grown to something close to a roar. The expectation of his experience that somehow his eyes would gradually become accustomed to the dark remained unfulfilled. He could still see nothing.

Then a noise somewhere in the trees up to his right made him stop in his tracks, straining to listen above the thunder of the falls. There it was again. A sound like the rustle of branches, the crunching of brittle pine needles underfoot. An animal, perhaps. Guy had said that there were deer and wild boar in the woods. And poachers. His mouth was dry and he could feel his heart pulsing in his throat, almost restricting his breathing.

He called out. "Hello? Hello, anyone there?"

The blast of a shotgun almost deafened him. He saw a momentary flash of searing light among the trees, and felt the force of the pellets as they passed within centimetres of his head.

"Jesus!" he shouted involuntarily. He began running, in no way wanting to present a sitting target for the second barrel. Panic impelled him recklessly into the dark. He had covered only a few meters before becoming aware that he was no longer on the road. He could hear the sound of someone crashing through the woods above him in pursuit, and wondered how the hell the shooter could see him in the dark when Enzo couldn't see him.

Almost as the thought went through his mind, his left leg tripped over the low wooden fence that ran along the side of the road, tipping him sideways. A second volley from the shotgun passed harmlessly over his head. But he was falling now, into the pitch black. Tumbling head over heels, making sporadic, jarring contact with the earth and rock of the hillside, before suddenly flying through space. Complete spatial disorientation felt almost like floating. Only the sound of the waterfall growing in deafening intensity provided him with any sense of his own movement, before he felt its spray in his face, and hit the pool at the foot of it with a force that took his breath away.

Now he was deaf as well as blind. Completely submerged, shocked by the extreme cold, and struggling desperately to hold his breath as he fought to break the surface. But even as he did, the force of the water falling on top of him forced him under again, and he felt his strength and energy being leeched away by icy liquid paralyzing muscles. In a moment of terrifying lucidity, he realized that if he lost consciousness he would never regain it. But it was slipping inexorably away, like sand through his fingers, the last moments of life before death.

Most people who return from near-death experiences talk about a blinding light, as of that at the end of a long tunnel of darkness. Enzo saw that light now. But there was no retreating from it. It sucked him toward it, filling his head and his mind, relentlessly, painfully, until it took him over completely.

If this were death, it brought no relief from physical sensation. The pain of the cold, the injuries sustained by his fall, were all acutely felt. He was shivering uncontrollably. He could hear his teeth chattering, and another, completely involuntary, sound coming from his throat. As if he was attempting to speak.

He heard a voice. "Man, another thirty seconds in there and you were a goner."

The light in his eyes shifted, and he saw the tumbling white water of the falls caught in the beam of a flashlight. Now he saw the face of his rescuer looming over him. A hard, expressionless face, with dark brows gathered in what looked like a frown, beneath a peaked cap pulled down low. It was Lucqui, the gardener. Enzo registered the barrel of a shotgun rising up over his left shoulder, where it was strapped to his back.

"Can you sit up?" He was having to shout above the roar of the water. Strong hands helped Enzo into a sitting position. "See if you can move your arms and legs. Don't want to go moving you any more if there's something broken."

Enzo tried his fingers, making fists with each hand, then bending and extending each arm. It was painful, but nothing seemed broken. Finally, he pulled his knees up into his chest, folding his arms around his shins in an embrace of self comfort, a fruitless search for warmth from his own body.

"Guess you're still in one piece, then. Come on, let's get you on your feet."

Powerful arms helped him through the pain barrier to raise him unsteadily to his feet. Almost immediately, his legs gave way beneath him, and he grabbed on to Lucqui to stop himself from falling, his right hand finding the barrel of the shotgun then sliding quickly down to feel the bite of cold metal on his skin. This gun had not been fired any time recently. So whoever had shot at Enzo, it wasn't Lucqui.

Finally, Enzo found his voice. "S..someone sh..shot at me."

"I know, I heard it."

"Wh..what the hell were you doing out here at this time of night?"

"Looking for poachers. And it's a good job for you I was. I was up the hill there when I saw your car rolling backwards down into the gully. You must have left the handbrake off."

"I didn't!" Enzo's denial seemed unnecessarily strenuous, even to him.

Lucqui was unconvinced. "You're lucky you didn't get your head blown off. Damned poachers! They shoot at anything that moves."

The only illumination in the kitchen came from a handful of strategically placed night lights, and so areas of it remained mired in shadow. But it was warm, and light from the hall fell in long yellow slabs through the glass across the marble table at its center. Enzo sat swaddled in blankets, sipping on piping hot chocolate, his hair hanging in damp strands over his shoulders. In a few minutes he would retreat to his room and stand under a hot shower until all vestiges of the deep chill that had penetrated every cell of his body were banished. But life and warmth had already returned to much of him, bringing with it more pain and a hot, stinging sensation on the skin of his face and hands.

He looked around as the doors slid open and Guy returned with the promised bottle of mirabelle and two shot glasses. He sat down opposite the Scotsman and placed them on the table between them, looking at him with concerned blue eyes. "Feeling any better now?"

Enzo nodded. "A bit."

Guy poured them each a stiff measure. "This'll help." He pushed a glass at Enzo, who lifted it to his lips and poured it back in a single gulp. It almost took his breath away as he felt the heat of it burning all the way down to his stomach. His face flushed. Guy grinned. "See what I mean?" He refilled Enzo's glass, then took a much smaller sip from his own.

Enzo looked at him. "How the hell could they see me in the dark like that, Guy, when I couldn't see them?"

But Guy just shrugged. "On a night like tonight they'd probably have been using night-sight goggles. Lucqui's got a pair himself." He took another sip of mirabelle. "They must have been having a bit of fun with you. You had a lucky escape, Enzo. Not to have been either shot, or drowned. It could have been a fatal accident."

Enzo knocked back his second glass, and banged it down on the table. "It was no accident, Guy. Someone deliberately tried to kill me tonight."

Chapter Thirty

The drizzle settled on them like a fine mist. A penetrating wet. The road, the forest, the drop to the pool at the foot of the falls, all seemed strangely unnatural in the sulphurous light of the morning after.

The tree had been moved off the road. Only a little debris remained as witness to it ever having been there. The revving of a powerful diesel engine filled the still air as the tractor on the bend winched Enzo's vehicle painfully up the scree. A breakdown truck with a flashing orange light was standing by to take it down to a garage in Thiers. Several other vehicles were parked at the roadside, including Dominique's blue van.

Her waterproof jacket shone wet in the dull morning light, her dark eyes troubled and searching his face with concern as they walked down toward the tractor, retracing Enzo's steps of the night before. He moved stiffly, although more freely now than when he had first woken. "You're not still thinking of going to Paris after this?" she said.

"Of course. What else am I going to do? Sit around here waiting for someone to try to kill me again?"

"You don't know that someone was trying to kill you, Enzo."

But he just dug his hands in his pockets and kept his thoughts to himself. "Well, anyway, I've not been wasting my morning while they cleared the road. I made a few phone calls. Arranged a few rendezvous."

"Jean Ransou?"

"Among others. I'm having lunch with Ransou tomorrow at the racetrack at Vincennes."

Dominique's eyes opened wide. "He agreed to meet you, just like that?"

"I didn't think he was going to be very cooperative at first. But the mention of the name Marc Fraysse changed everything."

She frowned. "Be *careful*, Enzo."

He nodded solemnly. "I will."

By the time they reached the bend in the road, Enzo's car was back on the tarmac, and the roar of the tractor had subsided. Enzo walked around his 2CV inspecting it with critical eyes. In fact, the damage was not as bad as he had feared. The paintwork was scratched, and the rear wheel arches and the lid of the trunk were dented in places. A mechanic in blue overalls was hooking it up to winch it on to his truck.

"What do you think?" Enzo nodded toward his battered car.

The mechanic shrugged indifferently. "I don't think there's much mechanical damage. The engine stalled, probably within a few minutes, and the lights drained the battery."

Dominique peered inside the car. "What about the handbrake?"

"When I first climbed down to take a look at it, the handbrake was in the off position. The idiot who was driving it must have got out without putting it on."

Enzo bristled. "I'm the idiot who was driving it, and I can assure you, I put the handbrake on before I got out of the car."

"If you say so, pal." He climbed into his cab to start up the winch.

Dominique glanced thoughtfully at Enzo. "You couldn't have."

Enzo restrained the urge to raise his voice. "Look at the incline of the road up there where the tree was," he said. "If I'd got out of the car without putting on the handbrake it would have started rolling backwards immediately. As it was, I was out of the car and over the other side of the tree before it began to move."

"So how come the handbrake was in the off position?"

His indignation was beginning to get the better of him. "Well, obviously someone was hiding in the woods, watching for my arrival, waiting to ambush me. I left the driver's door open. He must have slipped in and released the handbrake while I was climbing over the tree. And then he tried to shoot me."

"But why, Enzo? Who would want to kill you?"

"Whoever killed Marc Fraysse. Which only tells me that we must be getting pretty damned close to finding out who that is."

Chapter Thirty-one

Paris, France, October 2010

Enzo had not known what to expect of Jean Ransou, but the image that confronted him when they met outside the blue gates of the *hippodrome*, deep in the Bois de Vincennes on the eastern outskirts of Paris, was like that of a character who had just stepped out of a fifties French *noir* movie.

He was a big man, almost as wide as he was tall. He wore a black fedora tipped slightly forward at an angle on his head, and a long black coat with a cream silk scarf hanging loose at his neck. His black shoes were polished to an immaculate shine, so dazzling that had he wanted, he could have tipped his head forward to adjust the angle of his hat in the reflection. Black was the fashionable color in Paris, making the grey pallor of his face stark in contrast. A face that would turn heads in any crowd.

Pockmarked by adolescent acne, or perhaps childhood chickenpox, it was a wide, fleshy face flanked by gross, cauliflower ears with a broken nose at its center, squashed almost flat to one side. Fat, pale lips bore the scars of frequent splitting, and the whole gave the impression of a cake that had been left out in the rain.

Only his eyes betrayed the man behind the face. The palest of grey eyes that fixed Enzo in their compelling gaze, both wary and amused, but clearly intelligent. A faint smile parted his lips as they shook hands. "Started out life as a boxer," he said. "But I can see you've already worked that one out." His voice came from his throat and sounded like someone trying to shred stone with a cheese grater. "Wasn't any good at it, though. As you can see. Discovered that horses were more my game. Betting on them that is, not riding them." He laughed. "Might have kept my good looks if I'd found out sooner."

It was clearly a well-rehearsed opening gambit, and it probably impressed actors and politicians. Enzo was more cautious, allowing himself only the most perfunctory of smiles. Which did not go unnoticed. The amusement faded from Ransou's eyes.

"I'm only going to tell you this one time, Monsieur Macleod. Repeat anything I tell you today to anyone in the police or the judiciary, and I'll be sending my condolences to your family."

"Why did you agree to see me, then?"

"Because I want to see the bastard that murdered Marc Fraysse caught and hung up by his testicles till he drops off." The smile returned to his face and he slapped Enzo's back, guiding him through the turnstile toward the main entrance. "Come on, let's eat. I don't want to miss any of the racing."

Escalators zig-zagged them up from floor to floor through the vast echoing hallway of the main stand, a mammoth edifice of steel and glass. They climbed the last few steps to the open doorway of Le Prestige restaurant at the top of the building. A dinner-jacketed flunky almost bowed in deference to the man in black, ushering him and Enzo to a private table in a booth that looked out through panoramic windows across the racetrack below.

The oval circuit consisted of what looked like black gravel or ash. Tractors dragged giant rakes around it to drain a surface turned to sludge by the rain. The area contained by the track was grassy and peppered by parked cars and horse boxes. A huge screen conveyed flickering images of a live race in progress at Deauville.

A waiter in a white jacket brought them menus.

Enzo said, "Why are you so interested in finding Marc's murderer."

"Because I liked him, monsieur. He was one of the most famous men in France, but he had no airs or graces. He came from poor peasant stock in *la France profonde*, in the same way that I grew up in the *banlieus* of Paris, the son of a road sweeper and a Hungarian immigrant. He treated me with the same respect he treated all men, he made me laugh, and he cooked the most wonderful food I have ever tasted."

"He also owed you a lot of money, I think." Enzo watched carefully for a reaction. But there was none.

Ransou said simply, "He did."

Down on the track, several jockeys were out with their horses and sulkies, warming up for the competition ahead. It was to be a day of harness racing in the rain.

"He was a lost soul, monsieur. Eaten up by the urge to gamble, destroyed by his recklessness and his unfailing ability to lose."

"Exactly the sort of people you make your living from, I would have thought."

The grey eyes turned to steel. "Be careful, monsieur." He drew a long, slow breath, as if controlling some violent internal urge. "Marc Fraysse owed me more than a million. But I'd never have called it in."

"A million?" Enzo had realized that the debt probably ran to several hundred thousand, but the figure of a million plus was breathtaking. Men had killed for much less. "Why wouldn't you have called it in?"

"Because I regarded him as my friend. We met often when he came up to Paris. And the money he owed me...? Well, it wasn't real, was it? I mean, I didn't lend it to him. It was notional money. Winnings on a bet. I wasn't actually out of pocket." He laughed. "Besides, I had the restaurant as security. There was no way I was ever going to lose."

Enzo frowned. "Chez Fraysse? You had the auberge as security against his losses?"

"Yes. In a way I owned the best restaurant in France, even if only by proxy."

Enzo was stunned by the revelation.

On the far side of the track the first race was underway, riders manoeuvring their horses to achieve a prime position for their sulkies coming off the first bend. Ransou was momentarily distracted, raising binoculars to his eyes to see for himself how the order was shaking out. Enzo watched the TV coverage on the big screen. Black muck from the track was thrown up by the hooves of horses into the faces of the riders in their little buggies behind them. The jockeys' eyes were protected by goggles, but nothing could protect them from the horses' tails that slapped wet in their faces, along with whatever else might be involuntarily expelled from the animals' rears. There was nothing very glamorous about their profession.

"You like a flutter yourself, Monsieur Macleod?"

Enzo turned to find Ransou smiling at the disgust on his face. "No, Monsieur Ransou. I'm not a betting man."

"Oh? That's not what I heard."

Enzo tilted his head and cast a quizzical look at the ex-boxer. "What did you hear?"

"I heard that you bet you could solve the seven best known cold cases in France by applying new science to old evidence."

"Well, let's just say I only bet on a sure thing."

Ransou grinned. "Me too." He paused. "I'd have given you good odds on that."

Enzo was forced this time to smile. "I bet you would."

"Hah!" Ransou jabbed a finger in Enzo's direction. "There, you see? You're more of a betting man than you knew."

Enzo's reluctant smile developed into a grin. Ransou was a dangerous man, he knew. Certainly not one to cross. But there was, nonetheless, something irresistibly likeable about him. "So... when Marc died, you just wrote off the debt?"

Ransou wrinkled his face in mirthful amusement. "Good God, no. I called it in and it was paid off in full."

Enzo stared at him in amazement. "But... who? Who paid you?"

"His brother, Guy, of course. I had no qualms at all about taking the money off *him*." The first race came to an end, jockeys lashing sweating horses across the finish line below them. Ransou looked satisfied with the result, and picked up his menu. "Let's order, shall we? I'm starving. And I just earned lunch."

Chapter Thirty-two

It was always with a sense of dread these days that Enzo pushed open the heavy green door that led to the inner courtyard behind Raffin's apartment. And, as always, as it shut behind him, the sounds of the city's bustling sixth *arrondissement* grew hushed and distant. His own footsteps echoed back at him from the apartments that loomed on all sides, cobbles made slippery by the wet leaves shed from the old chestnut tree that provided such delicious summer shade.

He was haunted still by the memory of the shooting that had so nearly taken Raffin's life. He remembered the journalist lying bleeding in the hall outside his apartment, his blood on Enzo's hands, in more ways than one.

Now, as then, and almost every time he came, someone somewhere was practising the piano. A distant, clumsy rendition of Rachmaninoff. Daylight was fading fast, to be replaced by the cold yellow of electric light falling in squares and rectangles from apartment windows. He pushed open the door to the stairwell and began the weary climb to the first floor. He resented the fact that if he wanted to see his daughter nowadays, it meant an encounter with Raffin, too.

He and Raffin had never hit it off since the first moment they met. Only their collaboration on the resolution of the seven cold cases that Raffin had so carefully documented in his book, *Assassins Cachés*, kept relations between them civil. But now that Kirsty was living with him, even that was in danger of breaking down.

Raffin's greeting as he opened the door to him was cool, but polite. The two men shook hands, and Enzo stepped in out of the cold. He remembered entering this apartment for the first time, and his totally unexpected encounter with Charlotte, a serendipitous meeting that had changed his life.

Kirsty rose from the table as he followed Raffin into the sitting room, although sitting room was something of a misnomer. It contained only two uncomfortable leather armchairs, set so low that Enzo found great difficulty getting himself in and out of them. Neither Kirsty nor Raffin, it seemed, ever bothered. They appeared to spend their lives perched on even more uncomfortable chairs at the table, eating, reading, writing, drinking. Tall windows at one end of it looked down into the courtyard below.

"Papa." Kirsty threw her arms around his neck and gave him a long, lingering hug. Then he held her for a moment at arm's length, looking at her.

"Papa? What happened to 'dad'?"

She grinned. "Guess I must be turning into a *vrai française*."

"You look well," he told her. And she did. Gone was the pallor and the smudged shadows beneath her eyes that he had noticed at their last meeting. Her face seemed fuller somehow, slightly flushed, and her eyes shone.

Raffin watched them in brooding silence, and Enzo wondered briefly if he was jealous of their relationship. After years of estrangement, Enzo and Kirsty had rediscovered the affinity of father and daughter. Something, strangely, that had not suffered from the revelation that she had actually been fathered by his best friend. He had always been her father, and she his little girl. And nothing could change that.

She flicked long, dark hair out of her face, and folded her willowy figure back into the dining chair. "Sit down. Roger will crack open a bottle of something nice." She flicked a glance at Roger, and the journalist responded with a tiny nod of acquiescence and went in search of that something nice. "So how have you been?"

"Apart from being beaten up by one of Sophie's jealous suitors, and someone trying to blow my head off up on the Massif, everything's hunky dory." He grinned, and Kirsty was unsure if he was being serious or not. He heard Raffin laughing in the next room.

"Still in the wars, then?" His raised voice came through the open door.

"'Fraid so."

"How's it going? The Fraysse enquiry, I mean."

"It's slow, Roger. Hardly anything to go on. But I recovered his missing cellphone and the number of someone who arranged to meet him up at the old *buron* the day he was murdered."

Raffin appeared in the doorway, eyes wide with interest. "Really? Whose number?"

"I'm still working on that. But I did find out that he owed a Parisian bookie more than a million euros, and that he'd put up the restaurant as collateral."

Raffin whistled softly.

"And that's not to mention the affair he'd been having with the wife of his *second*."

"Jesus, Enzo! That's hardly what I would call *slow*." Raffin approached the table clutching a bottle and two glasses.

Enzo smiled. "Maybe it just feels like it up there on the plateau in the mist and rain." As Raffin put the bottle on the table, he noticed for the first time what it was. "Dom Pérignon 1995! What's the celebration?"

"A visit from my dad is always cause to celebrate," Kirsty said, a touch ingenuously. She seemed tense as Raffin popped the cork with a flourish, her smile a little strained.

Raffin raised the bottle, along with an eyebrow, in Kirsty's direction. But she shook her head.

"I'll stick with what I've got."

Raffin filled the two glasses with foaming champagne and handed one to Enzo before lifting his own. Kirsty refilled her glass from a bottle of Badoit sitting on the table beside her and raised it in a toast.

"Here's tae us, wha's like us? Damn few, and they're a' deid." A classic Scottish toast.

But Enzo didn't lift his glass. He glanced from one to the other. "What's going on?"

Kirsty's face colored slightly, and she cast a look at Raffin.

"We're getting married," Raffin said.

And Enzo's heart went still, as if someone had touched a button and put it on pause. He looked at Kirsty, who could hardly meet his eye. She had known, as had Raffin, that Enzo would not approve. Enzo made a huge mental effort to press the play button and get his heart beating again. He raised his glass and forced a smile. "Well, congratulations." And he and Raffin sipped their champagne, and Kirsty her water, in embarrassed silence. "Why?" he said, when he took the glass from his lips. "I mean, these days why bother? Lots of people just live together without ever getting married."

"Because I'm pregnant." Kirsty's words dropped like stones into the silence of the room. Enzo was not sure why he was quite so shocked. But he was. He stared at his daughter in disbelief. "It's a boy," she said. "So I'll be giving you a grandson." She made herself laugh. "Bet that makes you feel old."

Finally, he found his voice. "Yes," was all he could say. He raised his glass to his lips again and took a mouthful of foaming fizzy, giving himself a moment to recover his presence of mind. "Well, then, double congratulations are in order." In spite of everything he felt about him, he reached over to shake Raffin's hand, resisting the temptation to crush limp fingers in his stronger grip. And he leaned across the table to kiss his daughter's forehead. He slipped a hand through her hair to cradle the back of her head and draw her toward him until their foreheads touched. And he felt her hand close around his wrist and gently squeeze it.

Then he sat back in his chair to sip again on his champagne, his mind and his heart racing, memories crowding consciousness.

How was it possible? His little girl. She said, "So, anyway, it's made me think a bit. Being a mother, I mean."

"Think about what?"

"Family. Parenthood." She took a sip of her water and fixed him now in her gaze. "I missed you, dad. All those years when I was growing up."

And he felt tears of guilt and regret prick his eyes.

"I don't want that for my son. I want him to have his parents around him. And his grampa. His whole family." She hesitated, momentarily breaking eye contact until she summoned courage to meet his eye again. "And your son shouldn't have to suffer that, either."

"Kirsty…"

But she talked down his protest. "No, dad, listen to me. We're supposed to learn from our mistakes, right?"

Enzo refrained from correcting her. If the mistake was being repeated, it wasn't through any choice of his.

"You've got to speak to Charlotte, dad. You do." She looked at him earnestly, reaching out to wrap long, elegant fingers around his hand. "Call her. Please."

He squeezed her hand in his, staring at the table for a long moment, before looking up. "I already did. I'm meeting her tonight."

Chapter Thirty-three

The Café aux Deux Magots was the classic Parisian tourist *café* in the heart of Saint Germain des Près. It stood right on the boulevard, and had been made famous by its most celebrated client, the writer Ernest Hemingway. The American had spent his impoverished youth in the 1920s making a single coffee, or a beer, or a glass of wine last him all morning while he scribbled in his notebook in a corner of the *café*, penning the stories that would make him the most revered writer of his generation.

Enzo had supposed that Charlotte had chosen it because it would be full of tourists, busy and anonymous. It was easier, perhaps, to exchange angry words in such a place than in some less frequented establishment where their words would draw curious looks.

Enzo ordered a glass of red wine from a waiter in a long black apron who balanced his huge circular tray just above his left shoulder. The *café* was packed. Enzo never ceased to be amazed at how easy it was to be lonely in a crowd.

Charlotte was nearly twenty minutes late. Whatever his feelings about her might have been, the sight of her pushing through the crowds to join him at his table, still made his heart beat faster. She wore a long, black coat open over a woollen polo neck sweater and jeans. The rain glistened in sparkling droplets all over the black curls that tumbled about her shoulders.

She looked well as she leaned over to kiss him on each cheek, then drop into the chair opposite. Her face was flushed with the cold, her eyes dark and shining, the darkest eyes Enzo had ever known. Unfathomable pools that bewitched and hypnotised him. A smile split her face and she seemed genuinely happy to see him.

"How are you, Enzo? Still catching killers?"

"Trying to. How about you?"

"Oh, I don't try to catch them. Just talk them out of it. You know that."

But Enzo knew that wasn't strictly true. Her practise as a therapist was successful enough in its own right, but she had also trained in the States in forensic psychology, and still received the occasional call from the Quai des Orfèvres to help the police with some impenetrable crime. "What will you have to drink?"

"Kir."

He caught the waiter's attention and ordered a Kir and another glass of red.

"So what are you doing in Paris this time?"

Enzo shrugged, reluctant now to get to the point. "This and that."

She smiled at him knowingly. "That must be keeping you fully occupied."

He grinned, then sat back as the waiter delivered their glasses to the table. "Roger and Kirsty are getting married."

"I know."

He shouldn't have been surprised. He knew, after all, that Roger and Charlotte still had occasional contact, a relationship he had never understood. Former lovers who had broken up in acrimony, but still kept in touch. "And she's pregnant."

"I know that, too."

"I suppose Roger told you."

"No, Kirsty did."

Now he really was surprised. "You've seen her?"

"We had lunch the other day." She smiled. "Close your mouth, Enzo. Your jaw hanging open like that makes you look like an idiot."

"I didn't know you saw one another."

"We don't. She called me out of the blue." She sipped her Kir. "Why?"

"To tell me what a heartless, selfish bitch I am." And she laughed out loud at the look on his face. "Oh, not for the way I've been treating you." She paused now, and her smile faded. "For the way I'm treating my son." She caught and corrected herself. "*Our* son." She gazed sightlessly into her drink as she toyed with the glass on the table in front of her. "She told me things. About how she felt when you left. About how she hated and resented you. And how she never stopped loving you, or needing you. And how she had never felt complete until the day you held her again and told her you loved her, and she admitted that she loved you, too."

Enzo felt his eyes filling, and his throat burned.

"And she told me…" She looked up, startled to see his silent tears, and for a moment seemed almost choked herself. "She told me that you weren't really her dad. At least, not her birth father. But that it didn't make any difference. She still loved you, and needed you, and you would always be dad to her."

Enzo was finding it difficult to breathe. "I can't believe she told you all this."

Charlotte found a tiny, sad smile to turn up the corners of her mouth. "She wanted me to realize what it meant to have a father. As much as to realize what it meant not to have one." She paused. "She made a powerful case, Enzo. From experience, and from the heart. She said it was not my place to deny my son the right to his father."

Enzo's world shrank, then, to that tiny place in space and time that existed only across the table between them. The *café* was empty. There were no customers, no voices raised in laughter, no imperious waiters conveying trays of drinks above talking heads. He hardly dared ask. "And?"

"I think, perhaps, my mind and my body were both a little out of balance during those months of pregnancy. And I suppose Kirsty only made me feel what I'd already come to know in my heart." She drained her glass, and her eyes met his very directly. "He's your son, too."

His voice was barely a whisper. "What did you name him?"

She smiled, and in it she saw all the fondness for him that she somehow seemed determined to deny. "Laurent."

Charlotte's home and *cabinet* were in an old converted coal merchant's depot in the thirteenth *arrondissement*. The centerpiece was an indoor garden beneath a glass roof that soared three stories above it. It was here that she conducted her therapy sessions. Her kitchen, office, and sitting room were located in an apartment above the main entrance. Glass-walled bedrooms that looked down on the garden were accessed from railed catwalks built around the inside walls.

Their taxi drew up in the Rue des Tanneries outside the barred windows and grilled door of what had once been the coal merchant's offices. The street was dark and deserted, it's commercial and industrial properties padlocked and shuttered for the night. This was a *quartier* where once the white dust of innumerable tanneries had blanketed the streets like snow, and the waters of the nearby river Bièvre turned blood-red from the dye of Jean Gobelin's tapestry factory.

The rain pounded down on them as Charlotte unlocked the door and let them into a small entrance hall where they left their coats before climbing a narrow staircase to the kitchen above. "Janine?" she called as they got to the top of the stairs. A teenage girl of around eighteen or nineteen came down the steps from the sitting room as they entered the kitchen.

She smiled brightly. "Hi, Charlotte."

"Everything okay?"

"Yes. I fed him about an hour ago. So he's sleeping like a…" She laughed. "Well… like a baby."

Charlotte slipped her some notes. "That's great, thanks, Janine. I won't be needing you any more tonight."

The girl smiled. "Cool. Same time tomorrow, then?"

"Yes."

She smiled at Enzo, and he nodded as she passed him to head downstairs and out into the night. But, in truth, he wasn't paying much attention. His mind was filled with confusion, happiness, fear, trepidation, all rolled into one. He was barely aware of anything around him. *Laurent* was all he could keep thinking. *Lorenzo, Laurent.* Same name, different languages. She had named him after his father.

He followed her up into the sitting room, then down a handful of steps on to the walkway that led around to her bedroom. With the light on, he could see into it from here. Her bed, neatly made for once, and the white-painted cot at the foot of it.

"He sleeps with me," she said. "It took me a long time to get used to all his funny little noises. His breathing." She glanced at Enzo. "He snores like you, you know." She paused. "Now I don't think I could sleep without him."

He could hear the rain tapping out its tattoo on the glass overhead. The gentle sound of running water from the artificial stream in the garden below. Her voice echoing around all the hard, cold surfaces.

Before they reached her bedroom she stopped and turned to look at him. "This doesn't change anything, Enzo. Between you and me. We were good together, in those moments that we *were* together. And Laurent is the product of that passion. Which is not a bad thing. But I need to move on." Her words were like stones hurled with force. Each one struck its target, and he felt the pain of every one. Knowing that he would never make love to her again, or feel the soft touch of her lips on his, or the power of the lust that made her such a fierce and passionate lover.

"Is there someone else?"

She smiled, almost wistfully, and shook her head. "No. There is only one man in my life now."

He looked at her. The dark eyes below almost quizzical eyebrows. Full lips. Black curls cascading over square shoulders. And he knew that if he spent every waking moment with her for the rest of his life, he still wouldn't understand her.

The bedroom smelled of warm milk and perfumed baby powder. Laurent was lying on his back, swaddled in a cotton baby-grow and wrapped in blankets. His tiny pink face below a fuzz of black hair, was turned to one side, his little hands open, palm-side up, on either side of his head. His breathing was slow and regular.

Enzo gazed at his son with a sense of awe. Sometimes it was hard to believe that by making love you could make another human being. A part of you that would live on beyond you.

"Can I hold him?"

Without a word, she leaned over the cot and gently lifted the child from his blankets. She passed him carefully into Enzo's waiting arms, and he felt such a rush of emotion that for a moment he was afraid he might drop him.

The baby boy snuffled, and coughed and turned his head. He opened his eyes. Dark, impenetrable eyes like his mother's, and he looked up for the first time at his father. Enzo felt all the hairs stand up on the back of his neck, and a huge weight of responsibility descended suddenly upon his shoulders.

Chapter Thirty-four

The gold dome of the church at Les Invalides dominated the north end of the Avenue de Breteuil, the gateway to a complex of buildings originally built in the seventeenth century as a retreat for the veterans of French military campaigns. Later it had become home to a collection of army museums, and the final resting place of many of the country's war heros, including Napoleon Bonaparte himself.

The Michelin building was an ugly, modern, eight-story block set back behind black railings and stark, pollarded trees just a couple of hundred meters to the south.

Enzo walked quickly past the green neon light of the pharmacy next door, hands thrust into the pockets of his overcoat, head bowed by the rain. Pierre Mages stood waiting for him beneath a shining wet black umbrella outside the security booth at the gates. It had seemed like a convenient, and appropriate, place to meet. They shook hands, and Enzo looked up at the anonymous cream and black building which had so much influence on the eating habits of a nation. "Are we going in?"

Mages laughed. "Good God, no. I'm not welcome in there any more. And good riddance." He nodded toward the other side of the long, wide avenue. "I know a *café* not far from here."

The *café* he had in mind was several streets away, the windows of its steamy warm interior misted from the damp. Hardy smokers intent on shortening their lives sat under the canopy outside, wrapped in coats and scarves against the cold, and sipping on coffees which had long since lost their heat.

Mages found them a table by the window, and immediately rubbed a hole in the condensation with his hand to peer out at the grey, wet of the morning. "Have you had breakfast?"

Enzo nodded. Although, in fact, he had eaten nothing. He had barely slept, the image of that tiny face staring up into his, burned into his brain as if seared on to it with a branding iron. It had been a long night of alternating happiness and depression. But he forced himself to focus now. He was here to plumb the past, not fret about the future.

Mages ordered them each a coffee, plus a *pain au chocolat* for himself. Enzo looked at him closely for the first time. Dyed black hair was scraped thinly back over an almost bald pate. His complexion was pasty pale, loose flesh hanging around sad jowls. His suit seemed too big for him, as if he had lost weight. Enzo would have guessed that he was perhaps ten years older than himself. He said, "What on earth made you write the book? Surely you knew that Michelin wouldn't tolerate it?"

"Of course. But I was sick of it, Monsieur Macleod. I'd had fifteen years as an inspector, one of the monks of gastronomy, and three years as deputy director. You know, there is only so much food a human being can take."

"Most people would have envied you a job like that. Eating in the best restaurants, your employer picking up the tab."

Mages' laugh was without humour. "You have no idea, monsieur. Nobody does, unless they've done it. Eating huge meals twice a day, writing detailed reports on every mouthful, inspecting rooms, prices. Up and down hotel stairways. Always on the road. Always away from home. A damned lonely existence. And then back to Paris, stopping only long enough at the Service du Tourisme to file your reports, pick up your next assignment, and hit the road again. Oh, and of course, you always had to travel by road. Michelin makes tires after all. It wouldn't do for its inspectors to travel around the country on trains and planes."

He took a mouthful of coffee and nibbled on his *pain au chocolat*.

"Let me assure you, when you have eaten your way from one end of France to the other, in every kind of restaurant you can imagine, the last thing you ever want to see in front of you again is another plate of food. You start to hate it. Every dish a trial, every meal an ordeal.

"And, of course, you are sworn to secrecy. You can't even tell your friends what it is you do for a living. Not that it's what you could call a great living. I would have earned more as a bank clerk. And during my time there, the number of inspectors almost halved, which only meant more work for those of us who were left. More food. More goddamned food than you would ever want to eat in a lifetime."

Enzo watched him dip his *pain au chocolat* into his coffee. "You seem to have rediscovered your appetite."

Mages smiled. "This is a rare treat. Since I quit, my wife put me on a strict diet. I was a skinny young man when I married her. By the time I retired I had put on more than thirty kilos."

Enzo did a quick calculation. That was between sixty and seventy pounds.

"And that's not to mention the damage I've probably done to my arteries, wolfing down all those high cholesterol sauces made with butter and cream and *foie-gras*."

Enzo could almost have sworn that the grey skin around his eyes became tinged with green as he spoke. "So you enjoyed your job, then?"

The ex-Michelin inspector laughed heartily. "At first I loved it, Monsieur Macleod. I thought I'd died and gone to heaven. But, really, who would want to live in heaven. You can have too much of a good thing, and the endless routine of roads and restaurants becomes tedious to the point of *ennui*."

Enzo sipped on his coffee. "They fired you when the book came out?"

"No, they banned me from publishing it while I was still in their employ. Confessions of a Michelin inspector splashed in extracts all over the popular press was not the image they wanted for the *guide*."

"So you quit?"

"I did."

"And was the book a success?"

Mages shrugged. "Moderately. It created a bit of a stir when it first came out. But, you know, the media moves very quickly on to the next hot thing. There's nothing more redundant than yesterday's newspaper." He paused. "Or unsold books on a shelf. A meal that has gone cold. We sold a few, and remaindered a lot."

"You were still deputy director the year Marc Fraysse was murdered." Enzo watched him carefully.

"I was."

"You must have read Jean-Louis Graulet's piece giving air to the rumor that Fraysse was going to drop a star in that year's *guide*."

"I did."

"And?"

"And what?"

"Was it true?"

Pierre Mages looked Enzo very steadily in the eye. "Absolutely not. If Michelin had awarded four stars instead of three, monsieur, Marc Fraysse would have been in line for another."

Chapter Thirty-five

The restaurant, Au Gourmand, was in the aptly named Rue Molière just off the Avenue de l'Opéra, next door to an antique shop and opposite a realtor. In keeping with the shifting tastes of the French palate, it shared the street with a Japanese restaurant and a pizzeria.

Jean-Louis Graulet was waiting for him at a table by the window in this pocket-sized eatery that still catered for the theater going public of Paris. He rose to shake the Scotsman's hand and waved him into the seat opposite.

"It's a pleasure to meet you," he said. "I've read a great deal about you."

"All of it good, I hope."

Graulet smiled. "Almost none of it, actually. It seems that the French police and the political establishment are not very fond of you."

"Only because they don't like me showing up their mistakes. Much in the same way, I suppose, that a chef might resent you taking over his kitchen and humiliating him by preparing a better meal."

This time the food critic laughed out loud. "God forbid! I love to eat, monsieur. I hate to cook."

He was smaller than Enzo had been expecting. A thin, mean-faced man who did not look at all like someone who enjoyed his food. He had lively amber eyes, and for all that his facial features were not arranged in a particularly attractive way, he had a disarming smile. Enzo had come prepared not to like him, and found himself unexpectedly engaged.

He looked around at the pale yellow walls of the restaurant, the maroon chairs with their gold piping and monogrammed *Gs*, the books and bookshelves painted on the wall by the kitchen door. "Why did you pick this place to meet?"

"I've heard good things about it and want to review it in my blog. It used to be called the Barrière Poquelin, and was owned by Claude Verger. Cleverly named, don't you think? Barrière Molière might have been the obvious choice. But Molière was born Jean Baptiste Poquelin. That showed some originality. As did the food. It's where Bernard Loiseau cut his teeth and made his name before getting sucked into that dreadful place down at Saulieu."

Enzo couldn't resist a wry smile. "You're not here in disguise, then?"

He laughed. "No, monsieur, I am not. If I had been, how would you have recognised me?"

"I take it the owners already have."

"Oh, you can put money on it. But they'll be far too discreet to say so." He paused. "A glass of champagne?"

"I wouldn't say no."

Graulet caught the attention of a hovering waiter who was instantly at their table. He ordered two glasses of Veuve Clicquot and slipped on a pair of half-moon reading glasses as he lifted the menu. "I think I'll have the *Ouef de poule*," he said. "I'm interested to know what they mean by a contemporary version of Eggs Florentine." He ran his eye down to the main courses. "Ah, and in your honour, I think I am bound to try the *Selle d'agneau d'Ecosse*. I expect you have sampled a fair amount of Scottish lamb in your time."

"I have." Enzo looked at the menu. The lamb was marinated in hibiscus, and then cooked in a sauté pan. But Enzo had to smile. The menu described it as being *cuite au sautoir*. A nice pun, since a *sautoir* was both a sauté pan and a St. Andrew's Cross, the flag of Scotland. It was presented with gnocchi, preserved kumquats, and a reduction of the cooking juices. "Never had it served like this though." He ran his eye down the other choices and decided on seasonal vegetables in an open ravioli as a starter, and *civet de sanglier*, a stew of wild boar, for his main course.

"Bravo," Graulet said. "A perfect choice for a man who lives in the Lot. What wine would you like with it?" He passed Enzo the *carte des vins*.

"What about the Cahors? The Château Lagrazette."

"I wouldn't have expected you to pick anything else. It will go wonderfully well with the *sanglier* and the lamb." He removed his reading glasses and looked candidly at Enzo. "So what do you want to know about Marc Fraysse?"

"I want to know why you printed a rumor about him losing a star when it was patently untrue."

Graulet canted his head to one side. "Was it?"

"It was. And I got that from the horse's mouth."

"The horse, no doubt, being that manufacturer of pneumatic tires which likes to think of itself as being the ultimate arbiter of good taste."

Enzo tipped his head in acknowledgement.

"Hmmm. Well, monsieur, I think I can tell you without risk of contradiction that the rumor began with Fraysse himself."

Enzo frowned. "How's that possible?"

"Because the man was paranoid. You have no doubt heard the story of our little contretemps that cemented our mutual dislike?"

"Yes."

Graulet sipped his champagne thoughtfully. "I have to tell you that although I didn't like his food, there is no doubt that he was an extremely talented chef. But his cuisine owed far too much to the traditions of the eighteenth and nineteenth century. He introduced his own slant on it, I grant you. But he failed to bring it into the twenty-first century, unlike some of his contemporaries. The excellent Michel Bras, for example, who is unique in the way he has used natural regional ingredients to transform traditional dishes. Not to mention his presentation, which is pure art. Bras is *a*typical of the Michelin-starred chef, while Fraysse was just another hack as far as I'm concerned. Another typical anointee of the monks of Michelin."

"You didn't much like him, then."

For the first time, Graulet seemed annoyed. "It's not a question of whether *I* liked *him* or not. He disliked *me*. Because he saw in my assessment of him his own worst fears. He knew I was right, and deep down inside he was terrified that one day he would be found out."

They were interrupted by the waiter who came to take their order. When he had gone again, Enzo said, "So how did he start the rumor about himself?"

"By being afraid it was true. He lived in fear of losing a star, of the financial pain and personal humiliation that would bring. If you celebrate your success in public, you must expect that your failures will also be seen in the limelight. That winter he began phoning round all his friends in the business looking for reassurance. And in doing so sowed the seeds of doubt in the minds of others. The world of French cuisine is very small and claustrophobic, monsieur. And in the heat of the kitchen, a single microbic rumor can multiply to become raging food poisoning." He smiled. "Of course, when I heard it, I took great pleasure in printing it. A small modicum of revenge."

"Even though you knew it wasn't true."

"I knew no such thing."

For the first time since he had sat down with the man, Enzo began to experience the dislike he had expected from the beginning. And as their starters were delivered to the table, he said, "I thought it was the job of the journalist to report facts, not speculation."

But Graulet was unruffled. "Monsieur, in this business there is no such thing as *facts*. Only opinions. And although I am appalled by his murder, my opinion was, and remains, that Marc Fraysse did not merit one star, never mind three."

Chapter Thirty-six

Saint-Pierre, Puy de Dôme, France 2010

Enzo left Paris early on the Monday morning for the four-hour drive south, and reached Saint-Pierre shortly after ten. It was Toussaint, All Saints Day, a public holiday, and everywhere was deserted except for the cemeteries, where the living tended to the needs of the dead, scrubbing down tombs and gravestones and piling them high with flowers.

It was only when he pulled into the almost empty car park at the *auberge* that he remembered the hotel would be shut. The final meal of the season would have been served the night before, the last of the hotel guests departing just after *petit déjeuner* that morning. The few remaining cars, he guessed, probably belonged to staff. He knew that many of them, including the chefs, were being kept on for several days to clean and shut down the kitchen and the guest rooms for the winter.

He felt a chill in his bones as he waded through the leaves toward the front of the hotel. With the coming of November, the rain had stopped, but the mercury had tumbled, and bruised and brooding skies of pewter presaged the possibility of early snow. He did not relish the prospect.

As he rounded the corner of the building, he was stopped in his tracks by the sight of Sophie standing unhappily on the steps outside the main entrance, her suitcase at her feet.

He frowned his consternation. "Where are you going? I thought you didn't finish till the end of the week."

She could hardly meet his eye. "That was the plan. Until that little shit, Philippe, went and told Guy that I was your daughter."

Enzo sighed. With her cover blown it was likely his access to Guy and Elisabeth, and anyone or anything else, would be cut off. "Why did he do that?"

"We had a row."

"I thought I told you to keep away from him."

"I tried. But he seemed to think that knowing about you gave him some kind of leverage over me. I made it plain to him it didn't."

"So what happened?"

"Guy sacked me."

"Damn, Sophie!"

"I'm sorry, papa, but it's not my fault!" He saw a quiver in her lower lip. "Bertrand can't come and get me till the end of the week, and I've nowhere to stay."

He raised his eyes to the heavens. There was a good chance that all his work of the last week had been wasted. "We'll get a hotel room somewhere. I guess they'll want me out of mine, too."

"There aren't any hotel rooms, papa. All the hotels up here close down at this time of year, and the ski stations won't be open for another month yet. The nearest hotels are in Clermont Ferrand."

Enzo thought about it for a moment, then took out his cellphone.

"Who are you calling?"

"A friend."

Dominique arrived outside her apartment at almost the same moment as Enzo and Sophie. She drew her blue gendarmerie van into the kerbside and stepped out, still in uniform, to meet them. Both she and Enzo were restrained in their urge to be intimate in their greeting, and shook hands formally.

"This is my daughter," he said. "Sophie."

Dominique smiled and shook her hand warmly. "I've heard a lot about you."

Sophie flicked a curious look toward her father. "Have you?"

"I would never have guessed you were father and daughter. You don't look at all like him."

"She gets her good looks from her mother."

Sophie pulled a face. "Actually, if my hair wasn't dyed, you'd see that I do look quite like him. Same dark hair, same white stripe."

"Ah, so you inherited the Waardenburg."

Sophie cocked her eyebrow and threw her father another glance. "He *has* been telling you a lot."

Enzo shuffled uncomfortably. Dominique unlocked the front door and led them upstairs to her apartment on the third floor.

"I'm afraid I'm going to be short of somewhere to stay, too," Enzo said as Dominique opened the door to let them in. Tasha began barking immediately, bounding around the hallway with excitement, paws up on Enzo, almost knocking him over. He greeted her like a long lost friend, ruffling her neck and ears and dodging her tongue.

"I've only got one spare room, I'm afraid," Dominique said and she and Enzo exchanged looks.

He said quickly, "Maybe I could share with Sophie, then."

"Well, it *is* a double bed, and I suppose you two aren't exactly strangers."

Sophie pulled a face.

"Go on through to the sitting room, and I'll look out some clean sheets."

Tasha followed Enzo and Sophie into the front room. The log fire that had warmed Enzo and Dominique on their first night together was long dead. He looked from the window at the conurbation in the valley below, almost lost in the flatness of the cold, grey light. Sophie tugged on his arm and brought her face close to his.

"Papa!" she said in a stage whisper. "You're sleeping with her!"

He wasn't quite sure what to say, but denial didn't seem like an option. Her eyes were wide with disbelief.

"You are *impossible*, papa!"

"I'm human, Sophie."

She glared at him for a moment, but couldn't stop a half smile from sneaking around her lips. "Well, it's crazy for you to share with me, then." She paused. "And I don't want some big hairy man in my bed, anyway. Even if he is my father."

Dominique appeared in the doorway. "The room's through here, Sophie." And Sophie dragged her suitcase off after her, throwing the merest backward glance at Enzo. He sighed. His life, it seemed, was one long succession of women giving him grief.

Dominique reappeared after a few moments. She lowered her voice. "I suppose she's guessed, then?"

He nodded.

She smiled, half in regret. "Women have an instinct for these things."

"Yes. I know."

Dominique pushed the door closed and turned back to him, keeping her voice low. "I got word back this morning from the phone company. About the owner of that cellphone number. I was just about to head off to make an arrest when you called."

Enzo felt all his focus return suddenly to the murder of Marc Fraysse. "Whose was it?"

"Anne Crozes."

Chapter Thirty-seven

Anne and Georges Crozes lived in a converted stone farmhouse on the back road south out of Saint-Pierre, in a fold of the valley with hills rising all around it, dark evergreen and bleak winter brown. It was an impressive building, beautifully pointed, its roof recently remade with traditional *lauzes* tiles. It spoke of money and the share that the Crozes had enjoyed in the success of Chez Fraysse. There was only one vehicle sitting outside the house when they arrived. A black BMW. There was no sign of Anne's Scenic.

"Doesn't look like she's here," Enzo said.

Dominique pulled her van in behind the BMW. "We'll see. She's not at the hotel, I know that. Her contract for the season finished yesterday."

They stepped out into the chill air and heard the valley echo to the cawing of distant crows, the only sound to break the silence. Blue smoke rose straight up from the chimney and hung in strands like mist above the house. Away down in the valley, Enzo saw a hawk drop from the sky like a stone and knew that some unsuspecting creature was about to die.

Georges Crozes opened the door before they got to it. Enzo barely recognised him out of his chef's whites. He seemed less imposing somehow. A god in the kitchen, but an ordinary mortal in the real world. He wore torn old jeans that hung loose from narrow hips, and a grey sweatshirt that seemed to drown him.

He looked older, too, glancing from Dominique to Enzo, and glaring at the Scotsman. "What do you want?"

"Is Anne at home?" Dominique said.

"What do you want her for?"

"I'd like to speak to her."

"What's it got to do with him?" He flicked his head toward Enzo.

"He's helping with our inquiries."

He turned penetrating green eyes on Enzo. "Not get enough information from your little spy, then?"

So everyone knew about it. Enzo chose to ignore the barb. "Where is she, Georges?"

"I haven't the first idea. She doesn't tell me anything these days." And he thrust out his jaw as if challenging them to question his veracity.

Dominique said, "Okay, well tell her, when you see her, that I need to speak to her as a matter of urgency. And if she does not come to me, I will come back for her with a warrant."

Crozes' face darkened. "What's she done?"

"Just tell her, Georges."

He watched them all the way back to the van before closing the door. Enzo wondered what was going through his mind on the other side of it.

"What do you think?" Dominique said when they got back in the vehicle.

"I think he was very hostile."

She nodded. "Attack being the best form of defence. What do you reckon he knows?"

"A lot more than he's ever going to tell us."

Enzo's battered and bruised 2CV toiled its way back up the hill from Thiers. The mechanic at the garage had given it a clean bill of health, but still it didn't feel quite right, especially after driving the rental car in which he had made the return trip to

Paris, a sleek, fast Peugeot. Perhaps it was time, he thought, to get himself a new car. Or, as Sophie would say, a real car.

He turned off the main highway on to the private road that wound up through the trees to the *auberge*. He had left things in his room and knew that in going to get them he would probably also have to face the music with Guy and Elisabeth. A prospect he did not relish.

Up ahead he saw a car pulled into the parking area at the foot of the track leading up to the *buron*, and as he got nearer he realized that it was Anne Crozes' Renault Scenic. He drew in behind it and got out of his car, to stand listening in the silence. But all he heard was the ticking of his engine as it began to cool quickly in the cold, and the plaintive calls of the ubiquitous crows echoing around the woods. He checked the driver's door of the Scenic, but it was locked, and he peered up into the green gloom of the forest. Nothing moved.

He locked his own car and started off up the track. Ten breathless minutes later, he emerged from the darkness on to the open hillside and followed the path to the point where it doubled back, leading up to the plateau. Despite the cold, he was perspiring by the time he got to the top, and breathing hard. A solitary figure stood on the rise above the *buron,* gazing out across the valley to the east. He recognised the tall, thin, figure of Anne Crozes, but she had her back to him, and hadn't heard him coming. So he stood for a moment, watching her, and catching his breath, before climbing the last few meters.

She turned, startled, at the sound of his approach. What light there was from a sullen sky reflected dully on the tears that wet her cheeks. When she realized who it was, momentary fear turned to resignation and she hurriedly used the flats of her palms to wipe her cheeks dry. He stopped a little short of her, and they stood staring at each other in the unaccustomed still and silence of the plateau. The cold wrapped itself around them like icy fingers.

"You know the police are looking for you?" he said.

She nodded. "Georges called me on my cell." She searched his face. "I guess that means you know, then." It wasn't a question.

"We know that you arranged by text to meet him here on the day he died. Which puts you in the frame for his murder, Anne, especially since he had ended your affair just a matter of days before."

The tears came again. Silently. "I met him that afternoon, yes." She shook her head. "But I didn't kill him. I couldn't have. I loved him. I still do. And I always will."

"Why did he break it off with you?"

She bit her lower lip, pained still by some distant, haunting memory. "He said we had no future."

"Did he say why?"

"Not in so many words, no. He'd been behaving so strangely in those last weeks. He'd always been so much fun, but it was like it had all just been some kind of front he'd put on for me. Then the mask slipped, and he was this morose, unhappy creature. I hardly recognised him."

"Why did you want to meet him that day?"

"I thought if I could talk to him. Just sit him down and talk to him. Maybe he would open up, maybe he would tell me what was wrong, what it was that troubled him so much. And that if he did, I could win him back."

"And did he? Open up to you, I mean."

She shook her head disconsolately. "He was like a closed book. I couldn't read him, I couldn't get near him." She looked at Enzo with a sad plea for understanding in her eyes. "He seemed manic that afternoon. I'd never seen him behave so strangely. He'd been depressed before, but this time it verged almost on madness. A bizarre kind of elation. Like there was no way out but he didn't care any more. I knew he had gambling debts. I had no idea how much. But occasionally he would let things slip, and I would get a glimpse of a man I hardly knew. A man driven by something beyond his control. I think, in a way, that's really why he broke up with me. He didn't want me to see that man, and I don't think he could hide him any longer." She drew a long, trembling breath. "I had been so sure he believed he was going to lose the *auberge*. But he just stood there with a fire burning in his eyes, as if he had somehow risen above it, and it no longer mattered."

"Had he told you he feared to lose the hotel?"

"Not in so many words. It was just bits and pieces of things he said. Like disparate parts of a jigsaw. I was desperately trying to put them together."

"And do you think you got an accurate picture?"

"I think I got the picture of a man at the end of his rope. And the speculation about Michelin taking away his third star just seemed to tip him over the edge."

Enzo looked at her intently, a sense of everything he had learned about the dead man coming together in Anne Crozes' words. In the picture she was painting of a lost soul in search of redemption. "Do you think he was suicidal?"

"I had feared it, yes. He'd been so low. And he stood there that day in the entrance to the *buron*, tears streaming down his face like a baby, though to this day I'm not sure why." Her own tears returned. "But to me, he really was just a child. A little boy lost."

Perhaps, Enzo thought, the child she'd never had with Georges. Maybe Marc had aroused the mother in her as much as the lover.

"It wouldn't have surprised me to learn that he'd killed himself, monsieur. But murder!" He saw the anguish in her eyes as she caught and held him in her gaze. "Who would want to kill him? Why would anyone want to do that?"

And in that moment, Enzo thought that perhaps he knew exactly why.

Chapter Thirty-eight

It was well after *midi* by the time he got back down to Thiers, and there was no one at reception in the gendarmerie. He pressed a button marked *sonnez* on the counter top and heard a buzzer ringing distantly somewhere in the offices beyond. After several moments a gendarme, still chewing on his sandwich, appeared in the doorway and threw Enzo a sullen look. It was lunchtime, the sacred hour, and no one liked to be disturbed during it.

Dominique, too, was eating, sitting at her desk with a cloth napkin spread in front of her, slices of tomato on a plate, a *baguette* torn in half, and a small tub of *rillettes de porc*, the shredded leftovers of cooked meat and fat from the carcass of the pig. An open half bottle of red wine, and a half empty glass stood side by side at her right hand. She seemed surprised to see him.

"I thought you were going back to the hotel."

"I never got there. I met Anne Crozes *en route*. Or, at least, I saw her car parked at the foot of the track up to the *buron*, and found her up there."

"And you didn't bring her in?"

Enzo held up his hands. "Hey, that's not my job." He paused. "But anyway, I don't think she killed Fraysse."

"Maybe, maybe not. But she's a material witness and she withheld evidence from the police. Did she tell you anything?"

"She told me she met Fraysse on the afternoon of his murder. His mood had been bizarre, she said, almost elated. Manic, was the word she used." He took off his jacket and hung it over the back of the chair opposite. "Dominique, was there an insurance policy on Marc Fraysse's life?"

She thought for a moment. "Yes, I'm sure there was."

"Would you have a copy of it on file."

She shook her head. "No. But I could get the insurance company to send us one." She looked at him curiously. "What's on your mind?"

"Just a vague thought, Dominique. But if it was possible to get a look at that policy, it might turn into something more than a hunch."

He stood once more by the window, staring out at the start of what promised to be a long, bleak winter, while Dominique made the call. The sky was tinted purple, the air a sad ochre, and even as he watched, he saw the first tiny flakes of snow fall sparsely across the valley. Nothing that would lie, but still the sight of it sent a shiver through his bones.

Dominique came off the phone and spread some *rillettes* on a chunk of bread, topping it off with a slice of tomato. "They're going to fax it. Should be through in a few minutes." She took a bite and washed it down with a mouthful of wine.

The fax arrived five minutes later. Dominique watched Enzo carefully as he pored over the pages of the insurance policy on Marc Fraysse's life.

"What exactly are you looking for?"

He stood up, a light in his eyes. But he seemed a long way, away.

"Enzo?"

He blinked and looked at her as if waking from a dream. "This," he said, turning one of the pages toward her and stabbing a finger at a paragraph halfway down. And as she drew it toward her to read, he elucidated. "A suicide clause. To guard against the possibility of the insured killing himself to guarantee a payout to the beneficiary. In the event that Marc Fraysse had committed suicide, neither Elisabeth nor Guy would have received a penny."

◇◇◇

The kitchen was full of *stagiaires* scrubbing down counter tops, dismantling hotplates and grills to scour with wire brushes, sluicing water and disinfectant across the stippled floor, and scrubbing it with long-handled mops. The chatter of the young chefs died away, and curious eyes turned toward Enzo and Dominique as they made their way past the marble table toward Guy's office at the far side.

He saw them coming through the windows that offered him a panorama of his kitchen, and turned to face them with grim defiance as Enzo pushed open the door. Gone was all his bonhomie, and his sad blue eyes were heavy with disappointment. "I didn't extend you the hospitality of my hotel, Enzo, so that you could spy on me," he said.

"I wasn't spying on you."

"Then what was your daughter doing working in our kitchen?"

"She wants to train as a chef." Which was true, but didn't quite answer Guy Fraysse's question.

"Under a false name?"

"Merit was her mother's name. It is more convenient for her to use a French name. Most people can't pronounce Macleod."

It was clear that Guy did not believe a word of it, but saw the futility of pursuing it further. His eyes turned toward Dominique. "What do you want?"

But it was Enzo who replied. "Why did Marc invite the whole Paris press corps down here the day he died?"

Guy's eyes darted warily back toward Enzo. "I have no idea."

"I think you do, Guy."

"And I suppose you're going to tell me."

"We both know that Marc was in deep trouble. Whether or not he was actually going to lose a star is irrelevant. He thought he was. Add to that a gambling debt of more than a million that would take the sale of the auberge to pay off, and you have a man cornered by his addiction, plus his own paranoia."

The color was slowly draining from Guy's face.

"He believed he was on the point of losing everything he had spent his life to create. Chez Fraysse. His reputation. His public image. He faced ruin and humiliation. But he wasn't going to go out with a whimper, was he?"

"I have no idea what you're talking about."

"Yes, you do. He wanted to go out in a blaze of publicity, didn't he, Guy? He wanted all those journalists whom he'd spent his life cultivating, right here on the spot to cover his suicide. Everything was lost, but he was going to make one last, grand theatrical gesture. As flamboyant in death as he'd been in life."

Dominique said, "The only trouble was, the insurance wouldn't have paid out if he'd committed suicide."

"And *he* might not have cared," Enzo said. "But *you* did. And so did Elisabeth. Because, with Marc gone, and no insurance payout, you'd have lost everything, too. When you went up there that afternoon and found him dead in the *buron,* you knew that you faced ruin. That's why you doctored the scene to make it look like a murder, isn't it?" Enzo drew a deep breath. "Whose idea was it, Guy? Yours? Elisabeth's?"

But it wasn't a question that Guy was about to answer. He returned their stares, blue eyes clouded and surly. "I think," he said, "that you are going to have a helluva job trying to prove that."

And Enzo realized just how true that was.

Chapter Thirty-nine

Elisabeth Fraysse was nowhere to be found in the *auberge*, and none of the hotel's staff seemed to know where she was. Enzo walked Dominique through the reception area to the front door.

"She's bound to show up sooner or later," Dominique said. "But Guy's right. How on earth are we going to prove it?"

Enzo shook his head. "I have no idea."

"I'd better get back down to Thiers. I'm going to have to write up some kind of report, even although I can't draw any definitive conclusions." She hesitated. "There have been questions asked by divisional HQ about just how much cooperation I've been extending to you on this investigation. I guess someone at the gendarmerie has been shooting his mouth off."

"I'm sorry, Dominique, if I've got you into trouble."

She grinned. "Don't be. I can look after myself." She hesitated. "How did you get on in Paris?"

He briefed her on his encounters with the ex-Michelin man and Graulet. She listened in thoughtful silence.

"Actually, I meant with Charlotte."

And she immediately saw a wistful smile crease his eyes.

"I was introduced to my son for the first time."

Dominique's face lit up. "Oh, my God, Enzo, that's wonderful. How did you change her mind?"

"I didn't. My daughter did."

"Sophie?" Dominique was taken aback.

"No, Kirsty. It's ironic, really. My daughter, who's not really my daughter, was the only one who could make Charlotte see how important it was to her son that he had a father."

Dominique's eyebrows gathered in a frown. "Not really your daughter?"

He smiled sadly. "That's a story for another day." They passed through the revolving door out on to the step. "I'll go up and get my stuff from my room, and see you back down in Thiers."

She nodded, holding him in her dark eyes for a moment, intrigued and beguiled, and then reached up to touch his face with her fingertips before turning and hurrying down the steps toward her van.

He watched her go, and felt a pang of regret with the knowledge that their relationship, however nascent and intense, was destined to be stillborn.

He went back inside, then, and up to his room. It was clear to him immediately that someone had been through the few items he had left. Some shirts and underwear in a drawer, some books and papers in his canvas bag, were not as he had left them. He felt a bad taste in his mouth. He packed quickly and went back downstairs, leaving his keycard at the deserted reception, and headed out to the car park in search of his car.

As he rounded the east wing of the *auberge,* he almost collided with a large man wheeling a barrow full of garden refuse. It was Lucqui, his cap pulled down low on his brow, big hands and fingernails ingrained with the black, volcanic soil of the plateau. Enzo had not seen him since the night Lucqui had pulled him out of the stream below the waterfall. Lucqui barely acknowledged him as he wheeled his barrow past. But Enzo stopped, turning to call after him. "I never had the chance to say thank you, Lucqui."

Lucqui put down the barrow. "No thanks necessary. I'd have done the same for a dog."

Enzo raised a wry smile. "Well, that makes me feel all warm and fuzzy."

And for the first time since he'd met him he saw Lucqui smile.

"You wouldn't have seen Madame Fraysse, would you?"

The big gardener retreated behind his black eyes. "No." And he picked up the handles of his barrow. Then stopped and put them down again. "First of November, isn't it?"

"That's right."

"You'll probably find her at the cemetery, then. She always visits Marc at Toussaint."

The cemetery at Saint-Pierre was just outside the village, on a west-facing slope. It had an uninterrupted view of the Massif laid out below it, such a view to take with you to eternity that it must have seemed almost welcoming to those reaching a certain age of infirmity. But Marc Fraysse had been nowhere near that time when folk might start to think of death. He had taken his own *sortie de secours* far too early. A sad choice for a man with so much more to offer.

Enzo pushed open the gates in the high east wall, and wandered down among the tombs and headstones newly bedecked with fresh flowers, to the Fraysse family tomb on the lower slope. Elisabeth stood by the huge marble slab engraved in gold with the name of her late husband, his parents and grandparents, the bones of three generations lying together in the infinite darkness below. She turned at the sound of his footsteps on the gravel, and he saw the anger in her eyes as she turned away to gaze down again at her husband's tomb.

He stopped beside her, and without looking at him she said, "I remember the very first time I set eyes on him in the boat shed on the lake. He seemed so young. And innocent. Those beautiful big eyes of his fixing themselves on me, and casting their spell, even then." She shook her head. "For all his faults, Monsieur Macleod, and they were many, I never stopped loving him." And she turned, to fix him with steel cold eyes. "I don't like being spied on."

He nodded, and saw that those tiny *flocons* of snow he had seen earlier in Thiers were starting to fall now on the hill. But so light and insubstantial were they, an existence immeasurably ephemeral, that they vanished the moment they touched the ground. As did, in the grand scheme of things, the lives of the men and women lying here beneath it. He said, "I know that you and Guy faked Marc's murder to hide his suicide."

Her face turned almost instantly pale, and he saw the shock in her eyes, followed by resignation, and then something that seemed almost like relief. "Guy told you that?"

"I've just come from the hotel." Not a lie. But he knew she would put her own construction on it. "I know about the suicide clause in the life assurance policy. And Marc's gambling debt. I spoke to the man he owed the money to."

She closed her eyes and let out a long, slow breath, as if she had been holding it in all these years. "I'm glad," she said at length. "It was a secret almost impossible to bear. The tears I cried over those few words he left me. And still do." He saw those same tears well again in her eyes now. "I suppose I always understood why he did it. The debt, the rumors about losing a star. But it was typically selfish of him not to think, or care, how it would leave me, or Guy. He never could resist the grand gesture, the encore, the bow at the end of the show. It was always about him. No one else."

"Tell me how it happened."

She glanced at him, but her eyes flickered away, unable to hold his gaze. "The statement we gave the police was true, up to a point. Marc had gone off for his usual afternoon run, but failed to return on schedule. It was approaching prep time for the evening service, and when he didn't answer his cellphone, Guy went off to look for him. Which is when he found him dead inside the *buron*. He had shot himself, and left a note."

Enzo said, "A man intent on taking his own life wouldn't normally go to the trouble of burying his phone and his knife?"

She turned, almost startled. "You know about that?"

"I recovered them both. Do you want to tell me how that came about?"

"Guy buried the pouch and got rid of the gun. But not immediately. Not before he had come back down to the hotel and broken the news to me." She paused, lost for a moment in painful recollection. "I suppose I must have been pretty difficult for him to deal with. I was close to hysteria. It… it didn't seem possible that Marc was gone. Just like that. A flame extinguished. Vanished. Out of my life forever. Like he'd never even existed. But Guy was so calm. He forced me to sit down and face the reality. He'd only recently found out about the extent of the gambling debts himself. And he made me look at the suicide clause in the life policy. Not only had we lost Marc, we were going to lose everything else as well."

"So it was his idea to make it look like murder?"

She nodded. "He persuaded me to come back up to the *buron* with him. I couldn't go in. Couldn't get past the entrance. I sat outside on a rock and wept like I have never wept in my life. I suppose it didn't matter whether he had been murdered or taken his own life, my grief was just as great."

"And just as genuine."

She glanced at him through tear-filled eyes. "Yes." Her breath trembled as she breathed, trying to control herself, salvage something of her dignity. "Guy removed the suicide note and the gun, and buried the pouch to make it look like a robbery. He'd even had the presence of mind to take another pair of boots up with him, a size smaller than his own, to make another set of footprints in the mud."

Enzo then realized that the fifth set of prints must have belonged to Anne Crozes.

"That's when we called the police and waited for someone to come. It seemed like an eternity, trapped up there by our own deception, lost in guilt and grief for the man we both loved. I read his suicide note again and again. Words burned into my memory forever. I look at it still. On the anniversary of his death. On his birthday. At Toussaint. And the pain never diminishes."

"You still have it?" Enzo hardly dared to believe it was possible.

"Of course. They were his last words, Monsieur Macleod. How could I throw them away?"

◇◇◇

As they drove into the car park at the *auberge*, Enzo following Elisabeth Fraysse in her Mercedes Sports, he noticed that Guy's yellow Renault Trafic had gone. Although there were still one or two staff vehicles there, the hotel itself seemed deserted. Snow fell through the gloom like tiny vanishing fireflies, and the darkness gathering beyond the clouds gave witness to the coming night.

Enzo followed in the wake of the widow's grief, past the door of the suite he had occupied, before they stopped outside the door of Marc Fraysse's study. Elisabeth produced a key, and unlocked it, with the merest flicker of a glance at Enzo. There was no doubt that both Elisabeth and Guy knew exactly who had been in Marc's study, and when.

She crossed the room to his roll top bureau, pushing back the roller and turning on a desk lamp. The laptop computer and blotter, and the profusion of papers that lay scattered across the desktop, blazed in a pool of intense illumination. She reached into the light, a pale, long-fingered hand, speckled now with the first brown marks of age, and felt beneath a shelf to release some hidden catch. A drawer, which had seemed like a decorative panel, sprung open. Inside it lay Marc Fraysse's suicide note. Enzo realized how frustratingly close he had been to it every time he had sat at this desk. But how could he have known?

Elisabeth Fraysse laid her husband's last words on top of the computer and smoothed them out with the palm of her hand, an almost loving sweep of it across the curled sheet.

Enzo looked at it, intensely curious. He immediately recognised Marc's distinctive curlicued handwriting. The note was written on a flimsy sheet of stationery. The ink had already begun to fade, and the top third of the sheet was so badly stained by blood and rainwater that the words had been completely obliterated. The very bottom portion of it was equally disfigured.

Two words remained from the damaged portion at the top of the note … *things differently.*

It went on, *I have so many regrets. I just wish I could wipe out the past. I can offer apologies, but I know that forgiveness is more than I have the right to ask for. And in the end, apologies are only words, and words can't change anything. They can't take away the hurt. They can't wipe out the mistakes. And that's what I want to do. Just wipe it all out. I am so sorry.*

His signature was lost in the water and blood damage.

"May I see it?" Enzo held out his hand, a distant echo somewhere at the back of his mind of the perfume-stained suicide note left for Jack by Rita.

Elisabeth nodded, and Enzo took the note carefully between his fingers, turning it over, before holding it against the light of the lamp. He had half-hoped there might be some way to recover the lost words by holding them to the brightest source of light. But the lamp provided no illumination.

"I'd like to keep this for the moment if I may." And he stilled her objections before she could voice them by raising his hand. "I promise to return it to you."

"I doubt if you'll be allowed to, Monsieur Macleod. I am sure that the police will want to keep it as evidence."

He nodded grimly. "I'd also like a sample of one of Marc's handwritten menus, if I may?"

Her eyes searched his face, full of unasked questions, then she turned silently to the filing cabinet and drew out a menu to hand to him. She looked at him very directly, and he saw fear now in her eyes. "What will happen to us?"

"I imagine you'll be charged with defrauding the insurance company, and probably also obstruction of a police investigation, tampering with evidence, giving false statements." He shrugged helplessly. "Just as you understood why Marc killed himself, I understand why you covered it up, Madame Fraysse. But I'm afraid the law will not."

Dominique looked at the suicide note that Enzo had spread out on her desk in front of her. The blood that stained it was rust brown, the paper distorted by pools of blistered blue where the ink had run in the rainwater. She read it in silence then looked up at Enzo with searching eyes. "And she just confessed to everything?"

"She thought that Guy already had. It was like a damn had burst inside her, Dominique. Guilt and grief and fear given vent in a moment of absolute relief after seven years of deception. She *wanted* to tell me." He laid out the menu next to the note so that she could make the comparison herself. "He hand-wrote the menus every day, so we are not short of examples of his handwriting."

Dominique studied the two documents. "They certainly look identical. But I guess we'll need a handwriting expert to verify it." She shook her head then, perching on the edge of her desk and allowing herself a rueful smile. "So that's it. Not a murder at all. A suicide covered up to defraud the insurance company. How could we ever have guessed that?" She folded her arms. "There'll be charges, of course. Fraud. Obstruction. Tampering. Providing false statements to the authorities." She glanced at Enzo and immediately saw the doubt in his eyes. She was almost startled. "What?"

He shrugged. "I don't know."

She stood up again. "Yes, you do. You're not convinced, are you?"

He thought for a long moment before finally responding. "No," he said.

"Why not?"

"For one thing…" he picked up the suicide note and rubbed it gently between his thumb and fingertips, "…the quality of this paper."

She frowned. "I don't understand."

"Elisabeth told me that after Marc got his third star nothing was too good for him. He had high quality stationery specially watermarked with the logo of the *auberge*." He held up the note to the flickering fluorescent strip in the ceiling. "This is bog standard writing paper, not particularly good quality. And there's no watermark. Would it not be reasonable to assume that he would have used his best writing paper to record his last words?"

But he didn't give the gendarme too much time to dwell on that thought.

"He also habitually used a fountain pen. A very expensive fountain pen with which he wrote out his daily menus. Why didn't he use it to write his suicide note?"

"Didn't he?"

"Look at these together." Enzo laid the note out on the desk again, next to the menu. "See how the nib of the fountain pen used to write the menu creates a variation in the thickness of the up and down strokes? But the pen used to write the note doesn't. And it couldn't have been a ballpoint. Ballpoints use oil-based inks, which wouldn't have run when exposed to water. This was more likely to have been a rollerball pen, which uses water-based ink and wouldn't have produced any variation in the up and down strokes." He looked at Dominique. "He would almost certainly have written this note sitting at his roll-top desk in his private study. Why didn't he use his beloved fountain pen and his watermarked writing paper?"

Confusion had written itself all over Dominique's face. "You think it's a forgery, then?" She glanced once more the two sheets of paper lying side by side on her desk. "If it is, someone's done an amazing job."

But Enzo shook his head. "No, I'm pretty sure it's Marc Fraysse's own handwriting."

Dominique's frown deepened. "Then what on earth are you thinking?"

Enzo scratched his head. "Have the autopsy pics that the pathologist took of the dead man's hands arrived yet?"

"No. Are they that important?"

"I'd really like to look at them."

"Then I'll call him personally, and get him to fax them as soon as possible."

Enzo nodded. "And I have a big favor to ask."

She sighed. "What now?"

"Hold off on reporting any of this until I get back from Paris."

She seemed shocked. "You're going to Paris again?"

"I'll catch the night train from Clermont Ferrand and be back by tomorrow night." He hesitated, then lifted up the suicide note. "But I'll need to take this with me."

She gasped her frustration. "Enzo, I could be in so much trouble over this already."

He grinned. "I thought you told me you could look after yourself."

A smile spread reluctantly across her lips. "Don't you just hate it when someone uses your own words to back you into a corner?"

"That's why you should always choose your words very carefully in the first place."

She glared at him. "Bastard!"

"Is that a yes?"

Chapter Forty

Paris gave the impression of a flickering, monochrome movie from another age when he stepped off the train at the Gare de Lyon shortly after seven. A bitter north-easterly had driven the inhabitants of the city into winter coats, and hats, and scarves, and the Parisian penchant for blacks and greys seemed to have leeched all color from the seething mass of commuters that thronged the platforms. Summer was both a distant memory, and a far off prospect, and the winter months that loomed ahead had subdued the usually passionate populace. The dull murmur of voices was barely discernible over the constant announcements of departures and arrivals.

Enzo shouldered his way silently through the crowds, head lowered, and ran down the steps to the *métro*. His compartment was packed and uncomfortable, a human cattle truck filled with the warm, sour smell of body odour and cigarette breath. The twenty minute ride to the Gare du Nord seemed like an eternity.

Enzo was glad to step out of the station to breathe cold, fresh air again. He walked south on the Boulevard de Strasbourg, barely aware of the city around him, wrapped up in a confusion of thoughts. Of suicide notes and fountain pens, confessions and deceptions. And in amongst all of that, the sense of being close again to his son. Existing under the same sky, in the same city. He had an almost overwhelming urge to hold him.

At the Rue du Château d'Eau, he turned left and found the apartment block he was looking for around a hundred and fifty meters south-west on the opposite side of the street.

Raymond Marre was still in his dressing gown when he answered the door on the second floor landing. It took a moment or two before recognition banished his frown and he greeted Enzo like a long lost brother, kissing him on both cheeks and ushering him into the warmth of his apartment.

"*Mon dieu, mon ami, comment vas-tu*? It's been years. I'm just having breakfast. Will you join me?"

"With pleasure. I'm starving." Enzo discarded his coat and gloves, his face flushing with the heat after the cold outside, and followed Raymond into a small dining room which overlooked the street below through French windows. He watched the old man as he fussed to find another cup and saucer, and a plate for the *croissants*. The bag from the *boulanger* lay torn open on the table.

"I'm fortunate to have a neighbour who always fetches me fresh *croissants* in the morning. I'm not really a morning person. It's usually ten or later before I'm dressed and my brain is functioning." He grinned. "It gets harder and harder to kick-start it these days. How's my God-daughter?"

"Sophie's well, Raymond, and training to be a chef."

"Mmmmh, then you'll need to invite me to dinner sometime soon so I can sample her progress." He looked at Enzo. "And how are you?"

"I'm fine, Raymond."

Raymond had been Sophie's mother's mentor, an old hand in the *police scientifique* when Pascale was just starting out on her career in forensics. Enzo had asked him to be Sophie's God-father after Pascale died in childbirth. He was well into his seventies now, and long retired. He poured Enzo a coffee, and they ate in silence for some moments.

"So, what brings you to Paris? Still showing the French police how it should be done?"

Enzo smiled. "I'm trying to find out who killed Marc Fraysse."

"Ah." The old man's eyes twinkled. "I'm beginning to make connections already. Sophie, Fraysse, *haute cuisine*." He paused. "Figured it out yet?"

"Nearly. But I need your help. You spent several years working in the questioned documents lab."

Raymond looked doubtful. "It's a long time since I retired, Enzo. QD was my specialty, sure. But there have been a lot of scientific advances since my day."

"And you haven't kept up with them?"

"Of course I have. What else am I going to do all day?"

Enzo grinned. "And I'm assuming you still have some influence at the lab on the Ile de la Cité."

Raymond tipped his head to one side. "They tolerate the odd visit." Hard though he was trying to hide it, his interest was piqued. "What's your problem?"

Enzo went into his satchel and took out Fraysse's suicide note, safely sealed inside a clear plastic ziplock bag. He laid it on the table between them. "I want to know if it's possible to recover the words obliterated by the water damage and the blood."

Raymond picked it up and looked at it with thoughtful concentration, then he held it up to the light of the window. "Shouldn't be a problem."

"Really?"

"A video spectral comparator should do it. The VSC uses various light-filtering systems, infrared, ultraviolet and so on, to enhance effaced, faded, or stained writing."

"Even although the original text has been lost?"

"Sure. I mean, the writing's not actually lost, it's still there. You just can't see it."

"How does that work?"

"Visible and invisible radiant energy can excite inks to emit longer wavelengths of energy which make them luminesce. Of course, you still can't see it with the naked eye. But the comparator has an integration feature which allows you to adjust the exposure time of radiant energy entering a black and white video camera. Weak luminescence can be enhanced, in the same way as slowing the shutter speed on a conventional camera allows you to record images in low light. So the original writing will show up, even though it appears to have been wiped out."

Enzo glanced at the blood and water stains that seemed to have erased almost a third of the text on the page, and wondered what secrets the comparator might reveal. If any.

"And you would have access to a machine like this?"

"I believe the lab at the Quai de l'Horloge has the VSC6000."

"Yes, but that's not the question. Would they let you use it?"

The old forensic scientist sat back in his chair and laughed. "Enzo, Enzo, Enzo. Is the Pope a catholic?"

Chapter Forty-one

Charlotte was surprised to see him, although it was difficult to tell whether the surprise was pleasant or otherwise. An experienced psychologist, trained in the detection of the smallest *micro signes* in the faces of others, she was herself a master of obfuscation.

"I'm with a client just now. But Janine will bring Laurent through." She showed him into the combined office and sitting room, floor-to-ceiling windows looking down on to the Rue des Tanneries. A bank of computer monitors flickered on a long work table, and one of them showed a black-and-white image from a camera installed somewhere above the indoor garden below. A middle-aged man in a suit fidgeted nervously in a wicker chair by the little pool at the center of the garden. Charlotte's client. Her chair opposite remained empty.

He turned as Janine came up the steps from the gallery, carrying Laurent in her arms. "It's not long since he was fed," she said. "So he might be a little sleepy. I'll be along in the video room if you need me." The babysitter disappeared back down the steps, and he heard her footsteps retreating along the metal catwalk. He turned, holding the baby to his chest, and saw that Charlotte had resumed her place opposite the client.

He crossed to the settee, then, and sank into it, sliding Laurent down to cradle in his arms, the tiny pink face upturned toward his. Nonsense noises gurgled from the baby's mouth, and his wide open dark eyes stared up at Enzo in fascination. Enzo wondered if, even at that age, a child had any instinct about who his father might be. And decided that he probably didn't. Only time and exposure would provide that recognition. Still, the child seemed completely relaxed with him. And Enzo had his experience with Sophie to draw on. He was no stranger to babies and their needs.

He gave his son his right index finger, and the baby immediately seized it, clutching it tightly in impossibly tiny fingers, and holding on for dear life. Enzo grinned at him, and to his delight Laurent grinned back. A smile that turned to a chortle, and then a laugh. And Enzo laughed, too.

"What's so funny?"

Enzo looked up to see Charlotte breezing into the room. "I thought you were with a client."

"I got rid of him. What are you two laughing at?"

"Each other I think. He obviously figures it's pretty funny for his dad to have different colored eyes."

She perched on the edge of an armchair opposite and watched them for a moment. "Enzo, we never really had a chance the other night to talk about Kirsty."

He looked at her, surprised. "Kirsty?"

"And Roger."

And her ominous tone sent a chill of recollection through him. Kirsty was pregnant, and she and Roger were to be married. Revelations he had almost consciously chosen to bury.

"I imagine you're not very happy about it?"

"That would be an understatement. You know I've never liked Roger."

"And you know how much I dislike him."

"And yet you still see him."

"From time to time, yes. You know what they say about your enemy. Keep him always in plain view."

Enzo frowned. "Your enemy? Charlotte, he was your lover for eighteen months."

"Which is how I know." She paused. "He is a dark and dangerous man, Enzo. You need to do everything in your power to stop him from marrying Kirsty."

Enzo passed the fifteen minute *métro* ride from Gobelins to Pont Neuf on Line 7 lost in a deep despond. He remembered once before that Charlotte had warned him about Raffin. *There's something dark about Roger, Enzo*, she had said. *Something beyond touching. Something you wouldn't want to touch, even if you could.* Enzo had never witnessed that dark side. But he had seen him flirt with other women in Kirsty's presence, and experienced first hand an unpleasant and ruthless streak in him.

Kirsty, however, was her own person. He had no right to tell her what, or what not, to do. Not least because he had abandoned her to her mother at the tender age of twelve, to pursue a new life in France with Pascale. He had often wondered if, given the chance, he would do it all differently. But if he had, there would have been no Sophie, no Charlotte. No Laurent.

And Kirsty was an intelligent girl, sensible. She clearly saw something in Roger that her father didn't. But Charlotte must once have been beguiled by him, too. And only time and experience had led her to disillusionment. Kirsty had not had sufficient of either to arrive at that conclusion, and Enzo knew that there was nothing he could either say or do about it that would not lead him into conflict with her.

There was sleet in the air, blowing in on the edge of a northeast wind as he emerged from the *métro* at the Pont Neuf in the shadow of the decaying icon that was the Samaritaine building. The Ile de la Cité split the river in two, a classical skyline anchored to both banks by bridges at various points along its length, as if it might otherwise float away. On the far side was the headquarters of the Paris police, the Quai des Orfèvres. On the nearside, the forensic laboratories of the *police scientifique* at No. 3 Quai de l'Horloge. Enzo pulled up his collar and hurried off through the sleet.

Raymond Marre was waiting for him at the main entrance to see him through security, then lead him upstairs to an upper floor where the VSC6000 was housed in a small, windowless room. The machine itself wasn't much bigger than the average laser printer. It was connected to a computer terminal, keyboard and monitor. A gooseneck lamp on the desk cast light over a profusion of papers spread across its surface. Enzo spotted the suicide note in its ziplock bag among them.

"Well?" Enzo looked at him anxiously.

Raymond beamed. "It seems that for once the French *police scientifique* can actually do something for the great Enzo Macleod." He held up a sheet of photocopy paper. "Here it is, all cleaned up and perfectly readable. Although what illumination it might throw on your investigation probably only you can tell. It certainly doesn't mean anything to me."

Enzo took the sheet and read it in full. His immediate reaction was one of disappointment. There was nothing in the text recovered from the top or bottom of the note that added anything to what was already there. And no signature. He frowned.

"Doesn't make much sense to you either, I see," Raymond said. "I guess you'd need the missing pages to get anything more out of it."

Enzo looked at him, confused. "Missing pages?"

But even as he said it he understood for the first time exactly what he was holding in his hand.

Rows of dark blue police vans were lined up along the *quai* outside, and people with hoods pulled up, and umbrellas lowered against the sleet, hurried by, heads down. The Théatre de la Ville across the river was almost obscured by it.

Enzo fumbled in his pocket for his cellphone and hit the speed dial key for Dominique's cell. It was important she knew, and could move immediately. He felt his fingers stiffening in the cold as he waited for a reply. Eventually her messaging service kicked in and he left a quick message asking her to call him back immediately. He called the gendarmerie on the off-chance that she might be there and not have access to her cellphone. The duty officer replied and told him that Gendarme Chazal was not on duty until the following morning.

Enzo hung up, thought for a moment, then called Sophie. With a growing sense of disquiet, he listened as her phone rang unanswered. Eventually he heard her voice. "Hi, this is Sophie. Leave a message and I'll get back to you."

He said, "Sophie, call me as soon as you get this. It's important."

He slipped his cellphone into his pocket and checked the time. It was after 5.30 and the rush-hour, like the river, was in full flow. The city seemed to roar all around him, but the alarm bells of disquiet set in motion by those unanswered calls grew to such a crescendo in his mind that they began to blot everything else out. He knew he had to get back as soon as possible. There was a TGV high speed train leaving from the Gare de Lyon just after six. That would get him into Clermont Ferrand at nine-thirty, and back to Saint-Pierre by around ten.

He waved at an approaching taxi but it swept past him on the quay and vanished into the gathering gloom. In this weather, taxis would be like gold dust, and even if he got one, there was no guarantee it would get him through the traffic in time. There was no choice but to take the *métro*.

He turned and began running back along the quayside toward the Pont Neuf.

Chapter Forty-two

Clermont Ferrand, France, November 2010

By the time his train pulled slowly into the platform at Clermont Ferrand's central station in the Avenue de l'Union Soviétique, a sick sense of apprehension filled Enzo's gut like a dead weight.

He had called both Dominique and Sophie several times, leaving frustrated messages on each occasion with their respective answering services. Not one of his calls had been returned, and he knew by now that something was seriously wrong.

With a growing sense of despair, he had watched the sleet in Paris turn to snow as the train headed south, up on to the frozen central plateau. Big, fat, wet flakes flew at the train through the night like warp speed in a Star Trek movie. Even in the dark he could see that the countryside was blanketed now in white.

He hurried from the station out into deserted, snow-covered streets, only a few tire-tracks cutting through crisp, virgin white. Six inches of snow had accumulated on the roof of his 2CV. With gloved hands, he quickly cleared the windscreen and climbed in to turn the engine several times before it coughed and belched carbon monoxide into the night.

Crouched over the wheel, peering out into the dark, his Citröen slipped and slithered its way through side streets almost obliterated by the snow. Not until he reached the main road east, where ploughs and gritters had turned white snow to black slush, was he was able to pick up speed.

The ploughs had been out on the *autoroute*, too, spreading salt as they went, but the snow was already starting to lie again, and Enzo could only drive as fast as he dared, feeling the occasional slip of his wheels beneath him.

The roads deteriorated markedly when he turned off the motorway and began the long climb up to Thiers. The main highway snaked its way across the hillside, mitigating the worst of the incline, but still Enzo was finding it increasingly difficult to keep the car moving. His experience of driving in snow in Scotland had taught him to keep the car in second gear, or even third, to maximise traction. No sudden acceleration, or breaking.

He crawled at a snail's pace up the hill, ignoring traffic lights. To stop would have been fatal, and there were no other vehicles on the road. No sensible person was out on a night like this.

Almost at the top of the hill, snow still piling down between the buildings that towered above him on either side, he turned right along a level stretch of road toward Dominique's apartment. He immediately saw the cluster of blue and orange flashing lights gathered outside the building.

He slewed to a halt beside two gendarme vans and an ambulance. A couple of uniformed gendarmes stood among a gathering of curious neighbours sheltering under black umbrellas, stamping icy feet in the snow. Enzo jumped out and almost fell.

"What's happened here?"

One of the gendarmes turned, and Enzo immediately recognised him as the sandwich-chewing officer who had responded to his buzzer at lunchtime the previous day. He recognised Enzo, too. "Dominique was attacked in her apartment."

"Jesus!" Enzo felt his heart almost stop. "My daughter's up there, too."

And before either of the officers could stop him, he was past them, through the door, and pounding up the steps in the pale flicker of feeble yellow stair lights, his breath exploding in clouds ahead of him.

Dominique's apartment door lay wide open, bright light spilling out on to the dark of the landing. Another gendarme stood at the end of the hall, and beyond him two medics were crouched around the prone figure of a woman lying on the floor. Heads turned with Enzo's sudden arrival, and he saw Dominique's bloodied face as she pulled herself up on to one elbow. Her skin color was whiter than the snow falling outside her window, and her dark eyes filled with confusion.

"Enzo…" She reached a hand toward him.

He pushed between the medics and knelt beside her, taking her hand and squeezing it. "What happened? Are you okay?"

She seemed to be struggling to find words. One of the medics said, "She needs attention. She's concussed. There could be a fracture."

But she waved a dismissive hand. "I'll be alright. I just… I don't really remember what happened. I was coming back to the apartment. I opened the door, and… I guess someone must have struck me from behind. When I came to, it was something like four hours later, and I was lying in the hall. I managed to crawl in here and call the Samu."

With the help of the two medics, he got her to her feet, and then into a chair. One of them began cleansing the wound at the back of her head with a cotton pad and disinfectant, and she winced from the pain.

"Dominique, where's Sophie?"

"I don't know. Her boyfriend called this morning… Bertrand?" Enzo nodded. "Well, Bertrand called and said he was on his way to get her. He must have picked her up before I got back."

The gendarme at the door said, "There was no one else in the apartment."

Enzo frowned. "But if Bertrand picked her up, why's she not answering her phone?" He stood up and hurried through to the spare bedroom, and felt fear like cold fingers closing around his heart. Her suitcase was still there, clothes spread across the bed.

By the time he got back through to the sitting room, Dominique was on her feet and waving aside the attentions of the Samu.

He said, "Bertrand didn't pick her up. He must have been held up by the snow. All her stuff's still here."

Pain and confusion mixed with the blood on Dominique's face. "Then where is she?"

Enzo closed his eyes, trying to control his breathing. "I don't know for sure. But I think maybe I can guess."

He turned toward the door.

"Wait!" Dominique called after him, and as he turned back, she was reaching into her leather brief case. "I brought these with me from the gendarmerie so you could see them when you got back." She pulled out a large manilla envelope. "They're the pics of the hands taken at autopsy."

He hesitated just for a moment before turning back. She laid the photographs out on the coffee table and he knelt down to look at them, holding them between trembling fingers. A dead man's hands. Cold and white, and spattered by tiny droplets of blood blown back from the head wound that took his life.

He felt her eyes on him. She said, "What do you think?"

And in spite of everything, the professional in him calmed his panic and took control of his perception. He looked closely at the photographs. This was his area of expertise. And those tiny drops of blood were telling him everything he needed to know. "The pathologist wasn't wrong in his original assessment."

Dominique frowned. "You mean that Fraysse was murdered?"

Enzo nodded. "Guy and Elisabeth might have confessed to making his suicide look like murder, but the blood spatter says otherwise."

"How can you tell?"

"If he *had* shot himself, the blood droplets would be on the backs and tips of the trigger finger, the third and fourth fingers, and the front and tip of the thumb. Certainly on the gun hand. And they would appear in similar areas of the hand used to hold it steady. Which is common when you're turning a gun on yourself."

Dominique peered through her pain at the photographs. "I see what you mean. The blood spatter is on the back of both hands."

"Exactly. As if he had been facing his shooter, and raised his hands to protect himself."

"So he didn't kill himself."

"No, he was murdered. But I'd already guessed that."

"How?"

"From of a handful of words recovered from Marc Fraysse's supposed suicide note." He dropped the photographs and stood up suddenly. "I've got to go."

Dominique stood to go after him, but staggered, and grabbed a medic to stop herself from falling. "Enzo where? Where are you going?"

"The killer's got Sophie, Dominique. It's the only explanation."

She gasped her frustration. "I don't understand. Why? Who?"

"I won't know any of that for certain till I get up to the hotel."

The gendarme at the door caught his arm. "The *auberge* up at Saint-Pierre?"

"Yes." Enzo almost hissed it in his face.

"You can't go up there, monsieur. The road's closed. It's impassable."

Enzo tore his arm free. "Try stopping me."

Chapter Forty-three

Several times on the ascent out of Thiers, he thought he wouldn't make it. Wheels spinning sent his car slithering sideways, before catching and propelling him forward again.

The landscape caught in his headlamps was smothered in snow. And still it fell. Thick and wet.

He had left the town behind him now, and the road climbed less steeply, but was almost indistinguishable from everything else around it. Only the red and white stripes of the snow poles kept him from losing his way and ending up in a ditch. The falling snow almost obliterated his vision. Beyond his lights everything was black, like the fear in his heart that drove him on.

Twenty to twenty-five centimetres of snow had fallen in just a matter of hours, and he knew that when the road rose steeply toward the *auberge*, he was going to have to abandon his car. It would take a four-by-four to get him up there.

When he saw the stone pillars, marble plaques engraved with the Chez Fraysse logo at the road junction, he tried to keep the Citröen in third gear and turn gently without stalling it. Front wheels spinning, he only just succeeded in making the turn, and began to inch slowly up the incline. He thanked God for Lucqui's snow poles. Without them he would certainly have lost the road.

If there had been another vehicle up here ahead of him, then its tracks had long since been covered by fresh snow. Not even the faintest impression of them remained. For a moment Enzo began to doubt everything. Perhaps, somehow, he had got it all wrong. Maybe Bertrand had picked Sophie up after all, and the battery in her cellphone was simply dead. But if Bertrand had come for her, why were her things still at Dominique's apartment?

He was finding it difficult now to recognize the lie of the land. The dark of the pine forest pushed up out of the snow, branches laden and dipping under the weight of the wet snowfall. He thought the flat stretch cut away to his right might be the parking area at the foot of the track leading up to the *buron*, but he couldn't be sure.

Then his wheels began spinning hopelessly, the car drifting left toward the drop down to the stream below the waterfall. He tried to accelerate, but it only made things worse. He dropped down to second gear and stalled the engine. The car juddered to a halt.

"Damn!" he shouted at the night and slammed the steering wheel with the heels of both hands. No point in even trying to restart it. He would never get the tires to grip again from a first gear start. He pulled on the handbrake and reached into the glove shelf to retrieve his flashlight.

Before stepping out of the vehicle, he swithered about leaving the headlights on, and decided in the end that he would. They would provide illumination up into the darkness ahead for perhaps a couple of hundred meters, then reflected light beyond that.

The wet snow creaked underfoot like old floorboards as he began the long, difficult climb. As the light from his headlamps receded behind him, he became more and more reliant on the beam of his flashlight to guide him. His thighs ached from having to lift his feet so high for each step forward through the snow. Long before he got to the top, cold and exhaustion were sapping his strength.

Finally, as he reached the end of the road, and rounded the bend, the dark shape of the *auberge* loomed ahead of him. There was not a light anywhere to be seen.

Guy's yellow Trafic sat out front, several inches of snow gathered on the roof. There were no tracks in the snow. It had clearly been sitting there for some time.

From the front entrance, Enzo was unable to see if there were any other vehicles in the car park, so he made his way around the side of the hotel to direct a beam of light toward it. There were two vehicles parked beneath the plane trees. Elisabeth's Mercedes, and a mud-spattered Land Rover. Both with snow piled on their roofs. But no sign of tire tracks in or out. He returned to the front of the *auberge* and turned off his flashlight. He raised a hand to push the revolving door, and found himself sucked through it into interior darkness. He had no idea where the light switches might be located, but as his eyes grew accustomed to the gloom, he realized that emergency night lights were providing some kind of illumination, and the empty hotel began to take shape around him. Somewhere inside it, he knew, were at least three people, maybe more.

He did not want to use his flashlight and make himself an obvious target to anyone who might be waiting in the dark. So he contained himself until the dark outline of the reception desk took form, then began moving cautiously forward and into the corridor leading to the kitchen.

He found some switches just inside the sliding door and turned them on. Fluorescent strips flickered and flooded the kitchen with light. Cold, hard stainless steel, where so many three-star meals had been conceived and cooked, gleamed in the silence. But there was no one here. Guy's office, too, was empty. He went back out and wandered through the lounge and the two dining rooms. Tables and chairs were draped with dust covers for the winter. From the panoramic glass frontage, he could see the lights of Thiers twinkling in the valley below, the vast white plane of the central plateau vanishing into the night beyond.

The hotel was freezing cold, as if the heating had been turned off, and Enzo felt the chill of it seeping into his bones. He was about to head up the stairs when a sound from somewhere in the bowels of the building stopped him where he stood. Uncertain of what exactly it was he had heard, he listened intently for more. It could have been a voice. It could have been the creak of a door. But there was no further sound.

He moved slowly forward into the reception area once more, and this time noticed the line of a dark shadow down one side of the door to the *cave*. He approached it cautiously and realized that it was not shut. It lay a few centimetres ajar. With his heart in his throat he pulled it open, and felt a rush of cold, damp air in his face as he stepped inside.

The darkness here was profound, and he was obliged to turn on his flashlight. He raked its beam along the rows of dusty dull bottles resting in their racks below, before picking out the wooden steps that led down into the musty smell of dampness and stale wine that rose to greet him. He clutched the wooden rail at his left hand and made his way down to the stone flags that lined the floor. By the reflected glow of his flashlight, he could see icy water condensed in droplets on the bedrock walls, like cold sweat.

He sensed, more than heard, a presence in the cellar. Nothing that he could positively identify, but he knew that he was not alone. One careful step at a time, he moved along the near end of the rows, flashing light along each in turn, finding nothing but silent bottles and cold air misted by the damp.

Suddenly he was blinded by a light that seemed to come from nowhere, flashing confusion and fear into his brain. He half lifted a hand to shade his eyes, and at the far end of a canyon of wine saw Guy and Sophie. They were caught in the full glare of his own beam of light. Guy held an electric torch in a fist he made with his left hand, his arm wrapped tightly around Sophie's neck, the gun in his right hand almost touching her temple. She could hardly breathe, and Enzo could see the raw terror in her eyes. He felt his stomach lurch sickeningly at the thought that she might come to any harm.

"Hell, Enzo! You took your time." Guy's voice echoed around the *cave*. "Sophie and me got so damn cold waiting for you."

"For God's sake, man, let her go! What are you doing?"

"I knew she was the only thing that would bring you. Now the only people who know the truth are all down here in the wine cellar."

"You're wrong, Guy. It's over. Everyone knows now." But he could see in Guy's eyes, and hear in his voice, that all reason had left him. And that made him unpredictable, dangerous.

"When Elisabeth told me she had confessed everything to you, I knew it was only a matter of time before the real truth came out." It was as if he wasn't listening, or didn't want to hear. "Especially when I learned that she had given you the suicide note. I had no idea she'd kept it. It might have been good enough to fool her, but not some forensic expert. I knew that much." He paused to draw breath. "I suppose you've already figured it out?"

Enzo nodded. "It was a page of the letter that Marc wrote to you when he got his third star. He was making peace, asking for your forgiveness, wanting to wipe the slate clean. The words you left readable on the page were well-chosen. They could easily have been construed as the words of a man about to take his own life."

"Elisabeth thought so."

Enzo glanced anxiously at Sophie. Guy was a big man. His grip on her neck was powerful. He could break it with a single twist of his arm. She knew it, too, and was making no attempt to struggle. Thoughts tumbled over themselves in Enzo's mind, searching for clarity in confusion. He knew he had to keep Guy talking. "What I don't understand is why you went to all the trouble of faking the suicide, only then to make it look like murder."

Something close to a smile flitted over Guy's face. As if he believed he had been so clever. "To convince Elisabeth, of course. I needed her to believe Marc had killed himself, so that she would collaborate in making it look like murder. A murder that nobody could possibly solve."

"A murder that you committed."

"Yes, but she didn't know that. And nobody ever would as long as she believed it was suicide. Even if the murder story unravelled, she and I would be able to back each other up in telling the authorities he had killed himself."

"And why *did* you kill him?"

Guy let air escape through pursed lips. "You tell me, Enzo. You're the detective."

Enzo glanced at his daughter, then back to her captor. "You were going to lose everything." He paused to think. "What was he going to tell the Press that day? That he was going to sell up to pay off his debts?"

Guy's mirthless laughter resounded in the silence of the *cave*. "Of course he wasn't going to sell! Not the restaurant, anyway. He had too much of himself invested in it." He drew a long, quivering breath. "My little brother's problem, Enzo, was that he was too successful too soon. The future stretched ahead of him without any challenge. He was bored. So he found his excitement elsewhere. In his reckless gambling. In his affair with Anne. Only at the last did he realize he was on a course to self-destruction, that he was going to piss away everything he had worked for."

"So what *was* he going to tell the press?"

"Toward the end he had been seeing some psychotherapist in Paris." The word *psychotherapist* was laden with contempt. "She'd persuaded him that it wasn't too late to save the situation. That he could still put things right. Which is why he finished it with Anne. A clean break, a fresh start. Marc Fraysse on top again. But I only found out what he was intending to do when I took a call from an assessor at an auction house in Paris. The man wanted to arrange a time to come and value the wine." His voice trembled, still, with indignation. "*My* wine, Enzo. The *cave* didn't mean anything to Marc. He saw it only as a way of raising cash to pay off the goddamned debts. *His* debts. In theory he owned half of it, but it was *my* collection. *My* wine."

"So you confronted him?"

"Damn right, I did. Do you know what the bastard was going to do? Announce the closing of the restaurant during the winter. Tell them he was going to use those dead months to develop new dishes, new menus, shake everything and everyone up. Take the time to do some renovations. Chez Fraysee would be reborn in the spring." A snort of frustration and contempt exploded from his nostrils. "But it was all smoke and mirrors. A cover up. Renovations to mask a saving on overheads, new menus an excuse to reassess the wine, sell off the old to buy new."

It all became clear to Enzo. It was Marc's mercurial genius in the kitchen which had created the opportunity for success, but Guy's solid financial management that had built the Fraysse empire. And Guy's passion, Guy's obsession, which had amassed one of the most prestigious and valuable collections of wine in the whole of France. And his little brother was going to take it away from him. "So you killed him to save your wine?"

"To save it all, Enzo. Come on! He was an addict, a gambler. He'd put his restaurant—*our* restaurant—in hock to a bookie. He had fresh cards in his hand, ready for a new play. But sooner or later he'd lose, crash again. Destined to fail." Guy shook his head and Enzo saw tears glistening in his eyes. Even at this distance. "The irony of it was, the only dispensable part of he empire was Marc himself. He might have been the creator, but in the end we didn't need him any more." He waved his hand toward the ceiling. "Look how successful we've been without him."

"And Elisabeth?"

"She had no idea. She really did think he'd killed himself."

Enzo felt the cold rising up into his legs through the flagstones beneath his feet. His hand trembled. "So what are you going to do now? Kill me and Sophie? Because that's not going to do you any good, Guy. Like I said, it's over." And he reached very carefully into his inside pocket to take out the photocopy of the restored 'suicide' note that Raymond had given him. He shook it open and held it up. "That's the page of your letter, made fully legible by a machine called a VSC6000. The police already have it in their possession. And the photographs of blood spatter on the back of Marc's hands taken at autopsy prove beyond doubt that he was murdered, and didn't commit suicide. Killing us won't make any difference now, Guy." But he could see fear and indecision behind the tears, a man on the edge. He had embarked on a certain course and, like a runaway truck on a dangerous descent, there was no guarantee he could stop himself. Enzo couldn't afford to wait and find out.

He flicked a switch, plunging Guy and Sophie into darkness, then ducked quickly out of the beam of Guy's flashlight. Guy's voice rose in panic. "What are you doing? I'll kill her, Enzo, I will." He started dragging her along the end of the racks flashing the beam of his electric torch up and down the rows. Then he froze at the sound of breaking glass. "For God's sake, Enzo, what was that?"

Enzo's voice boomed out of the darkness. "A St. Emilion Grand Cru, 2005, Guy. Worth what… a hundred and fifty euros?"

"Stop it! I swear I'll kill her."

"Harm a single hair on her head, and I'll break every fucking bottle in this *cave*." The menace in his voice in no way reflected the uncertainty in his heart. But he'd made his play. He had to see it through now. The sound of more breaking glass echoed around the glistening bedrock. "That was a Crozes Hermitages. Oh, and here's a good one. Lynch Bages. Must be more than a thousand euros in this one." Enzo dashed it on the floor. The smell of wine, like fresh blood, filled the air. And he went running down the aisle between the racks pulling out bottles at random, letting them smash on the floor behind him. "Are you dying a little bit with every bottle, Guy?" he shouted.

Guy's shriek of anguish filled the cellar, and the deafening report of a gunshot stopped Enzo in his tracks. Guy's flashlight swung around the end of the row, catching Enzo full in it's beam. Guy still held Sophie by the neck, but Enzo could see the panic in his eyes as he directed his torch toward the broken glass and priceless wine that pooled on the floor. He no longer had the gun at Sophie's head, and she used the moment to drive an elbow hard into his gut.

He grunted in pain and cursed, the beam of his flashlight crazily criss-crossing the *cave* as Sophie struggled to break free. Then it fell from his hand and rolled away across the floor. He swung a fist blindly in her direction, catching her on the cheekbone and sending her spinning away in the darkness to fall semi-conscious to the flags.

Enzo made his move, trying to cover the four or five meters between them before Guy had a chance to recover. But Guy was quick to swing the gun in his direction. And even by the reflected light of the fallen flashlight, Enzo could see the intent in his eyes. He knew, in that moment, there was nothing he could do to stop him from pulling the trigger.

The sound of the shot reverberated around the walls, and Enzo staggered two steps back, clutching his chest, wondering why he could feel no pain. He looked down and saw there was no blood on his hand as Guy toppled backwards, crashing into a row of wine bottles and sending the rack tipping over to smash its precious cargo and spill its contents over the floor. Priceless wine washed all around him. Worthless now.

The bullet wound was almost in the center of Guy's chest. His head was pushed forward by the rack that semi-supported his fallen body. His eyes were wide open, staring at the wound, as if in disbelief. But he was quite dead.

The *cave* was suddenly flooded with light. Enzo turned to see Elisabeth standing on the top step, the gun she had used to shoot her husband's killer and one-time lover still trembling in her hand. "I never knew," was all she said.

It had taken a plough to clear the road up to the *auberge* and make it accessible for the phalanx of police vehicles and ambulances that was gathered now at the front entrance of the hotel. Blue and orange lights flashed out of sync, casting alternating color tints across the virgin snow that lay thick all around.

It had stopped snowing now, and with a clearing sky temperatures were plunging, forming a hard crust on the snow, and ice in the tire tracks up the hill.

Forensics officers from the *police scientifique* were still meticulously photographing the scene in the *cave* before the waiting medics could remove the body. Enzo had already briefed the first gendarmes on the scene, but he knew that a long night of interrogation and official statements lay ahead.

Sophie's cheek, where Guy had struck her, was swollen and already darkening. One of the Samu had washed and dressed the broken skin where blood had been drawn. She was shaken, but otherwise alright.

She stood on the top step, wrapped in a blanket, her father's arm around her, still slightly dazed, shocked by the trauma of the last hours. Enzo could feel her trembling against his body.

They moved aside to allow two officers to lead an ashen Elisabeth Fraysse to a waiting van. She glanced at them both, but passed without a word. Enzo and Sophie watched the gendarmes put her in the back of the van, and saw for the first time that she was handcuffed.

"It's so sad," Sophie said. "What will happen to her?"

"I've no idea. But I can't imagine that anything could be worse than what she's already suffered."

"She saved our lives."

Enzo nodded. "She did. And killed the murderer of the only man she ever really loved. A man she was prepared to forgive anything. Even his affair with a hotel receptionist."

Sophie said, "It's a terrible thing, papa, when two brothers fall out like that. When hate is stronger than blood."

Enzo raised his eyes toward the firmament, and saw a nearly full moon rising over the pine clad hills. "It is," he said.

Epilogue

Glasgow, Scotland, November 2010

It was milder here than up in the frozen wastes of central France. The Gulf Stream brought lower temperatures, but more rain. And it was raining now. A fine rain, like mist, that the Scots called *smirr*.

Enzo stood on the hillside, gazing out over the roofs of rain-streaked tenements toward the slate grey of the river Clyde, silent, rusting cranes rising all around it. They were like dinosaurs from a lost age when men built boats that sailed out from the firth and around the world. An age long gone.

The grass was winter withered, dead now, like the men and women buried beneath it all across the hill, a skyline broken by marble plinths and granite crosses.

It was more than half-an-hour since Enzo had ventured up through the dead leaves, feet crunching on the gravel, and he had stood growing cold before the grave of his father long enough now to have lost the feeling in his feet and his hands. He could hear the distant rumble of traffic from Maryhill Road down below.

It was strange how little he felt. In truth, he knew that his father was not really here. Not the man he had known, and respected, and loved. A man whose integrity, and honesty, and sense of justice had been a bright guiding light in his life. The man was long gone, only his bones lay here. And if he lived on at all, it was in Enzo, and in Jack.

How, he wondered, was it possible that brothers who had sprung from the same loins could be so irreconcilably different? Surely to God, sharing a father gave them more in common than could ever separate them. And yet more than thirty years of silence gave witness to the contrary.

He heard footsteps on the gravel and turned to face a stranger. An older man, balding and grey, and only very faintly familiar. He was so much thinner than Enzo remembered. Diminished, somehow, by age. His long, dark coat, glistening in the rain, hung loosely from narrow shoulders.

"Hello, Jack." Enzo's own voice sounded strangely distant to him. "I wasn't sure you would come."

Jack nodded. "Neither was I."

They stood for a long time, then, neither sure what to say next.

"How's Fiona?"

"Died five years ago, Enzo. Cancer."

And unaccountably, Enzo felt tears fill his eyes. "Jesus, Jack! I'm sorry. I didn't know." All those years of anger and pride. And where did it all end? In death. Where all things end, leaving nothing but regret for wasted lives. "I'm sorry for everything, Jack. I really am."

Jack looked at him for what felt like an eternity, and for the first time in his life, Enzo saw his father in his brother's eyes. Jack bit his lower lip. His voice was barely a whisper. "So am I."

Enzo held out his hand. The older man looked at it for a moment, then stepped forward, and in a spontaneous gesture that neither of them could ever have imagined, they embraced. Enzo closed his eyes and knew that he held a part of his father in his arms, a part of himself. And if Sophie and Kirsty had grown up never knowing their uncle, then certainly Laurent would not.

To receive a free catalog of Poisoned Pen Press titles, please contact us in one of the following ways:

Phone: 1-800-421-3976
Facsimile: 1-480-949-1707
Email: info@poisonedpenpress.com
Website: www.poisonedpenpress.com

Poisoned Pen Press
6962 E. First Ave. Ste. 103
Scottsdale, AZ 85251